TALES OF THE DISTRICT
Life in the Nation's Capital in a Time of Terror

A novel by Rachel King, author of

Don't Kill in Our Names:
*Families of Murder Victims Speak
Out Against the Death Penalty*

&

Capital Consequences:
*Families of the Condemned
Tell Their Stories*

Activist Media, Washington, D.C.

Contents

Part I – Dan and Claudia – Fall 2002

1. Hill Life

Dan Canavan sat in a room full of Democratic House staffers searching for the words to convince the skeptical group that their member of Congress should take a vote that most considered political suicide. Why he bothered, he couldn't say. Hope sprang eternal, and maybe one day the Democrats would decide to act like Democrats again, and give up the notion that if they just acted more like Republicans they could regain the majority.

Dan's navy blue suit and polished shoes contrasted starkly with the jeans and T-shirts worn by his audience. It was Friday, casual day, a risky choice for a meeting, since most staffers were thinking about their weekends instead of listening to Dan.

Dan was a lobbyist for OutReach, the country's largest gay rights organization, with a membership of almost half a million. It was his job to convince the Republican-controlled Congress that it should oppose SOFA – the Sanctity of Families Act – a mean-spirited piece of legislation that cut off federal funds to any state that legalized gay marriage.

"You've got to stand firm on this issue. It's a matter of principle," Dan beseeched the assembled group, but his voice rang hollow, even to himself. "Gay people vote, too. We're going to score this vote. All of our members will know how your members voted on this issue, and they'll remember when they go to the polls next month."

"Give me a break," cooed Ken Parker, the head lawyer for the Democratic staff of the House Judiciary Committee, who reported to Ranking Member Bobby Reynolds. Tall, dark-haired, and handsome, Parker appeared frequently as a talking head on Washington talk shows. "Your members are going to vote for Democrats over Republicans, regardless of this vote. You can't expect our Democrats in the Bible Belt to vote against SOFA. It would be political suicide."

"There are gay people in the South, too," Dan retorted.

"Only they don't know it," another staffer joked. People laughed tentatively, looking to see Dan's reaction.

Dan kept his cool and joked, "Some of them know it. Why 'dya think they need those sodomy laws down in Georgia? They need to control the ho-mo-sex-uals."

Dan's light-hearted joking hid his frustration. He was fighting a losing battle.

Ken continued, "If it was a close vote, if you had any chance at all of winning, I'd ask the Chairman to whip it, but there's no way in hell you're going to win. Why should our members stick their necks out to vote against a bill that's going to pass anyway?"

Dan couldn't argue with Ken's logic, but his position wasn't principled. Dan stopped himself from saying, "Because it's the right thing to do." He had been in Washington too long to think that members of Congress cast their votes because it was the right thing to do.

The day, which had started out so promising, had turned out to be a failure. Dan who had stopped smoking six months earlier, still craved Virginia Slims, the kind his mother smoked when he was a kid, whenever he was frustrated. He walked to the CVS after the meeting, swearing under his breath, which startled several homeless people, and made his way to the counter, gazing longingly at the display, which contained dozens of options. Like a lion before it devours its prey, Dan paused, long enough to decide to buy a peanut butter and chocolate protein bar instead. Pleased with his abstinence, he quickly left the store before changing his mind.

There wasn't much left to do that day. He had already written a letter to each member of the Judiciary Committee, which he would send by blast fax so that it arrived before the scheduled Tuesday hearing.

He was heading to the Metro by 8:30, earlier than he had left work in weeks. He took out his cellphone and scrolled down to the entry for Claudia Connors, his neighbor and best friend. They lived at Tulip Lane Cohousing, or TLC, an intentional community in Takoma Park, Maryland. Claudia was also single, so the two spent most evenings eating late dinners and processing their stressful jobs, and their lack of love lives.

"Middle Eastern take-out or Paul's Place?" he asked.

"How about soy cheese pizza?" she replied. "If you're not too tired we could watch "Erin Brokovich. I'm in need of inspiration."

"Your place or mine?"

"Let's see, should we watch on your 10-year-old 12-inch screen or my brand new, state-of-the-art, high-definition, LCD, large screen digital TV?"

By 9:30 they were settled in front of the television with a large vegan pizza and a six-pack of Coronas, ready to escape from the craziness of their work lives. Dan took the comfortable red sofa and Claudia stretched out her 5-foot-10-inch frame on an old Lazy Boy recliner that she had bought for a steal at Value Village, where most of her clients shopped. Although Claudia had a dining room, and a countertop in the kitchen with barstools, they always seemed to end up eating in the living room watching TV. They didn't always watch movies. If they got home from work in time, they watched PBS News Hour. Dan had a crush on Jim Lehrer, and dreamed of one day being interviewed by him.

"How was your day?" she asked with her mouth full of pizza.

"Same old thing. I'm trying to bang down the doors of the Democrats and not making much progress."

"Maybe you should try the Republicans," she joked.

"That's funny. OutReach can't even get meetings with some of the Republican committee members. One member told my boss there was no need to meet with her because there weren't any gays in her district."

Claudia laughed.

"How was your day?" Dan asked wanting to change the subject.

"I got a few criminals back on the street," Claudia joked. Her tone turned serious. "I also got a disturbing phone call from a woman who hasn't heard from her husband in three days. She thinks he may have been arrested and detained incommunicado. The FBI had been at their house interviewing him, but when she called the agent to try to get information, he wouldn't return her calls."

Dan shook his head, not wanting more worries than the ones already occupying his mind. "Let's not talk about work anymore. I need a break."

Claudia put in the DVD and turned off the lights. Dan stretched out on her long blue sofa where he had more than once woken up in the morning.

Claudia placed an afghan blanket over him, tucking in the sides. "Do you want me to wake you up if you fall asleep?"

Dan shook his head. "Not unless you're worried about what the neighbors will say when they see me leave in the morning."

"Not to worry. The neighbors already know about us."

2. Tulip Lane Cohousing Community

Claudia lugged her dry erase markers and bottle of water into the Common House and began arranging the hard plastic chairs into a semicircle. Normally an optimistic person, she dreaded this meeting where they would be discussing work-share policy, a contentious issue in the community. She had even biked to the food co-op to buy vegan, whole-wheat, fruit-juice sweetened, carob chip cookies hoping to woo her community into agreement.

She loved her community with its well-tended grounds, modern apartments and large, airy Common House. It had saved her life when she had moved to the District three years ago, running away from a failed relationship in Seattle. It had been a refuge from the intense loneliness of a broken heart. She had grown to love most of the people, a collection of 60 adults and 20 children, who lived, more or less companionably, in 40 separate condos that they called units. What she didn't always love were the meetings. When they had first formed their community they met once or twice a week, thankfully now it was only every other week, but even that sometimes felt like too much.

The problem, or the challenge, as Claudia preferred to think of it, was the decision-making process. They made all decisions by consensus, which meant that they all had to agree on any decision, or at least they all had to agree to disagree. Claudia was "President" of the Tulip Lane

Cohousing Community — a dubious title for a group of strong-willed, highly educated, extremely opinionated people who disliked authority. As a lawyer, and an experienced mediator and facilitator, Claudia was more successful than most at helping the group achieve consensus. But even with Claudia's talent, the decision-making process was extremely slow. The community had lived together for three years and had yet to agree on a pet policy. Some had compared the community's decision-making process to herding cats.

Besides the regular committee reports — reports about the state of the facility and reports about the happenings of the members — the main agenda item for the meeting was the work-share policy. Since its inception, the community had been struggling with its work-share policy, whether to require its members, none of whom wanted to be told what to do but all of whom had visions of how things should be done, to participate in work around the community. Claudia had heard her neighbors debating the policy endlessly, sometimes arguing into the early morning and occasionally exchanging heated "words," as her grandmother used to say. Agreement was unlikely.

Residents started to arrive. She searched the crowd for Dan, who was often the voice of reason at these meetings. By 3:30, there was still no sign of him, so she started without him.

"Greetings, friends," she began. Scattered hellos and good afternoons reverberated from the group. She smiled warmly. "Has everyone had a chance to review the agenda?" She didn't want any changes made to the already contentious agenda, but it was her standard practice to get group buy-in on the agenda before she began a meeting.

Aimee Shipley, a twenty-something white woman with long wavy brown hair and silver hoop pierced rings in her lip and eyebrow, raised her hand and jerked it up and down, like a fish pulling line from a rod.

Claudia considered pretending that she hadn't seen Aimee, but she knew Aimee would just interrupt her if she didn't call on her. She nodded at her. "What is it, Aimee?" she asked, trying to sound patient.

"I'd like to add something to the agenda," Aimee said, with a tone of entitlement.

The group stirred collectively. Aimee was known for introducing contentious topics.

"I'd like us to discuss the fact that the president is considering going to war again," she emphasized. A few people groaned but Aimee persisted. "As I was saying, our country is considering declaring war on a country that has done absolutely nothing to us and I want to know what we are going to do about it."

"Here, here," chimed a few voices.

"Not again," Frances Perkins murmured, loud enough for Claudia to hear. Frances' mother had been a labor organizer in the days when you could get shot for doing that kind of thing. Frances had grown up in the wake of Vietnam and had protested that war before getting involved in feminism. She worked for the Service Employees International Union organizing Latina hotel workers. Frances disapproved of this new brand of activists who dressed in black and wore outrageous hairstyles as they threw rocks at windows of the World Bank and IMF. She couldn't see the point of that. Causing property damage for no reason was not going to bring anyone over to her way of thinking. Frances herself had been arrested more times than she could count, but it was for a clear purpose, like protesting when the factories wouldn't let the workers strike.

Claudia was frequently playing referee between the two women. She believed the two didn't get along because they were exactly alike. But she knew better than to suggest that to either of them. She chose her words carefully, not wanting to appear insensitive. "Just because we have set aside time to discuss work-share policy this afternoon, it doesn't mean we don't care about the president's plan to go to war." Then, without meaning to say it, she added, "Frankly, we can at least have some control over our work-share policy. I'm not sure the president and Congress care about our opinion on invading Iraq."

As soon as she made the remark she regretted it. First of all, she doubted its veracity. Influencing work-share policy seemed on par with influencing the president's foreign policy. Plus, it was the perfect set-up for Aimee to begin her tirade.

"That is precisely the problem with this country," Aimee said glaring at Frances. "No one takes responsibility for anything. We let the president do whatever he wants and then tell ourselves there's nothing we can do about it."

Aimee's self-righteous attitude grated on Claudia's nerves. The idea that this twenty-something upstart considered herself the moral conscience of the community galled her. Claudia sighed. She recognized Aimee as a younger version of herself. When had she started caring more about getting through an agenda than protesting war?

Josh Horowitz, who dressed like it was still the sixties, wearing a full beard, frizzy brown hair, tattered jeans, and a Grateful Dead T-shirt, raised his hand. Claudia called on him, hoping he would say something to bring the meeting back on track.

Josh stood up as though speaking to a congregation. "Friends, let us not turn against each other during this difficult time." He tugged on his beard, a nervous habit. "We need to pull together. Aimee, let me assure you that everyone in this room cares deeply about whether we go to war, but we still have to make decisions about how to run our community. There will always be outside issues that seem more pressing than work share, which is precisely why after three years we still don't have a work-share policy."

Several members nodded in agreement.

Aimee responded, "I just don't see how we can avoid talking about the war. It's going to affect our lives whether we like it or not."

Claudia interrupted, "I'll tell you what. I'll add the war to the end of the agenda and if we get through everything else, we'll talk about it."

"OK," Aimee grudgingly agreed. Frances rolled her eyes in disapproval.

Claudia turned the meeting over to Josh to present the newest version of the work-share proposal. Just then, Sarah Khadonry burst into the room yelling, "Emad's been arrested!"

Claudia and Emad had been friends for years, and most recently had been involved in a peace group organizing against the war in Afghanistan. They had spent many hours discussing politics, especially the situation in the Middle East. Emad had grown up in Saudi Arabia, but had come to the United States to attend graduate school at American University. He met Sarah there, and she converted to Islam, much to her family's dismay. They married and now had a three-year-old daughter, Semya. Sarah and Emad had asked Claudia to be Semya's Godmother, an honor that she had gladly accepted.

Claudia snapped to attention like a doctor awakened in the night by an emergency call. "When was he arrested?"

"This morning. An FBI agent and a D.C. cop came to our house and got him out of bed." Sarah was nearly hysterical. "I don't know what to do."

"Where was he taken?" Claudia asked.

"I don't know, but one agent left a card," Sarah said, handing it to Claudia.

"I'll go try to find out what's going on," Claudia said. She grabbed Sarah's hand. "Josh, will you take over the meeting for me?" She ran out of the room without waiting for an answer.

3. Seeking Comfort

Dan was sipping his favorite drink, a soymilk latte, at the Daily Grind and reading *The Nation* when Claudia called to tell him about Emad's arrest. He had skipped the community meeting, which he did frequently because they drove him crazy, so he missed the news of Emad's arrest. He folded the magazine under his arm and grabbed a cab for the First Precinct. He wanted to help, even though everything he knew about criminal law he had learned by watching reruns of "Hill Street Blues." But he figured he could at least flash his bar card and drop a few names of members of Congress.

Dan knew Emad from years of working on Capitol Hill. Emad worked on immigrant's rights, not gay rights, but they traveled in the same circles and frequently called each other for advice. Although Emad and his family did not live at TLC, they visited regularly.

When Dan arrived, Sarah was resting on a chair in the waiting area, her eyes swollen from crying, her face filled with fear. Claudia was arguing with a police officer standing behind a counter. Dan couldn't tell who was winning.

"I'm a friend of Mr. Khadonry's and I'm an assistant federal defender. I have a right to speak with him," Claudia said. Dan knew she was on the verge of losing her temper and wondered if he should intervene or let fate take its course.

"All I know is that we are holding him under a federal warrant. We're not authorized to give out any information other than what I've told you. If this were a D.C. case I could help you, but you know how the feds are…" He didn't have a chance to finish his thought before Claudia interrupted.

"Am I in the United States of America?" Claudia snapped. "What the hell is going on here? I've never been denied information about a client before. This is absolutely outrageous. I want to speak to your supervisor."

"I am the shift supervisor," he said smugly. Dan decided the situation could use a mediator.

"Hello officer, I'm Dan Canavan. I'm an attorney and a friend of Ms. Connors."

The officer nodded.

"Can you tell us when we will be able to get information about Mr. Khadonry," he asked calmly.

The officer scanned a piece of paper. "He's scheduled for arraignment Monday at 9 a.m. It's a public proceeding. You're welcome to go."

"You've got to be kidding me," Claudia snapped. "I'm not leaving here until I see Mr. Khadonry."

Dan groaned. Claudia had just destroyed any chance they had of seeing Emad. Dan tried again. "Is there any way we could see him? Just for a few minutes?" Dan asked. "I've never had a problem seeing clients before," he added, which wasn't exactly a lie. He had once represented a group of Methodist ministers who had been arrested for protesting the church's decision to excommunicate a lesbian minister and in that case, he had been permitted to go inside the cell to visit his clients.

"Things are different now," the officer said. "When was the last time you represented a terrorist?" he asked.

"He's not a terrorist," Claudia's voice could have cut steel.

"Says you," the officer said. "According to the feds he is."

Sarah, who had been watching without saying anything, began to wail.

"We're not getting anywhere," Dan said, touching Claudia on the shoulder. "Let's get out of here."

Claudia looked like she was going to protest, but she backed down. She went to Sarah and wrapped her arms around her while the woman sobbed. "I'm so sorry," she said.

They picked up Semya from a neighbor and drove mother and daughter home. Dan and Claudia helped the two get inside and fixed Sarah a cup of tea. Drowsy with sleep, Semya asked Claudia where her papa was. Claudia dissolved in tears. Dan said, "Your daddy is not here right now, but we'll do everything we can to bring him home."

This seemed to be enough explanation for the child. Claudia offered to spend the night, but Sarah told her to go home.

On the way home, Dan suggested going to Arucala, one of their favorite restaurants. Dan, whose mother was Italian, believed that good food and wine could make most things better. "Sure fine," Claudia said, her thoughts a million miles away.

He asked for an outside table to enjoy the warm evening, and ordered a bottle of Chianti. Claudia was on her third glass before the food arrived.

"I can't believe they wouldn't let me see him," she said for at least the tenth time that evening. "It's outrageous. Poor Sarah. How is she going to explain to Semya that her daddy is in jail? Of course he wouldn't be in jail if he had a decent lawyer."

Dan knew after two years of friendship that the best thing for Claudia when she was upset was to let her talk until she had talked herself out. He used to try to think of things to cheer her up or talk rationally to her, but that only irritated her.

He ate his dinner and listened half-heartedly. Claudia wasn't eating. She hadn't eaten anything since breakfast and was on her fourth glass of wine. She'd likely fall asleep soon.

"I'm sorry," she said. "I've been babbling non-stop. Tell me something, anything to take my mind off this."

"Rita Jane comes this week," he said. Rita Jane was his childhood best friend. They had attended Catholic school together in Washington. Rita Jane went to New York after graduation to attend NYU and had never looked back, visiting Washington only at Christmas or when her parents succeeded at guilting her into a visit. Now, twenty years later she was moving back to Washington. Dan had arranged for her to sublet a unit at TLC from Amanda, who was spending a year in India. Dan was looking forward to having her back, but wondered how the two women in his life would get along. They were both strong willed and high maintenance. Rita Jane was prone to jealousy, and might not like the fact that he had a new best friend. One thing was certain — between the two of them, he'd never be lonely. He probably wouldn't have time to meet a boyfriend, either.

"I can't wait to meet her," Claudia said. Claudia had already met most of Dan's close friends, but she had been out of town the only time Rita Jane had visited Tulip Lane Cohousing.

"You two will love each other," Dan said, wondering if it would be true.

Claudia took a bite of her meal and pushed the food around on her plate. His food was all gone and he gazed at hers half hoping that she would offer him some and half hoping that she would not.

"I'm afraid, Dan," she said. "I'm really afraid. It's never been this bad before. I fear for our country."

Sometimes Dan also feared that the country was going in a dangerous direction and trying to change it was like using a teaspoon to bail the ocean. He didn't want to have that discussion now. Claudia was prone to melancholy when drunk.

"Come on, let me take you home," Dan said, helping her out of her chair and putting her arm around his shoulder.

Claudia was quiet on the drive home. Her eyes were closed. Dan parked on the street next to her unit. He wanted to carry her upstairs and put her to bed without waking her, but at 5-foot-10, Claudia was too tall for him to carry.

"We're home," Dan said cheerfully. "Someone needs to get to bed."

With her arms wrapped around him, leaning heavily on Dan, Claudia managed to make it to her apartment. He helped her into her room, sat her on her bed, took off her shoes and jacket, and turned down the covers.

"Stay with me, Dan," she said. "I don't want to be alone tonight."

Dan didn't particularly want to be alone, either. He brushed his teeth with the spare toothbrush he kept in her guest bathroom and stripped down to his jockey shorts. When he returned from the bathroom, Claudia was wearing shorts and a T-shirt with a large picture of an eye and the words, "An eye for an eye makes the whole world blind."

It seemed strange to be preparing for bed like an old married couple. They had slept in the same bed before on weekend trips where the hotel only had rooms with one bed. He had fallen asleep on her couch before, many times, usually staying up late to watch the "Daily Show" or a DVD that they had rented from Video Americana. But he had never gone to bed with her like this before.

They got into bed and held each other. Dan was in that dreamy stage just before sleep when Claudia started crying again. "I feel so helpless. It's so wrong and there's nothing I can do." He stroked her hair to comfort her and whispered, "It'll be alright. I promise." "I'm afraid. I've never been so afraid before," she said.

He kissed her on the cheek and then on her eyes and nose and before he knew what he was doing, on her lips. She kissed him back. At first it was a friendly kiss, but then they kissed deeper and Dan, to his surprise, found himself becoming aroused.

He had never made love with a woman before, having come out as gay while he was in high school. Desire, curiosity, and need drove him and he touched her and she touched him back, stroking him and arousing him more. Her tall thin body and flat chest seemed more boy than woman, a thought that made him harder.

"Do you have a condom," he whispered urgently.

"I'm a lesbian," she said. "I don't keep condoms around the house. But it doesn't matter. It's a safe time of the month."

He contemplated getting up to see if he had a condom in his jacket pocket, but feared it would break the mood. He didn't want to break the moment. He wanted to go through with what he had started, as much out of curiosity as desire. He could smell his own body odor, mixed with Claudia's. She was soft. It seemed strange to touch someone with so little body hair. After a few minutes he forgot what he was doing and succumbed to the experience that was so familiar and also so strange. They moved fiercely, joined together from desperation, each seeking relief until the release and then they fell into sleep, a journey each had to make alone.

4. Rita Jane Moves to Town

Claudia and Amanda Jones were sitting on patio chairs discussing the work-share task force meeting that had met to incorporate suggestions from the previous week's community meeting when Rita Jane and Dan approached. Several other adults were sitting on patio furniture reading novels, chatting, or supervising children playing in the play area, enjoying the warm day.

"You must be Rita Jane." Amanda said holding out her hand. Amanda was petite and black, a striking contrast to Claudia, whose mother described her build as "Swedish Olympic Swimmer."

"Hello, Amanda," Dan greeting her, kissing both cheeks. "This is RJ."

Amanda stood up and hugged Rita Jane, "My new tenant."

Claudia held back, waiting for Dan to make the introduction. She felt uncertain. She and Dan hadn't spoken since their evening together. She was still processing the event, figuring out what it meant. Certainly it would not happen again. It had been a moment of coming together, of finding comfort. It was rather insignificant really, it shouldn't change anything, but she knew from past experience that sex had a way of changing relationships. Dan was her north star, the thing that anchored her, that kept her connected. She felt as though she were wandering in the wilderness with a broken compass. She wanted it back the way it had been.

Dan put his arm around Rita Jane and steered her toward Claudia. "Claudia Conner, I'd like you to meet Rita Jane Spencer."

"I'm so glad to finally meet you," Rita Jane said.

Claudia extended her hand, "Dan has told me so much about you. I feel like I know you already. Welcome to TLC."

When they shook hands, Claudia felt a jolt of recognition, like a feeling of déjà vu. She had wondered how she would feel about Rita Jane, concerned that she might feel jealous of her close friendship with Dan, but there was something about Rita Jane's demeanor – her slightly sad, but kind expression, that reassured Claudia that they would get along. Also, Claudia had always been partial to redheads, and Rita Jane had the loveliest head of auburn hair, wild and thick, long enough to entwine small animals.

"What's happening with Emad?" Dan asked.

"We're still waiting to get a bail hearing date scheduled. I've been to see him a few times. Sarah goes every day, of course. She's a mess." I am, too, she wanted to say, but Dan hadn't asked her how she was doing.

"You'll get her out," Amanda told Claudia. She said to Rita Jane, "If I were in jail, I'd want her as my lawyer. Look guys, as much as I'd love to stay here and nosh with you, I gotta' go back and finish packing. Do you wanna' see your new place, Rita Jane?" Amanda nodded at Claudia and Dan, "You two can come, too, of course, not that you haven't seen the place before."

"I've got things to do," Dan said. "I'll leave her in your capable hands." It wasn't clear if he was talking to Amanda or Claudia. Claudia didn't want Dan to go. She missed him. She wanted to run after him, force a conversation, but her heart and head were too mixed up. She would wait until the time was right, then she'd know what to say.

They showed Rita Jane inside the Common House first. Claudia loved showing people this part of TLC, where people came together to play, work, eat. It was a grand room filled with years of memories of people living together, caring about each other, and undertaking, gallantly, a social experiment of creating a community together. Claudia felt a flush of pride watching Rita Jane admire, with her artist eyes, the large open room with a thirty-foot ceiling, floor-to-ceiling windows, skylights, and a light-colored hardwood floor. There were several nooks in the room with overstuffed couches, large pillows, and comfortable chairs next to built-in bookcases. In one corner of the room, a ladder climbed up to a small loft. "It's beautiful," Rita Jane said to no one in particular.

"Thank you. We like it." Claudia spoke slowly with her Texas twang. "And I'm sure you'll like it, too. The people are wonderful – very supportive. We do have a lot of meetings, which are sometimes challenging."

Amanda interrupted, "That's the understatement of the year."

"As I was saying," Claudia cut Amanda off before she could complain further. "We place a high premium on communication. Meetings are a necessity when you live closely with so many people. Besides, Amanda loves living here. She's just having separation anxiety about leaving us to go to India for a year. She's trying to convince herself she won't miss us when she's gone."

"Oh, is that what I'm doing, Ms. Psychoanalyst?" Amanda retorted. "Whatever you say, girlfriend."

Clematis festooned the entrance to Amanda's walk-in unit with dazzling purple and pink star-shaped flowers. A small garden displayed pink hydrangeas and bright red cockscomb still in bloom. The four small rooms were decorated with exotic tapestries and rugs. Amanda had obviously traveled extensively. A shelf in the living room was devoted to elephants of all shapes and sizes. Masks from Africa and paintings with bold, bright colors filled the walls, and the bed had a purple canopy enclosing it. The scent of jasmine incense perfumed the air.

"I'm leaving for India for a year, maybe two," Amanda said casually, as though traveling to India was a run-of-the-mill-kind of thing to do. "My boyfriend is into yoga and meditation. He's going to an ashram in Rishikesh to study with his guru. I'm going to teach English to children who are illiterate."

"I'll probably come home at least once for a visit, but if you don't want me to sleep on the floor I can stay someplace else. I'd just as soon leave my stuff here, but if you want, I can put it in storage."

"You seem awfully casual about picking up and going across the world for a year," Rita Jane observed.

"Amanda never stays still for long. I think she was a gypsy in another life," Claudia said.

"The politically correct term is Roma," Amanda interrupted her.

"It's fine with me if you leave your things. You have such beautiful art work. I don't have many things anymore. I purged myself when I left New York."

Claudia and Amanda exchanged glances but neither of them said anything.

"You'll love it here," Claudia said.

"Let's celebrate with a cappuccino," Amanda suggested.

"Are you leaving the espresso maker, too?" Rita Jane asked hopefully.

"Absolutely."

They took their large mugs out on the back deck and sat at a small Italian tiled table. "How lovely," Rita Jane sighed. A bird feeder hung from a maple tree, its leaves changing to a brilliant burgundy. Several starlings pecked greedily at the sunflower seeds. The air was moist and fresh from a rainfall during the night.

"Those pigs can go through an entire feederful in one day," Amanda said. "They aren't even pretty. I can't seem to get any interesting birds to visit. My mother says it's because I use the wrong kind of bird seed."

"You should listen to your momma," Claudia said.

"Aren't you going to miss this place?" Rita Jane asked. "Why are you going to India?"

"Hell, no, I can't wait to get away from here," she laughed.

"Knock it off, girl," Claudia said. "You're scaring her. Besides its not true."

"I'm sorry," Amanda said to Rita Jane. "Once you get to know me you'll learn I'm a bit prone to hyperbole. It's not bad living here, although I guess I do have my own love-hate relationship with the place. I love the people, although I wish there were a few more that looked like me," she said, looking at her bare, dark-skinned arms. "But they have good hearts. But contrary to what Claudia says, the meetings do drive me crazy. We talk, and talk, and talk, but rarely make decisions. Maybe it's a white thing. I don't know. Do me a favor, Rita Jane, and figure out the work-share policy before I return." She sipped her coffee. "Anyway, I cope by traveling. That keeps me sane."

"We discuss other things, too," Claudia said, annoyed with Amanda who had a lot of nerve to criticize the community when she spent half of her life traveling in other parts of the world.

"Of course we do," Amanda said giving Claudia a patronizing smile. "Anyway, enough about us. What about you? Are you going to tell us why you left New York to come back to D.C.?"

Rita Jane looked as though she was deciding how to answer the question. "Things weren't going well in New York." She laughed. "That's an understatement. I lost my job. I broke up with my fiancée. I was tired of the New York art scene. I guess I was ready for a change." She hesitated, and then added, "I'm thinking about having a baby."

The remark grabbed Claudia's attention. Dan had never mentioned that Rita Jane wanted a baby. Claudia's ears perked up. From Dan's description of Rita Jane, she hadn't figured her to be the motherly type. Claudia had thought about children, but had chosen to focus on her career instead. She kept thinking that one day she would have a child, but now that she was 40, it didn't seem likely. Claudia wondered if Rita Jane was planning on adopting. She had a number of single friends who had adopted children, although privately Claudia thought they were crazy to raise a child alone.

"Oh girl, that's great." Amanda said. "I love kids. Don't necessarily want any of my own, but I love other people's kids."

"This seems like a good place to raise kids," Rita Jane said, with a question in her voice.

"It is. There are lots of kids and everyone looks out for them." She hesitated briefly then continued in a less enthusiastic tone. "But we have had problems with some of the neighborhood kids."

"There you go again scaring her," Claudia admonished. "We don't have any more problems than any other urban community."

"What kinds of problems?" Rita Jane asked.

"Graffiti, vandalism, stealing mail," Amanda replied. "One nine-year-old, who lives in the neighborhood, even walked into someone's unit when the owners were home and stole $400 and a camera."

"What happened to the kid?"

"Nothing," Amanda said. "The police went to the house to investigate, but the mother wouldn't let them talk to the boy. The cop thought she put him up to stealing to feed her drug habit. The police didn't do anything."

"The kid's lucky he didn't get shot," Rita Jane remarked.

"These kids aren't dumb," Amanda explained. "They know the people who live here are a bunch of do-gooders and peaceniks. Not the kind of people to have guns at home or to shoot trespassing children."

"That kind of thing goes on in any city," Claudia said. "Believe me, I know. I'm a public defender. Crime is everywhere."

Amanda ignored her. "There's also racial tension. Most of the folks who live at TLC are white and most of the neighborhood is black. Since TLC was built the property values have increased, which the neighbors like, but that also means that property taxes have gone up, which they don't like."

"There's plenty of crime in New York," Rita Jane said. "And plenty of racial tension. I appreciate you giving me the "full disclosure," but it doesn't change my mind about wanting to live here. Honestly, I'm more worried about the sniper who is shooting people around the area. My mother's been sending me articles."

"Thankfully the sniper seems to be operating mostly in the suburbs," Amanda said. "Now that we've finished the business, let's toast Rita Jane's arrival. To Rita Jane, may she have a happy, productive year."

They clinked their mugs together. "Now, Rita Jane," Amanda said, "When exactly were you thinking about having a kid? I mean, this place is a little small for a kid."

"Don't worry," Rita Jane assured her. "I'm not having one any time soon."

"That's cool," Amanda said.

5. A Proposition

To celebrate her return to the District, Rita Jane and Dan ordered garlic eggplant and Mu Shu vegetables from the bad Chinese restaurant around the corner from TLC. On the way back to Dan's place, they stopped at the Value Liquor Store for a bottle of wine.

"What's your best bottle of cheap wine?" Rita Jane asked the skinny, Indian man who greeted her as she walked into the store.

"All our wine is good, ma'am," he said.

"I'm not old enough to be called ma'am," Rita Jane mumbled to Dan.

"You don't look a day over 38," Dan assured her.

"Can you tell me what you like, ma'am?" the clerk asked patiently.

"That word," Rita Jane muttered. "White, I guess. I prefer quantity to quality."

He chuckled. "That's a good one, ma'am." He retrieved a two-liter bottle of Cabot Pinot Grigio from the walk-in cooler. "This is a good buy. It's on sale, too."

"Thank you, sir," she said. He smiled at her, evidently not bothered by being called sir.

After the food, and after a few glasses of wine, they took the rest of the bottle out on the back deck and sat in Dan's hanging swing. He put his arm around her and she snuggled up next to him. The warm autumn air felt sweet. The two friends reminisced about their high schools days, swapping stories with fondness — twenty years had rubbed away the hard edges of their memories. Dan looked forward to re-exploring the city with his old friend, and introducing her to his new friends. He had worried that Rita Jane's return might put a strain on his friendship with Claudia, but he and Claudia had done that without Rita Jane's help.

He listened as Rita Jane shared her feelings about returning to D.C. The wine helped quiet his anxiety about Emad's arrest, and his estrangement with Claudia. They had nearly made it through the two-liter bottle when Rita Jane turned to him and said, "Dan. Let's have a kid."

Dan choked on his wine. He was speechless, which was unusual for him.

"I'm flattered, but you know I don't like girls."

"I don't want to have sex with you," she said defensively.

"That's a relief."

"Dan, I'm serious. Let's you and me have a kid. We don't have to have sex to have a child. We could use a turkey baster."

"That could be fun."

"I've been thinking about this for a long time. We both want to have kids. We've been talking about it for decades but neither one of us is close to making it happen. I'm almost 40."

Dan smiled at her sympathetically. He squeezed her hand and neither of them spoke. In the background, kids were playing a nighttime game of wiffle ball.

"Is there any chance you and Sean will get back together?" He had heard the breakup story many times, but that's what best friends were for.

"Never. I gave that jerk the best years of my life. He knew I wanted kids. He said he wanted children, too. We even tried to get pregnant for over a year. I bought a thermometer and took my temperature all the time and charted my cycles. Whenever I was ovulating we made sure to have sex at least once."

"How romantic."

"We used to visit his niece and nephew in Westchester. I loved playing with them. I brought them presents." The tears stuck in her throat. "I bought Louie his first bike." A few tears escaped. "They loved me. They called me Auntie Rita."

"I bet you were a good aunt," Dan said, stroking her tangled red hair.

"But then, out of the blue, he announced that he wanted to devote his life to his art and didn't want children." The tears were falling in earnest now.

"You poor baby." Dan hugged her and held her close. "You'll meet someone else. You know you will. You're gorgeous. You're funny. You're nice, most of the time." He laughed. "You're smart."

"I'm not gorgeous. I'm fat and my face is puffy from crying all the time. I'm sick of waiting for some man to come along and rescue me. I want to take charge of my life. Besides I don't think I'll meet anyone I'd rather raise a child with more than you."

Dan laughed. "It is tempting, I admit. But it's too messy."

"Life is messy."

"I can't even imagine how we would do it. Would we live together? We'd drive each other crazy. And how would we raise a child together if we didn't?"

"Oh, I don't know," Rita Jane said in exasperation. "I haven't figured out all the details. We could live here or we could buy a duplex somewhere and each have our own place. We could figure it out."

"But don't you want to get married and have a child with someone you love?"

"I love you," Rita Jane said fervently.

Dan sighed. "Not that kind of love. You know what I mean."

"Romantic love is overrated," she responded. "Who says being in love is necessary for raising children? It's probably an impediment if you really think about it. I can't imagine anyone whom I would trust more than you."

Dan had to admit that the idea had some merit. He squeezed her hand. "I promise I'll think about it."

Rita Jane put her head on his shoulder and they rocked silently for a long time.

6. Moving Day

Claudia undressed and stood on the cold, tiled bathroom floor inspecting her body in the mirror. Slender, with long blonde hair, she was good-looking in a wholesome sort of aging cheerleader way. She liked her looks well enough, but resented the aging process. Nearsighted since junior high, she was now experiencing the beginning stages of farsightedness as well. Her thighs were still sculpted from her days playing basketball and field hockey at Chapel Hill, but a small pouch was growing around her middle. She examined her almost non-existent breasts. As an athlete, she never minded being flat-chested. She always felt sorry for large-breasted women who flopped around on the court or field. Now she found herself wishing for slightly larger breasts to counterbalance her growing stomach.

She stepped into the tub filled with scalding, bubbly water so hot that it turned her skin bright red. She lifted one foot then the other seeking a reprieve from the heat then eased her way down until the lower half of her body was submerged. She thought about adding cold water but didn't. She leaned back against a terrycloth bathtub pillow with a rainbow print that she had bought at the Seattle Gay Pride festival three years ago.

As the heat and steam enveloped her, she thought of the coming day. Rita Jane had not reacted when Dan had introduced them. Apparently he had not told Rita Jane about their encounter. Either that or Rita Jane was a very good actor.

She left her house in time to walk to Paul's Place to pick up coffee and cinnamon rolls before arriving at Dan's by nine.

Dan greeted her with a quick peck on the cheek. He seemed so normal around her, more interested in the bag of cinnamon rolls and coffee than in her. She resented how shaken the experience had left her. She had been looking for comfort, she supposed, but the experience left her feeling empty. She missed Dan.

Dan returned with plates and napkins. "Unfortunately, the princess is not quite ready to go yet. Although she's been here less than three days, she has managed to unpack most of her stuff. She wanted to show me her newest paintings and her newest thrift store clothing acquisitions. You know how girls are."

Claudia wasn't sure she did know how straight girls were. She had assumed that Rita Jane would be packed and ready to go. She didn't say anything, but mentally calculated all the other things she wanted to accomplish during the day.

"So, how're you doing?" Dan asked. "I haven't seen much of you lately."

So we're going to go the superficial route, Claudia thought. "I'm okay. Work's busy. You know the usual. And you?"

He didn't meet her eyes. "The same. Any news on Emad's case?"

"No. He still hasn't had a bail hearing yet." Neither said anything. She heard Rita Jane walking around upstairs, out of earshot. "Did you tell her about us?"

"No way," he said.

"I didn't think so. Are you going to tell her?"

"I don't know. What's there to tell?"

Their conversation was interrupted by Rita Jane bounding down the stairs. She ran to Claudia and hugged her. "Thank you so much for coming to help."

Carrying several loads, it took less than an hour to move Rita Jane's boxes into Amanda's apartment. As she worked, Claudia stewed over Dan's words. What's there to tell? What did he mean by that? Did he mean that he wasn't sure how to explain what had happened or that the experience was so insignificant it was not worth mentioning? She suspected it was the former. Dan was not a cruel person. At least she had never thought he was. Maybe she didn't really know him. Could it be that he was blaming her? Anger coursed through her. How dare he blame her? He had initiated it. She'd been drinking. He'd been totally sober.

She willed herself to stay in the present moment and concentrate on helping Rita Jane. I'm here to help her, not to confront Dan. I can talk to him later if I need to.

As Claudia brought in the last box, Rita Jane was standing in the middle of the living room surveying her possessions. She gestured to the stack of boxes in the middle of the living room, "So this is my life, these few boxes. What does it all mean? What does any of it matter, anyway?"

Dan laughed, "You're not having an early mid-life crisis, are you? You always were precocious."

Claudia couldn't tell whether Rita Jane was seriously upset or just being melodramatic. Rita Jane continued her speech, "I want to do something that matters. That is lasting." She turned to Claudia. "I want to be a mother. I've asked Dan to have a child with me."

Claudia blanched. Her breath caught in her throat. She felt lightheaded. She looked at Dan. He looked at her with a pained expression, his eyes sending her a silent apology.

Claudia tried to hide her surprise, but Rita Jane saw her expression. "He hasn't agreed or anything, I just asked him."

Rita Jane asked Dan, "Is it okay that I told her?"

"Too late to do anything about it now," he replied.

Claudia recovered herself like the good trial lawyer she was. "It's an interesting idea," she said. Her mother had always taught her if you can't find anything else to say, you could at least say that something is interesting.

Claudia had intended to stay and help unpack, but abruptly said, "I've got to go. I'll see you two later."

Claudia saw Rita Jane give Dan a questioning look as she closed the door behind her.

7. Paul's Place

Dan disliked cooking almost as much as he disliked Republicans, so after they had spent the morning moving in, he took Rita Jane to Paul's Place, his home away from home, for lunch. Voted "Best Cheap Eats" by the *City Paper* for each of its two years, the owner, Paul Petrovich, had retired as chief counsel for the Democrats on the House Judiciary Committee after Gingrich and the Republicans declared their "Contract with America," or "Contract on America" as the Democrats preferred to call it. Paul's Place served a diverse menu of homemade food, ranging from tofu cakes to double bacon cheeseburgers, all at reasonable prices. Paul invented daily specials incorporating the political events of the day into their titles. That day's specials were "The Pelosi Burger," a double-bacon cheeseburger with avocado named after Minority Whip Nancy Pelosi in honor of her comments criticizing the President's plan to go to war in Iraq.

Dan knew that Rita Jane would like Paul's Place. She loved art deco and Paul had renovated the old pharmacy and restored its original features. The ceiling was made of tin with an embossed pattern of ivy that formed a square. He had restored the old soda fountain with a long countertop, chrome barstools and red cushions, and an old-fashioned milkshake machine.

"I love this place," Rita Jane said. "Look at that milkshake machine. I want a milkshake. Oh, look at these great stools. Can we sit at the counter?"

They sat on the stools and Dan looked around for Paul. He spotted him in the corner talking with a customer. Dan had been talking up Rita Jane to Paul for weeks. He had described Rita Jane as an Irish fireball — with pale skin, gorgeous red hair and sparkling blue eyes. He had even brought in some of Rita Jane's paintings for Paul to see. Maybe if Rita Jane had a boyfriend, she'd forget about her idea of having a kid with him.

At 43, Paul had the body of a marathon runner and the looks of a CPA. Wiry and muscular, he always walked as though he were running late to an important meeting. His hair, what little still remained, was dirty blond and he wore wire-rimmed glasses.

Dan hoped he had not gone overboard with his matchmaking efforts. Though he loved her dearly, Rita Jane was not looking her best. She hadn't done anything with her hair, her eyes were puffy from crying and lack of sleep and she was wearing gray sweatpants covered with splashes of paint. Plus, she had gained weight and her normally thin waistline was now a small, but noticeable, roll of fat.

Paul slapped Dan on the back and thrust his hand toward Rita Jane. "You must be Rita Jane. I'm Paul Petrovich. Nice to meet you. Dan's been talking about you for weeks."

"Oh he has, has he? Should I be nervous?" Dan was pleased to see that Rita Jane appeared to be flirting a little.

"Only good stuff. Although he did tell me a few of your high school exploits from your days at Sacred Heart. But I promise I'll never tell anyone."

"You brat!" Rita Jane said punching Dan lightly on the shoulder.

"The usual?" Paul asked. Dan nodded and Paul poured Dan a Diet Coke from the soda fountain, placing it in front of him.

"And for the lady?"

"I'd like a milkshake, please. What kind do you recommend?"

"The house specialty is ginger milkshakes. People come from all over the city for them."

"Sounds good."

Paul stepped into a walk-in cooler and removed a large plastic tub of snow-white ice cream. He added milk and vanilla, and, using a small grater, ground up fresh ginger and added it to the mix. "Are you ready to order?" Paul called over his shoulder.

"I'll get the usual," Dan called to Paul. "I get a veggie burger on a croissant with sweet potato French fries. But everything here is good," he explained to Rita Jane.

Paul added a fresh cherry to the milkshake and set it in front of Rita Jane who immediately tasted it. "This is the most delicious thing I have ever tasted," she said in her melodramatic way.

"Thanks," Paul said, clearly pleased. "What would you like to eat?"

"Since Dan's getting a burger, I'll get one, too. Can I get the special?"

"A woman after my own heart," Paul said. "I never meet women who like to eat meat anymore," he said, then immediately looked embarrassed. "I mean, everyone is a vegetarian, or they're all trying to lose weight."

Rita Jane didn't seem offended by the remark. "You've been hanging out with the wrong crowd," she said, giving him a flirtatious smile.

Dan laughed and rolled his eyes, pleased that the two seemed to be hitting it off.

After Paul left, Rita Jane said, "I should probably eat less meat," squeezing her stomach. "I've let myself go since the breakup. I've been indulging in comfort food. Right after Sean told me he didn't want kids I went to the all-night diner and ordered a bacon cheeseburger with fries. And here I am, what's it been nine months, and I'm still eating them."

"It's not like you've ever had a healthy diet anyway," Dan said. "You've always eaten cheeseburgers."

"But I've never had to worry about my weight before," she pouted.

"Welcome to your forties," Dan said.

"I'm not 40 yet."

"If you stop eating meat, those pounds will drop right off." Dan studied her face for a reaction, but if she was upset he couldn't tell. "But you look great anyway."

"Now I know you're lying," she said slurping her milkshake with a straw. It's embarrassing, really, to be coming back to D.C. twenty years later, single, childless, with nothing to show for the last two decades of my life except for the 20 pounds of stomach."

"Please," Dan said. "Give me a break. You've done plenty with your life. Change is good. D.C. is good."

"Take Paul, for example," Dan said, hoping to coax her out of her mood. "He's a great guy."

"He seems nice," Rita Jane agreed. "How long have you been friends?"

"I've known him since I've been working on the Hill. We first met when he was chief counsel for the House Judiciary Committee, in the good old days when the Democrats ran this town."

"Is he a lawyer?"

"I'm afraid so. Once the Republicans took control of the House he couldn't stand it anymore. He lost his opulent office and was relegated to a cramped closet in the basement of the Rayburn Building. He couldn't get anything done that he cared about. He finally decided to quit and open this place."

"Does he have a girlfriend?" Good, Dan thought. Maybe she's interested.

"No. He did. He was engaged to another staffer but they broke up after he left the Hill."

"Hmm," Rita Jane murmured.

Paul brought their meals. "Refill?" Paul asked. Dan nodded. "What about you, Rita Jane?"

"I better not," Rita Jane said wistfully. "Can I get a Diet Coke?"

Paul returned with the drinks. "Dan tells me you're an artist. He showed me your work and I was very impressed. I was wondering if you'd like to have a show here. Every month I feature the work of a different local artist. I've got shows booked through the year, but nothing after that." Dan had been lobbying Paul to show Rita Jane's work thinking it might help pull her out of her slump. But Paul hadn't given him a firm commitment.

"Oh my God, that would be great!" Rita Jane exclaimed.

"I even have an idea for a new series," she said. "I was reading in the paper today about Bush's color-coded terrorist alerts. I thought I'd call the series 'The Color of Fear.' What do you think?"

"That's brilliant," Paul said. "I wonder if anyone has done that yet."

"Not that I know of," Rita Jane replied, "but I'm not really familiar with the D.C. art scene."

"Do you want to pick a date now or let me know later?"

"How about March — for my birthday? It'll be a good way to celebrate."

"Great, I'll put you on the calendar."

Dan nodded at Paul and mouthed, "Thank you," relieved that Rita Jane would have something to focus on in the coming months besides her baby obsession.

8. Settling In

Claudia had felt bad about the awkward scene at Rita Jane's. She had been badly shaken by Rita Jane's announcement she wanted to have a child with Dan, but wasn't sure why. She supposed she was a bit jealous. She missed Dan and wanted their separation ended. It had been easier when there were just the two of them, but like it or not, Rita Jane was now on the scene. Claudia decided to stop by and see how she was doing in her new apartment.

Rita Jane's door was open and the small space was crowded with items spread over every available surface. All of the boxes were open but none were fully unpacked. Being highly organized, Claudia felt uncomfortable with the clutter. Rita Jane was sitting in the middle of the mess contemplating a cobalt blue glass pitcher.

"Hi, I brought you some Chinese food. It's not that good, but it's filling."

"Aren't you kind," Rita Jane said. "I think I had some of that the other night. It wasn't too bad."

Claudia cleared away some space on the table for the food and asked, "Can I help you unpack?"

Rita Jane looked as though Claudia had told her she had won the lottery. "Would you do that? I hate unpacking. Or rather, I start unpacking and end up thinking about every object – where I got it and what it means to me – then I go through a whole debate about where to put it. Anyway, you can see what happens." She spread her arms encompassing the room. "It never gets done."

"Well, I'm the right person for the job. I'm a get-down-to-business kind of girl." Claudia plopped down on the floor next to Rita Jane who handed her the pitcher. "See this? My grandmother Rita brought this back from Germany when she visited in the 1950s."

"It's very nice," Claudia said turning the heavy object over. "Are you named after your grandmother?"

"Yes, both of my grandmothers, actually: Rita and Jane."

Claudia began unpacking a box filled mostly with ceramics, and porcelain teacups. She passed them to Rita Jane who gave her the story behind each object. Teacups collected on travels to Asia, family heirlooms, stuff she picked up in secondhand stores. Rita Jane loved beautiful objects. After telling the story behind each treasure, she consulted Claudia as to where she should put it. Rita Jane had been right, it was a slow process, but the two fell into a companionable rhythm.

At the very bottom of the box Rita Jane pulled out her high school yearbook. "Oh, I've got to show you Dan's senior picture. He was such a hunk."

Claudia remembered that the two had gone to the same private high school. Rita Jane flipped open to the page, "Wasn't he cute?"

Claudia read the caption, "To Rita Jane, the funniest person I know. I hope we are always friends. Love, Dan."

"He was cute." Claudia was pretty sure she knew the answer but she asked anyway, "Did you two ever date? I mean were you ever involved?"

"No." Rita Jane looked lovingly at the picture. "I wish we could be involved. That would be so much easier. I mean, I love him and he loves me. But he's gay. You know he's never been with a woman. That's pretty amazing really. A lot of gay guys have sex with women at some point."

"Hum." Claudia didn't know what to say. She started to understand more Dan's reluctance to tell her. Was Rita Jane in love with Dan?

"Enough about me," Rita Jane said. "And no, I'm not in love with Dan, if that's what you're thinking. I love him, but it's more like he's my brother. I was an only child and I think I kind of made him into a brother. What I meant about wishing we could be involved is just that I wish I would meet someone like Dan, whom I loved as much as I love him."

Claudia nodded. "I know what you mean."

Rita Jane smiled. "Tell me your story. How did you end up at TLC?"

Claudia stopped unwrapping for a moment and tucked her long hair behind her ears. "Well, it's kind of a convoluted tale," she began. "I had been part of a cohousing community in Seattle. My partner, Claire, and I had been two of the founding members. But then we broke up — or rather she broke up with me. She left me for another woman. A friend of ours from the community. It broke my heart. I tried to stay on. I had helped found the community and didn't want to leave, but after a few months I knew I had to get on with my life. It was too painful to see them together."

Claudia paused and Rita Jane reached over and touched her on the shoulder. "That's rough," she said. "It must have been so hard for you."

Claudia nodded, and to her surprise felt tears coming on. She pushed them back. "There's a happy ending. One night, while surfing on the Internet, I found TLC's website. I called the next day and learned they were still accepting members. A month later, Bob and I were on the road headed east."

"Bob?"

"My car."

"That's quite a story," Rita Jane said.

"Yeah, sometimes I can't even believe it myself. But it turned out to be the perfect thing for me to do. I love it here and it has been much easier to start a new life without the constant reminders of Claire."

"Whatever happened to Claire? If you don't mind me asking," Rita Jane said.

"Oh, after about a year, she and her little tart broke up. She wanted me to move back to Seattle but I said no way. Once the trust was broken I could never go back."

"Were you glad when they broke up?" Rita Jane asked.

"A little bit, at first, but then I felt sorry for Claire. I want her to be happy, and I know she is happier when she has a girlfriend. I don't want her anymore, but I hope she finds someone else to love."

Neither of them said anything for a few moments, in respect for the intimacy that had been shared. Then Rita Jane asked, "Have you ever been with a man?"

Claudia was taken aback, unsure why Rita Jane was asking. "Yes, I had always been with men before Claire. And I had a brief affair with someone in D.C."

Claudia waited, hoping Rita Jane would let it go at that. Fortunately, she did.

"Well, he was a lucky guy," Rita Jane concluded.

9. Columbus Day Barbecue

The annual TLC Columbus Day Barbecue brought together people from the neighborhood for an evening of grilled food, games and political speeches. Paul, who lived down the block from TLC, came every year, with his award-winning barbecue sauce that made the vegetarians rethink their eating habits. Dan served as the vegetarian grill master, serving up tofu pups and veggie burgers, but he secretly missed the wafting smells of roasting meat, which stirred memories of childhood and summertime.

Claudia and Rita Jane were talking together on a bench in the corner of the piazza. This pleased Dan, but it made things more complicated. Dan hadn't told Rita Jane about that night with Claudia. But what was there to tell? He and Claudia had been good friends for two years and one night they drank too much and went to bed together. It was such a common story as to be cliché. The fact that they were both gay did make the situation a bit unusual he supposed. If Rita Jane learned about the incident it would only boost her crazy idea of them having a child together. She'd say that if he could have sex with one woman, why not another one? Rita Jane had said she didn't want to have sex with him, but he wondered. He sometimes thought that she wished they were a couple. Having sex with Rita Jane would be like having sex with one of his sisters. He hadn't disliked sex with Claudia, it simply felt odd and he didn't really understand why he had done it in the first place. He wanted to blame it on alcohol, but truthfully, Claudia had been drunk. He had been sober. She had asked him to spend the night, but he was the one who had initiated sex. Freud would have had a good time analyzing this situation.

But that one night of intimacy had extracted a large emotional price. Since then, they were polite with each other, but had not spoken about it. Neither knew what to say. He had even wondered about his sexuality for the first time since he was in high school. He had always considered himself a 6 on the Kinsey scale — completely homosexual. But what if he was really bisexual? If so, why not just be with women? Lord knows it would make some parts of his life easier. And if he was going to be with a woman, why not be with Rita Jane? Or Claudia for that matter? He loved them both. Maybe he should have a child with Rita Jane. He wasn't having much luck meeting a man who wanted to have a family and children.

He regretted that he had ever opened that Pandora's box. He knew he was gay. So why had he slept with Claudia? That was the question he couldn't answer.

Rita Jane noticed him and rushed over. "I'm having so much fun," she said, hugging him. "I love your neighbors."

Dan kissed her perfunctorily on the cheek. "I'm glad. I saw you talking to Claudia," he said trying to sound nonchalant.

"She told me about her friend, Emad. She's very worried about him. It sounds like a completely bogus charge. I can't believe he is in jail on something like that. Anyway, she seems really nice and very dedicated to her job."

Dan didn't say anything. Claudia was nice, which made the situation that much more awkward.

Various neighbors clustered around Rita Jane, eager to meet the newcomer. Rita Jane loved the attention. He felt the echo of a memory from high school when Rita Jane had been the popular one and he had been the fat kid. That was twenty years ago. He was no longer the overweight kid who was confused about his sexuality. He had lots of friends and didn't need to compete with Rita Jane.

Rita Jane had sat down next to Paul and Dan overheard their conversation. "Will people eat that stuff?" she asked Paul. "I thought they were all veggies."

Paul said, "My barbecue sauce separates out the real vegetarians. The closet meat eaters can't resist it."

"It smells divine," Rita Jane said. "Although I have to admit hanging out with all these vegetarians is making me re-think the meat thing."

"I knew it! They're brainwashing you. Thank God I arrived just in time. One bite of my barbecued ribs and you'll swear off vegetarianism forever."

"She'll see the light," Dan interrupted. "Want a beer?" he asked Paul.

Paul nodded and Dan opened a Corona Light and handed it to him.

"When do the speeches begin?" Paul asked.

"Soon," Dan said.

People were wearing shorts and T-shirts, enjoying the end of the Indian summer. Aimee dragged an apple crate into the middle of the piazza. "It's time for the speeches," she announced, mounting the box. "I'll go first." She wore tight jeans and a snug T-shirt. She pushed her long hair behind her ears and cleared her throat.

"This ought to be good," Dan said under his breath.

"On this day, our country takes time to honor a man, Christopher Columbus, who history claims was a brave explorer. When Columbus landed in the Americas, it was the beginning of European conquest and colonization of the native people who lived here. Ultimately, the native people were largely destroyed by disease and war, and although many descendants of those cultures survive today, they are weakened, having been decimated by the foreign invaders. Today we commit to working for justice and a new America. Instead of honoring the colonists, we pay tribute to the Native Americans who opened their country to our ancestors, and from whom we must learn how to honor and protect the earth."

She stepped off the crate to applause and accolades. She curtsied, revealing her cleavage. Paul gave her a high five. Dan thought his eyes lingered a little too long on her body. He couldn't imagine what Paul saw in her. Besides being a troublemaker and a know-it-all, she was barely half Paul's age.

Aimee tapped Paul on the shoulder. "You're next, handsome."

Paul handed Dan his beer. "Mind this for me, please." He stepped onto the crate and looked back and forth surveying the crowd. "Maybe Columbus wasn't the nicest guy around, but hey, that was a long time ago. We need to focus on today's problems. Our present problem is yet another war, although this one will be outside of the Americas. I urge all of you to oppose this war and all the rest of Bush's aggressive, undemocratic policies."

He stepped off the box and took back his beer. "That wasn't too lame," Aimee teased.

Paul pointed to a handsome man wearing loose fitting white clothes and a headdress accompanied by a large, smiling woman and a young girl. "Rizwan, you're much more articulate then I am. Let's hear from you."

Rizwan, a local activist and friend of Emad's walked to the center of the crowd and bowed slightly. "Neighbors, let me first thank you for inviting my family once again to this auspicious occasion. We are truly honored to share this meal with you."

A few people cheered.

"These are difficult times, my friends. Difficult indeed. Many in my community live in fear. As you know, my brother Emad was arrested a week ago. He was detained for two days before he was allowed to see a lawyer or anyone in his family. The government says he is a terrorist, but you know Emad. He is a good man. He is a family man. He has been your neighbor. He loves this country. My family left our country to get away from these types of abuse. I am sorry to see that we are once again forced to live in fear of a tyrannical government."

Rizwan paused for a moment and took a sip of his drink. "Now our country is preparing to invade Iraq. Friends, I am no friend of Saddam Hussein, but if the United States invades Iraq it will only make more enemies. There is a meeting at the Peace Center next Saturday. Anyone who is interested in speaking out against another war, please join us.

He bowed again and returned to a large woman wearing a headscarf and holding a small girl.

Dan jabbed Rita Jane in the ribs and said out loud, "I think it's time that we hear from the newest member of our community."

"Good idea," Paul said.

"I'll pass," Rita Jane said.

"You can't. If you're picked you've got to go."

"I don't have anything to say," she pleaded.

Dan rolled his eyes. "You'll have to improvise."

Rita Jane stood on the crate and smiled. Rita Jane was a born entertainer. She came alive on a stage, even an apple crate. "For those of you who don't know me, I'm Rita Jane. I'm renting Amanda's place and I just want to say that I am so happy to have found such a great place to live with such wonderful people. I don't have a lot to say about Columbus, but I'm glad that I live in a community where people care so much about the world. That's all." Dan smiled. That was his Rita Jane, charming the audience.

She hopped off the box and walked over to him. "That wasn't too bad, was it?"

"Bad — you were great!" Paul said. He stabbed a hunk of ribs with a long, two-pronged fork.

Dan loaded up a large plastic platter with tofu hotdogs, barbecued tempeh and grilled zucchini, eggplant, onion and red and green peppers. "Dinner's ready." He said, glancing at Paul, "At least for the vegetarians."

* * *

After dinner, there were games of bocce, croquet and badminton. Paul offered to teach Rita Jane how to play bocce, which pleased Dan. Dan played croquet. As much as he tried to act otherwise, Dan was fiercely competitive. He hated to lose. Through most of the game, he was neck and neck with Claudia until the end when he whacked his ball into hers and sent it flying off the course and into a clump of dried up daisies. Claudia glared at him.

"What a gentlemen. You sure know how to use your balls"

Dan didn't say anything. He stopped himself from calling her a spoilsport. He had grown up with five sisters and was used to women being overly sensitive. Of course he wanted to win. Who wouldn't send their competitor's ball away if given the chance?

Rita Jane bounded over with a blue ribbon that declared her the winner of the Columbus Day bocce tournament. "That's great. You won your first time playing," Dan exclaimed, pleased to see her and Paul spending time together.

Rita Jane grinned. "No thanks to me. If I hadn't been on the same team as Paul I would have lost. And it looks like you won over here."

"Claudia gave me a run for my money," Dan said, "but I salvaged victory on the last hole, knocking her ball out of the course."

Rita Jane punched him on his shoulder. "Why'dya do that, you meanie?"

"It's a game, for Christ's sake. The object is to win," he said testily.

"She probably let you win," Rita Jane said.

"No she didn't," Dan said. "Claudia likes to win more than anyone I know." He smiled at Claudia, but she didn't look amused.

"I was just teasing you," Rita Jane said, "Lighten up." Dan cringed. He wanted to lighten up, but he wasn't sure he knew how. Maybe if he told Rita Jane about Claudia, he'd be less anxious. He'd tell her tomorrow. For now, he just wanted another beer.

He grabbed one from the cooler and saw Aimee and Paul leaving together, hand in hand. Shit, Dan thought. It's too late.

10. Defending Emad

To her astonishment, Claudia had been unable to get Emad out of jail over the weekend, and feared that defending him was going to be a much harder task than she had thought. At the weekend arraignment, the judge had temporarily appointed the federal defender to represent Emad, with the appointment to be reviewed in a month. Emad was not indigent, so normally he would not qualify for the public defender. However, the family had contacted a number of firms and had been unable to pay the large retainers they were asking. Given the seriousness of the charges, the judge did not want Emad to go unrepresented. Claudia's supervisor had agreed to let Claudia continue representing Emad, and had even lightened her caseload so she would have plenty of time to devote to the case.

Claudia knew she could get Emad out of jail. She just needed to find the right words to convince the judge that Emad was a nice, normal, family man, not a terrorist.

Everything had to be perfect for the hearing. She dressed and undressed several times before settling on her best power suit — a blue silk pantsuit with thin white pin stripes. She felt a thrill of excitement mingled with dread. She loved challenging cases, but she had never represented an accused terrorist or, for that matter, a friend. Emad was charged with providing material aid to terrorists under the USA PATRIOT Act that had passed in the wake of the September 11 attacks and was the government's favorite new weapon in its "war on terror."

She arrived at the federal courthouse early with time to visit her client before the hearing started. Plus, she liked to arrive in the courtroom before the prosecutor did. The government had most of the advantages in criminal cases, so she tried to make sure that she was better prepared than the prosecutor. Arriving early made her feel in control.

She went in the side door of the courthouse, avoiding a throng of reporters that she suspected were there for the hearing. She jogged down the stairs two at a time and entered the holding area where prisoners who had court hearings spent the day waiting their turn.

"Morning counselor," said Officer Peters, the transport officer. "Are you here to see Mr. Khadonry?" Claudia appreciated Officer Peters' treatment of her clients. Most other officers would have made a crack about him being a terrorist. Peters gave her clients the benefit of the doubt.

Emad looked like he hadn't slept in 48 hours. Huge bags hung below his eye sockets, and his skin had lost its usual healthy glow making his wrinkles more pronounced. He smiled weakly at her.

"I read the papers," Emad said, handing her the charging document. "They say I gave money to a terrorist organization. I gave money to Widows and Orphans, an organization that provides support for the families of Hamas who die in the war. The money goes to feeding and clothing hungry children. If that is terrorism, then I am proud to be a terrorist," he said.

"I agree, the case is weak, but I'd rather discuss it sometime when we have more privacy. Today, my job is to get you out of jail. Your bail has been set at $500,000, which is unheard of for a man with no criminal record and strong ties to the community. I arranged with Sarah for you to post your home as collateral, which is valued at $489,000, and Sarah believes your family can send the remainder in cash."

"Yes," he nodded. "Will the judge agree to it?"

In any other case, Claudia would have been sure that those bail arrangements would have been sufficient to get her client released, but she felt like she didn't know the rules of this new game. She didn't want Emad to get his hopes up.

"You have to prepare yourself emotionally," she said. "The prosecutor is going to say things that are hard to hear. He's going to use the T word. Don't lose your cool. Don't let him goad you on. Let me do the talking unless the judge addresses you directly."

By the time the hearing started, self-righteous anger coursed through her veins, as injustice always enraged her. How could she convince the judge that her client was in jail because he was an Arab? If he'd been an Irishman living in Boston who had sent money to the IRA, the U.S. government would not be prosecuting him. She herself had given money to the African National Congress in the days when they were fighting apartheid. He was an Arab from Jordan fighting for his cause – how was that any different?

Federal District Court Judge Scott Taylor walked into the courtroom and everyone stood up. A former public defender, he bent over backward to prove he wasn't pro-defense. Strike two was Jim Allen, the Assistant U.S. Attorney assigned to the case, who was her least favorite prosecutor, which was saying a lot because Claudia generally disliked all prosecutors. Jim was a tough-on-crime kind of guy.

"You may proceed, Ms. Connors," the judge nodded at her.

"Your honor. Mr. Emad meets all the qualifications to be released on bail. He is not a danger to the community and he is not a flight risk. He has lived in the District for 20 years. He is employed. He owns his own home and he works full-time. He has a family and is well respected in the community. He doesn't have any criminal record. He can post his home as collateral for the bail and pay the remainder in cash.

"If Mr. Khadonry is so flush, why is the public defender agency representing him?" the Judge asked.

"Your honor, he attempted to retain private counsel over the weekend, but he couldn't find anyone willing to take his case for less than $100,000. He does not have that kind of money available. Under the circumstances, our office is representing him until he can retain private counsel. Also, Mr. Khadonry is a personal friend."

"Your honor, may I be heard?" Jim Allen whined. "With all due respect to my colleague, friend or no friend, this man is a terrorist. He has provided material support to Al-Qaeda. He is just as responsible for 9/11 as the murderers that flew the planes."

"Objection," Claudia said, reminding herself to stay calm. Allen wanted her to lose her cool and the reporters would have a field day if she did. "The prosecutor is making ad-hominem attacks against my client. There is no evidence to support any of these allegations. He has not put forward a single fact to suggest any connection with Al-Qaeda."

She glared at Allen and saw him smirking. "Your honor," he said obsequiously, "Much of the indictment is based on confidential information. The grand jury proceeding has been sealed because it contains information that, if made public, would compromise our national security."

Allen was at his most slimy. His arrogance enraged her. She was in danger of losing her temper. "Your honor, this is outrageous. We do not live in a police state. The prosecution is required to give me the information necessary to defend my client."

"Well, actually, your honor, we do have the authority to keep some information confidential if it is going to compromise national security. Ms. Connors should know that if she keeps up with the law."

"Under the circumstances, Ms. Connors, I'm going to deny bail. You're free to make another application in the future, but I want assurances that Mr. Khadonry is not a security risk."

Anger roiled through her. She wanted to scream. She wanted to grab Emad and run with him out of the room. Emad was not a terrorist. "I'm sorry," she said to her client as the transport officer escorted him out of the room in handcuffs and leg chains.

As soon as she opened the courtroom door, a throng of reporters descended on her. "Ms. Connors, would you like to comment on Judge Taylor's denial of Emad Khadonry's bail?"

Claudia rarely granted press interviews. The media never reported stories in a way that was beneficial to her clients. However, this was

not a legal battle, it was a political one, and she had to get public sentiment on her side.

"I believe it is a tragic day for our country when a law-abiding citizen
can be held on half-a-million dollars bail without being informed of the
nature of the charges against him."

11. Dan Learns a Secret

Dan spent most Wednesdays at the Meet Market, the premier meeting
spot for gay men seeking a refuge from the nightclubs haunted by the
twenty-something crowd. Wednesdays the DJ played songs of the '70s
and '80s and some people, certainly not Dan, wore bell-bottoms and
wide leather belts with fringes or other appropriate attire from that era.
Dan wore black jeans and a black muscle T-shirt.

Dan sought escape in dancing. Claudia had not managed to get' Emad
out of jail and the two of them had still not spoken about "that night." Nor
had Dan told Rita Jane about the "incident" with Claudia. He hoped that
the hot sexual energy of the club would distract him from his worries.

A sense of optimism buoyed Dan as he surveyed the crowded room,
ever hopeful that maybe this night he would meet "the one." Realisti-
cally, he knew that he had a better chance of finding sex than love at
the Meet Market, but he held out hope. One of his best friends had met
his partner here and now they were in the process of adopting a baby. It
could happen to him, too.

The Market, as everyone called it, had been a warehouse in a previous incarnation. Now its gaily-painted walls were decorated with all the
colors of the rainbow. The sign at the entranceway read: "Men looking
for men meet at the Market."

On the blue dance floor, men gyrated, with varying degrees of grace,
to a loud pop beat. The room reeked of sweat and desire. After determin-
ing that there wasn't anyone he was interested in, he made his way to
the bar, where the bartender placed a large glass of Diet Coke in front of
him. Dan never drank alcohol at bars, not wanting alcohol to cloud his judgment about sex. He had known too many people who had died that way.

A very handsome tall blond, who looked like he had just stepped off a
Viking ship, sidled up beside him.

"Are you a local?" he asked Dan.

"Yes. Are you a foreign invader?" Dan asked, knowing the answer.
Only someone who lived outside the District would start a conversation
by asking if you were a local. A Washingtonian would ask what you did
for work before asking you your name.

The Viking laughed. "I guess you could say that. I'm from Minnesota.
I came with our local Pride group for our annual lobby day."

"Great," Dan said. "Are you having any success?"

"Some. Our delegation is either all with us or to the right of Attila the Hun."

"I know all too well."

If he asked the guy's name that would mean a longer conversation and he didn't want to narrow his options so early in the evening. But the man seemed nice enough, and Dan had come to the Market to meet people, so what was the harm?

"I'm John Anderson, by the way," the man said sticking out his hand in greeting.

"Dan Canavan." John wore an outfit, which was similar to Dan's, but his T-shirt was red instead of black. As they shook hands, Dan noticed John's well-built arms and felt a shiver of excitement.

"Would you like to sit down?" John asked. The two searched around the crowded room and found two metal stools in a corner by a large window that opened to an outside deck. A warm summer breeze cooled the split pea-soup air, calming their nervousness. Between the noise from the street and the pounding of the music, they had to scream to hear each other.

"Do you work on the Hill?" John yelled.

Dan nodded. "I'm a lobbyist."

"Are you one of those high-powered movers and shakers?"

"Not really. I work for OutReach. We're a nonprofit, so we don't have a lot of money. But we do okay. We move and shake it up a little."

"I know OutReach." John leaned backwards in his chair. Dan admired his flat stomach. This guy was hot. He looked at John's face so as not to be rude. John continued, "You guys are great. I give you money all the time. What issues are you working on?"

Dan reached for some pretzels in the small metal bowl on the table. "We work on all kinds of issues, but the main thing I'm working on now is opposing SOFA, the Sanctity of Family Act."

"I know what SOFA is," John said with a slight tone of annoyance. "That bill is so outrageous. We finally start to make a little progress in the states and the feds interfere. Personally, I don't understand the hype about some of the things we're fighting for. Like marriage. It's so passé. But if straight people can marry, we should be able to, too."

Dan cringed. He hated it when people downplayed the importance of gay marriage. Dan's life mission was making gay marriage legal. "It's not hype, it's about legal rights: inheritance, health insurance, end-of-life decisions, raising children, everything important."

John put up his hand, "Hey, calm down. I know the drill. I told you, I agree, gay people should have the right. Personally, I think marriage is a bit passé."

Typical, Dan thought. I'm looking for a man who wants to get married and have kids and I'm spending time talking to a guy who lives halfway across the country and doesn't believe in marriage. Lighten up Dan. It's only a conversation.

"I want to get married," Dan declared. "I mean, if I meet the right person. But then again, I grew up Catholic, so I probably can't help myself."

John laughed. "I grew up on a commune. My parents didn't believe in marriage or religion. They named me after John Anderson, the third party presidential candidate. Things were rather loose in my family. That probably explains my feelings about marriage."

Dan, who thought that everyone who lived in the middle of the country belonged to some Protestant sect, was surprised to learn there were communes in Minnesota. But he kept his thoughts to himself and said, "It's amazing how much of that early childhood conditioning stays with you."

Dan excused himself to go to the bathroom. Standing at the urinal, Dan gave himself a pep talk. He knew the likely course of the evening. He had decisions to make. Did he want to continue to flirt with John? Did he want to go home with him? John seemed nice enough, but he reminded himself that his goal was to be in a committed relationship. John didn't fit the bill. But what's wrong with a little sex in the meantime? Dan looked down the line of urinals. There was a very young man with an eager expression on his face and a splotchy, overweight, balding man. John looked very good in comparison.

"Dancing Queen" came on over the loudspeaker and most of the sitters joined the dancers on the floor. John moved gracefully for a tall man and Dan lost himself in the sea of bodies. The tempo picked up with "Staying Alive." John grabbed Dan by his hip, rubbing against him. The hot lights and contact were arousing Dan. By the time the DJ played "YMCA" everyone was on the floor, moving their arms in unison forming the letters of the song. Dan forgot about Emad.

When everyone started lining up to do the Macarena, John asked, "Want to go somewhere else?"

Despite his ambivalence about casual sex, Dan agreed.

When they got to the room, the sheets on the king-sized bed had been turned down and two squares of chocolate had been placed on the pillow. John opened a small refrigerator filled with tiny bottles of liquor and overpriced candy bars.

"Can I offer you a drink?"

Dan flopped down on the overstuffed couch and pondered the question. Now that he had made the decision to sleep with John, his no-alcohol rule technically no longer applied. John walked towards him with a questioning expression on his face. Dan noticed his cologne – he was trying to place the fragrance – and decided against alcohol.

"Water would be great."

John took two bottles of water from the mini-bar and handed one to Dan. He let his fingers linger on Dan's hand as he passed him the bottle. He sat down next to Dan, close enough so that Dan noticed John's taut thighs. He took a large swallow of cold water, contemplating his next move.

That day's paper was open to a picture of James Weymouth, Chairman of the House Judiciary Committee. "Turn that paper over," Dan said. "I can't get it up looking at that guy. He's my nemesis."

"Really, why's that?" John asked.

"Just that he's bad on every single issue I care about."

"I met him. He seemed nice."

"You know him?" Dan asked, astounded. "How do you know him? He's one of the most powerful men in Washington." Maybe John was more than just a backwater hick from a Minnesota commune.

"I follow politics a little, but I don't know who is chair of what committee," John said, sounding a little embarrassed.

"He's been in Congress several terms but he's only been chairman since last election," Dan explained.

"He's gay." John said matter-of-factly as if everyone knew it.

"What are you talking about?" Dan asked, wondering if John was crazy. He stared at him in utter disbelief. "He's married. He has three blond children."

"He's in the closet," John said.

"I'd say he's in more than a closet!" Dan looked at John intently, trying to ascertain if he was joking. "How do you know this? Are you messing with me?"

"I slept with him," John said. Dan was speechless, a condition he didn't experience often. John continued, "I was at Ole Miss for a conference on endangered species. He was there making his token appearance as the Congressman of the First District." John cocked his head, reminiscing. "We both took a side trip to Faulkner's House then had dinner together and one thing led to another. He's a nice guy."

"He's a nice guy alright if you ignore his politics," Dan said sarcastically. "He's letting the Republicans ram SOFA through the House." Dan paused, "Although I admit, I did think it was a little strange that he never became a sponsor."

Dan's mind was racing with possibilities: exposing Weymouth on Fox News, giving the *Post* an exclusive story or maybe even giving the story to the *Times*. This could mean the end of Weymouth if he exposed it right before the election.

"Have you told anyone about this – anyone who's influential?" Dan asked.

"No," John said. "I don't believe in sleeping and telling."

"Of course not," Dan said with a tone that suggested he would never think of such an idea. "I'm surprised he slept with you. I'd think he'd be afraid of blackmail."

"I'm just a hick from Minnesota. I'd never heard of him." John flashed a broad smile. "Plus, he could tell I'm a nice guy."

But I'm not, Dan thought. "Do you have any proof of this affair?"

John looked at him suspiciously. "Why do you ask? What are you going to do with it?"

Dan considered what tack to take. "Listen, he's chairman of the committee with jurisdiction over the biggest issue threatening our community, and he's doing nothing to stop it."

John shrugged. "He can't be perceived being in favor of gay rights. It would be political suicide," he said, stating the obvious.

"So instead he gets elected on the homophobe platform while he's in the closet." Dan's voice rose, "What kind of hypocrisy is that?"

John looked thoughtful. "I suppose you're right." He leaned back on the couch and reached over to touch Dan on the shoulder. "This wasn't exactly what I had in mind when I invited you over."

Dan's mind snapped back to the moment. "I'm sorry," Dan reached over and squeezed John's hand. "I can't think about sex right now." He laughed, "I guess I am thinking about sex. I mean, I can't think about doing it myself, I'm too distracted." He gave John his best don't-be-mad-at-me look. "You have to understand, this is the most amazing news of my political career." Trying to steer the conversation back to Weymouth, he asked, "Do you have any proof or not?" he sounded pushy even to himself.

John thought for a moment. "I have a letter — a note really. We slept together twice. He left me a note in my hotel room: "Thanks for a wonderful time. Love, Jim.""

"Not much to go on," Dan said. "Why'd you keep it?" Dan asked, assuming an unsavory motive.

John shrugged. "I'm a romantic. I keep all that kind of stuff."

Dan hesitated momentarily, self-conscious about what he was asking. "Would you show it to me?"

John frowned. "I don't believe in outing people. If he wants to remain in the closet, that's his business."

Dan prepared to launch into a diatribe about the importance of the issue, but he stopped himself. Bullying John wasn't going to get him what he wanted. Besides, what could he do with a note? "I understand. I'm not sure it's worth much anyway," Dan said, trying to hide his disappointment.

Dan stood up. "I should go. Look, I'm sorry that we got off course. I'm such a political junky. You can't know what this news means to me."

John nodded, "I think I have an idea."

Dan reached into his back pocket. "Here's my card. Give me a call if you come to town again." He wanted to add, or if you want to mail me something, but he didn't.

John reached over and took the card. "I'm sorry," he said. "I shouldn't have told you."

"Don't be ridiculous," Dan exclaimed. "Don't be sorry. I wouldn't have missed this for the world. At least it will give me something to laugh about. I'm the one that's sorry that I'm so caught up with my work I can't let it go."

"I'm glad there are people like you doing what you do," John said.

Dan let himself out of the room, his mind buzzing.

12. Election Results

Esme Root, a stalwart denizen of the TLC community, hosted election night parties. Her lovely home with a wide-open first floor was decorated with her work and the work of other artists. Esme answered the door wearing a long, purple silk caftan with a gold link chain around her waist, looking like she belonged in the royal court of Louis XIV. Claudia and Rita Jane arrived together, and were greeted with the sad news that the Republicans were sweeping the mid-term elections.

"We're going to need more than that, girls," Esme sighed referring to the two bottles of wine Claudia had brought. "The bad guys are winning, again. Fortunately for me I've begun looking into emigrating to Canada. There's an artist commune there, and I hear there is a need for sculptors."

Claudia felt like a crow in a pen of peacocks next to Rita Jane and Esme. Arriving straight from work, she was wearing a boring, black pant suit, while Rita Jane had on a red mini skirt, black fish net tights, an intricately embroidered peasant blouse and a black silk jacket studded with rhinestones.

Esme embraced them both, "Dan is beside himself, of course."

Claudia had barely paid attention to the elections this year because she had been so engrossed with more important matters – representing Emad. She had still not managed to get her client out of jail, a fact that irked her daily.

Rita Jane was arranging appetizers on one of Esme's enormous ceramic trays when Paul arrived, wearing tan khaki pants, a button-down shirt, and a jacket. He kissed all three women, but his eyes lingered on Rita Jane's legs, "You look great," he said to her.

Claudia agreed with Paul's assessment. Rita Jane did look great. Claudia hadn't seen her wear anything except sweats and jeans since moving to TLC. Rita Jane said thank you without revealing whether she appreciated the compliment.

The large screen TV was turned to CNN, which aired a running commentary as the election results poured in across the country.

Dan, Frances, Aimee, and Frank, Esme's husband, were in the living room glued to CNN.

"It's worse than we feared. The Republicans are gaining ground. It looks like they're going to hold the Senate and gain a few more seats," Dan informed them before gulping down the rest of his Corona.

"I think we can officially declare this event a wake, my dear," Frank said to Esme.

Esme passed around a tray of whole-wheat pita breads with ceramic bowls of hummus and baba ghanouj. Claudia was too depressed to eat. The last Republican-controlled Congress had passed the PATRIOT Act and detention of suspected "terrorists" without trial or access to legal counsel. Things were not looking good for Emad.

She half watched the election returns distracted by worrying about her case and watching Paul flirt with Rita Jane. She barely heard Esme announce dinner. Everyone moved over to the dining area, except Dan, who refused to leave his vigil. To Claudia's surprise, Rita Jane left Paul and sat down next to her.

"Tell us about your case," Frank said, pouring Claudia a glass of white wine.

"It's a disaster. It'll just make you more depressed."

Rita Jane gave her a cute pout and patted her on the shoulder. "If it'll help you to talk about it, we'll listen."

The remark cheered Claudia.

"Yes, please do talk about it," Frank said, "I'm thinking of using it in my political science class as a case study."

"He's charged with providing material support to terrorists under the PATRIOT Act because he sent money to a charitable organization, Widows and Orphans. Widows and Orphans provides financial support to family members of people who have died in the Palestinian conflict, some of whom were suicide bombers. The U.S. government claims the organization is a front for Hamas, and may have ties to Al-Qaeda."

"Is it true?" Frank asked.

"I can't tell. The government won't provide me with the financial records, claiming they're classified. It's impossible for me to figure out what connection there may be."

"That's outrageous," Aimee said. "There has been a direct pipeline for years between the Boston elite and the IRA, which is as much, if not more, of a terrorist organization than Hamas. But since half the members of Congress are Irish, I guess that's not considered terrorism."

"I know," Claudia said. "I even made that argument in court, but it's a bit like saying you can't prosecute one person for shoplifting because you haven't prosecuted everyone. It's not a winning argument."

Aimee harrumphed.

"You're not going to win this case in court anyway," Paul said. "This is a political issue. The only way you are going to win is if you get public opinion on your side. We need to raise money for a public education campaign."

"Right. In case you hadn't noticed, there's not a lot of support for accused terrorists these days," Claudia said.

"People don't know what's going on," Esme said. "There's too much happening. Everybody's attention has been focused on the snipers. Thank God they were arrested. People can't keep track of everything. You've got to do something to draw attention to your issue."

"Like what?" Aimee said. "You have to run around naked shooting people to get the media to cover your issue these days."

"Are nude demonstrations the next thing on your agenda?" Frances asked Aimee.

"I hadn't thought of it, but now that you've suggested it I'll bring it up at our next meeting," Aimee replied.

Claudia wasn't in the mood to hear the two of them bicker and was relieved when Esme suggested, "Why don't the two of you organize an event together?"

"That's less likely than Bush hosting Osama bin Laden at the White House," Paul said, laughing.

"I think it's a great idea," Esme said. "I could solicit artists to donate work and we could make it a fundraiser to help cover Emad's legal expenses. Rita Jane could help me — that way she'd get to know other artists in the community."

"I'll cater the event," Paul offered.

"What do you say, Rita Jane?" Esme asked.

"Sure. My show is opening in March at Paul's Place. We could do it then. I'll donate my proceeds to the cause."

"You'd do that?" Claudia asked incredulously. As far as she could tell, Rita Jane had very little money. Through tears, Claudia said, "I can't believe you would do that for a person you've never met." The act of generosity buoyed her spirits. Things were looking up.

Dan returned from the living room with the sobering news that the Republicans had picked up three seats in Texas.

"SOFA will pass without a hitch," Dan said. "Should I kill myself now or later?"

"You can't kill yourself now," Esme said. "We have too much work to do. Rita Jane and I are going to have a fundraising event for Emad. We need your excellent organizing skills to pull it together."

"I wouldn't worry about raising money for Emad's defense. They'll probably deport him without a trial," Dan said.

"What a horrible thing to say," Rita Jane said.

"Ignore him." Paul said. "He's got the post-election blues. It can last a long time, sometimes weeks and months."

"Sometimes years," Dan said. "Every election I tell myself it can't get any worse, and every two years it does."

"Well, as you said, there's always suicide," Claudia said, more harshly than she had intended.

"Touché," Dan said.

13. Going to Any Lengths

Claudia watched her client walk along the corridor to the attorney visiting room. Normally a vibrant man, Emad shuffled slowly. He had lost 20 pounds since being in prison due to the fact that prison officials refused to provide him vegetarian food. Claudia had argued with the prison officials all the way up to the warden about providing vegetarian alternatives for her client and had even filed a motion in federal court arguing that the jail must accommodate her client's religious beliefs and provide a vegetarian diet, but the request was denied because Islam did not require its adherents to be vegetarians.

The prison smelled like antiseptic mixed with men's locker room. Apparent order masked chaos and violence. Claudia rarely felt uncomfortable with her clients, whom she usually trusted, something she couldn't say for the guards. Many guards treated her clients decently, but some did not. She worried that Emad's terrorism charge would make him a target for bullies.

Claudia wished she had some good news for her client. Things were not going well in his case. She had written a beautifully compelling (she thought) motion to force the government to turn over the financial records of Widows and Orphans and any other alleged "terrorist" organizations, but so far it had not been granted. She had racked her brain for new arguments to get Emad out of jail, again with no success.

Meanwhile, Emad languished at the federal holding facility in Virginia and Claudia felt helpless and discouraged when she went to visit her client.

"Salamo Alaikom," Emad greeted her smiling graciously, which only increased Claudia's feelings of guilt over her failure to help him. "How's life on the outside?"

"The world is falling apart I'm afraid. The Republicans picked up even more seats in Congress. I shudder to think what they'll do next."

Emad nodded. His dark brown eyes twinkled. "Sometimes things have to get worse before they get better."

"Yes, but how much worse can they get?" Claudia whined.

"Unfortunately, quite a bit."

"Things aren't going well with your case, either, I'm afraid. The government won't give me the financial records of Widows and Orphans. I don't know how I can possibly defend you without them."

"Why don't you contact Widows and Orphans?" Emad suggested. "You could send a letter requesting the records on my behalf. I'll write it and you send it and I'm sure they'll give you whatever you need. In fact, I was going to ask you to mail some letters to my family for me. We could write the letter now and you could mail them all."

Claudia had never mailed a letter for a client before and she briefly considered the possibility that she should not do so. On the other hand, she had never represented a friend before. Nor had she represented a client whose family lived in Jordan. How else would Emad be able to mail letters to his family? The prison certainly wouldn't do it, nor would Emad be permitted to give anything to his wife to mail. "There's nothing illegal in here," she asked jokingly taking the letter addressed to someone in Jordan.

"Of course not," Emad assured her.

Emad struggled to hold a pen in his handcuffed hand. There was a small steel surface that served as a desk in the cramped visiting room that was no bigger than a closet. The upper half of the booth had Plexiglas windows, which enabled the guards to watch their visit. A video camera was mounted on the ceiling above them.

"Is your wife getting in to see you?" Claudia asked.

"She tries to come once or twice a week, but it is hard for her. She gets very upset seeing me in here."

He handed her the finished letter. "Send it to this address," Emad instructed. "Thank you so much, my friend. You are so good to represent me."

"You're welcome," Claudia said. "It's my job," she added.

"I know," he said, "But you have gone above and beyond what a lawyer would do for a client."

"If I am such a great lawyer, why are you still in jail?" she thought to herself.

On her way back to her office, she mailed the letters by registered mail. There was a message waiting for her from Sarah, who sounded desperate, "I need to see you right away. I don't feel comfortable talking over the phone."

Claudia returned the call and they made arrangements to meet at 5:30.

Sarah arrived wearing a black pants suit. Tufts of hair peeked out from her headscarf. Her pocketbook was open revealing scraps of paper, a checkbook, a worn wallet, and a cosmetic case. Her eyes were red-rimmed with the faintest smudge of mascara.

Claudia came from behind the desk to hug her. "You better close this," she said taking the purse from Sarah. "You don't want to lose your valuables."

"Thanks," Sarah said dismissively "My purse is like my life, disorganized and falling apart." She smiled at Claudia, "Thank you for meeting with me on such short notice. We need your help to communicate with Emad's relatives in Jordan."

"What kind of help do you need?" Claudia asked.

"I need you to explain to them what is going on. My Arabic is spotty and they don't speak a lick of English, but I can translate for you."

"Why don't you explain to them yourself?"

"Because I know they'll have questions that I won't be able to answer. Is this a problem?" Sarah asked defensively. "Don't you usually communicate with your clients' families?"

"Yes, but I speak to them directly that way I know what is being said and my clients are there, which protects the attorney/client relationship."

Exasperated, Sarah replied, "Surely you've had other clients that didn't speak English, or whose families didn't speak English?"

"Yes."

"That's the situation here," Sarah said.

"Fine," Claudia said not wanting to argue with Sarah. "When do you want to make this call?"

"Right now, if possible. It's late there, but it's okay to wake them up. This way we'll be sure to find them at home."

Claudia wondered if Sarah's motive for calling was that she feared her phone line was being bugged. Claudia felt uncomfortable, but wasn't sure why. The idea briefly crossed her mind that Sarah was using her to communicate an illicit plan to her in-laws, but she quickly discarded the idea. Sarah and Emad were her friends. She didn't believe that either one of them was involved in any terrorist activity. Her fears were groundless.

She pushed the phone in Sarah's direction. Sarah punched in a long series of numbers and was quickly speaking Arabic with someone – presumably her in-laws. After a minute or so, Sarah said, "They are very grateful for everything you are doing for Emad," she said, then punched in the speakerphone setting and asked Claudia to explain what was happening in the case.

Claudia explained the charges and walked through the ramifications of what might happen if Emad were convicted. It certainly seemed that Sarah was translating what Claudia was saying, although Claudia had no way to know for sure. When Sarah finished explaining what Claudia had said, Sarah asked her, "They want to know if you work for the government."

Claudia sighed deeply. She was tired and hungry and didn't feel like explaining the role of a public defender. "In a manner of speaking, yes, but I am on Emad's side. Can you explain the role of a public defender to them?" Claudia asked.

"I tried, but they want to know how they can trust you if you work for the government."

Annoyed, Claudia reminded herself that these people were scared to death for their son. With effort, she said patiently, "Tell them if the family can come up with the money I am happy to help you hire a private lawyer."

Sarah spoke for several minutes. Claudia looked at her watch, eager for the call to be over. She had other files to read, but couldn't work with Sarah in the office. Finally Sarah hung up. "Thank Allah that is over with. I've been dreading that call all week."

"I meant what I said about the private lawyer. I won't take it personally if you want someone else to represent Emad. In fact, Emad may have to get another lawyer if the judge determines he can afford it."

"We don't want anyone else. We want you. But it is difficult for Emad's parents to understand. His father is a doctor and his mother is a college professor. They are middle class, but they can't come up with the $50,000 retainer. Besides, Emad is worried that if his family gives him financial support that they may become targets."

That thought hadn't occurred to Claudia, but it wasn't completely far-fetched to think that Emad's family might be at risk. Or maybe they were involved themselves in supporting Widows and Orphans.

"We might be able to get someone to take the case pro bono, which means you wouldn't have to pay for it. It's a high-profile case. Some attorneys would love the publicity."

"We're very happy with you," Sarah repeated.

Changing the subject, she asked, "How do you think Emad is doing? I saw him today and he didn't look well."

"He's not eating much. That is pretty normal for him — he doesn't eat when he's upset. But I think he's doing okay, all things considered." Sarah's eyes watered and her voice wavered, "The one I'm worried about is Semya. Every night she asks for her Papa. I keep telling her he'll come home soon, but I'm starting to think that's never going to happen."

Claudia pushed a box of Kleenex across the desk to Sarah.

"To make matters worse, my family is being simply horrible. They never wanted me to marry Emad anyway. When I converted to Islam they were horrified. When my mother found out that Emad had been arrested, she advised me to divorce him. Can you believe that? They think I should leave my husband because the government has charged him with some trumped-up nonsense. Do they think I would discard my wedding vows so quickly?"

Claudia went around to the front of her desk and put her arm around Sarah. "There are lots of other people who care, you know. TLC made a public statement of support of Emad and you know what it's like to get us to agree on anything. Esme is organizing an art show to raise money for his case and Dan's artist friend who just moved to town is going to donate a whole bunch of paintings to it. Even Frances Perkins and Aimee are working on the event and you know how much they despise each other."

"Everyone is so kind." Sarah broke down, sobbing. "It's been so hard. I can't tell you how hard it is to get out of bed each day. Reporters call early in the morning and late at night. If I don't answer the phone they just call back. If it weren't for Semya I would probably stay in bed and never leave the house."

Claudia squeezed her. "You have to stay strong. It's going to be alright. We're going to beat this case, and we're going to get him out of jail," she said, as though saying it might make it come true.

14. The Package

The Wednesday before Thanksgiving, when most of Washington had shut down for the holiday, Dan was sitting at his desk puzzling over his latest vote count. The committee vote on SOFA, originally scheduled to be held before the elections, had been held over until after the elections, December at the earliest and possibly not until the next Congress. Dan was running through the list of committee members for at least the hundredth time – 20 Republicans and 17 Democrats. He had all of the Democratic votes except for two undecided. He had one Republican – Larson from Connecticut – who was going to vote against it. If he got all the Democrats he'd lose by one vote. If he could get all the Democrats and one more Republican they could kill the bill in committee. He still hadn't told anyone about Weymouth, even though it was killing him. He was surprised at his own discretion and wondered why he was feeling so loyal to John Anderson, whom he would likely never see again.

He needed caffeine to clear his head. He walked to Caribou Coffee and ordered a double espresso, black. Maybe he should just go confront Weymouth one-on-one with what he knew, trying to guilt him into doing the right thing.

"Too bad, you just missed that cute FedEx man," Becky the receptionist said as he returned to the office. "He left a package from one of those Midwestern states that start with an M. I put it in your box."

"Minnesota?" Dan asked. He ran to his mailbox, tore off the FedEx packaging and pulled out a small manila envelope, which he carefully opened. Inside was the note:

Dear Dan,

I thought a lot about what you said and decided you were right. I've sent you the note. (I kept a copy for myself.) Do what you think is right.

Best of luck,
John

"Yes!" Dan shrieked. He ran into the conference room, where his colleagues were gathering for a pre-Thanksgiving lunch. The room was decorated in chic high tech with a long table trimmed in chrome and high-backed black executive chairs. Several of the other lobbyists were already there: Siobhan, a cute blonde from Alabama who took her girlfriend to her high school senior prom; Eric, a lanky Nigerian whose idea of a good time was running 50 miles; and Samantha, who was wearing a shear black dress with a lapel pin that read, "Straight but not narrow."

"You'll never guess what I know!" he yelled, not giving anyone a chance to guess. "Weymouth is queer!"

"No way," they shouted gleefully. The feeling of euphoria that suffused Dan was better than sex or falling in love for the first time.

Dan explained his encounter with the blond Viking and how he had come to get the note in the mail.

"It did always seem odd that he never sponsored SOFA," Siobhan said. "But who would have thought?"

Lenora, the director of OutReach, and a woman who most aptly fit the definition of Amazon, entered the room. "What's all the excitement?" she asked smiling broadly. "Did Dan finally get laid?"

"Better than that," Dan repeated the story to Lenora, who listened raptly. By the end of his tale her smile had disappeared. Dan felt the slightest tinge of apprehension. Lenora could be scary when she was angry.

"What exactly are you going to do with this information?" she asked. "Blackmail the guy? Publicly out him?"

"No," Dan said thoughtfully. "I've thought about it a lot the last month."

"You've known for a month and haven't told us," Siobhan ribbed him. "How did you manage that?"

"I didn't think he wanted me to tell anyone so I didn't." He looked at Lenora with a smug expression. "But it's been killing me," he confessed. "Anyway, I've decided that I'll request a personal meeting and bring the note with me. Then I'll ask him why he's moving this homophobic piece-of-crap bill through his committee."

"What will you do if he does nothing?"

"I've thought of that, too," Dan said. "But I haven't come up with an answer. I probably won't do anything, because this note is hardly proof of a homosexual affair. It's not like a video or something juicy. I don't want to ruin his career — I just want him to know that I know the truth about him."

"How're you going to get a meeting with him alone? He's always surrounded by staffers."

"I know his chief counsel. I'll tell him that I have something highly personal that I want to talk to the congressman about. Once Weymouth hears that he'll suspect what it's about and he'll agree to meet with me because he'll be afraid that I'll out him."

"Do you want me to come with you?" Lenora asked. "I know him pretty well."

"I've considered that, too, but I think it's better if it's just him and me."

"I wouldn't want to interfere with your male bonding," Lenora said.

15. Dan Meets Dave

For weeks, Paul had been telling Dan about a nice gay doctor who had recently moved to Washington. Finally he had arranged for Dan to meet Dave, convinced that the two would hit it off.

Dan didn't know whether to laugh or cry when he walked into Paul's Place and spotted Paul talking with a very ordinary-looking man with a long receding hairline and thick glasses, wearing corduroys and a cardigan sweater, reminding him of Mr. Rogers, a sweet image, but not exactly sexy. Dan thought about leaving and calling Paul to say that something had come up, but Paul spotted him and waved him over.

"Dan Canavan, this is Dave Austin."

When Dave smiled his eyes lit up and dimples appeared on his cheeks.

"I've got to run to the kitchen," Paul said avoiding the evil eye that Dan was trying to give him.

"Please join me," Dave offered. "Paul's told me so much about you. I'm so happy to meet you."

Since he had to eat dinner anyway, he might as well eat it with Dave, even though he could never in a million years imagine going out with him.

"Tell me about your job," Dave said, after they had ordered dinner and were sipping wine. "I'm fascinated by life on the Hill. Do you meet with important and famous people?"

"Sometimes, although the most important meetings are not usually with the members themselves, but with their chief advisor. I make it a point to know who that person is."

Dave listened so intently that before he knew it, Dan was telling him the story about how he had met John Anderson and learned about Weymouth and then receiving the note in the mail. "You can't tell anyone," Dan said. "I can't even believe I told this to you."

"I'm a shrink. People always tell me their secrets. I'm used to keeping them private. What are you going to do with the note?" Dave asked, changing the subject. "That poses an ethical dilemma for you. Do you think its okay to expose someone's sexual identity for the sake of a good cause?"

"I don't know what I think about that," Dan said. "It doesn't really matter in this case, though. The note is not sufficient to prove that Weymouth is gay. If it were a videotape or something like that, then I'd really have to decide what to do. As it stands now, I just want Weymouth to know that I know his secret. I'm hoping to guilt him into doing the right thing."

Dave's face revealed neither judgment nor approval. Perhaps to see if he could get a reaction, Dan said, "If I had better proof, I'd probably out him."

Dave nodded, but said nothing.

Dan continued as though in confessional, "I don't know if that's the right thing to do or not, but knowing me, that's what I'd likely do."

"It would be a hard decision," Dave agreed.

They were interrupted by Paul arriving with two bowls of tofu-carob mousse, another house specialty. "On the house," he said. "To celebrate new friendships."

Dan took a bite, savoring the silky texture. Between the red wine and the good food, Dave was starting to look somewhat handsome.

"Tell me about your job."

"I'm a child psychiatrist. I work with troubled youth. I moved here from Boston to work at the juvenile detention facility."

"That explains why you're such a good listener," Dan said.

"Thank you, that means a lot to me," Dave said. "I don't always get a lot of praise in my profession. People suspect that men who want to work with children, especially gay men, must be pedophiles or something."

"You must like children," Dan said, fishing to see if Dave would divulge his opinions on parenthood.

"I do." Dave said. Dan hadn't discussed Rita Jane's proposal with anyone and Dave seemed like the perfect person to listen without judgment.

"My childhood best friend, Rita Jane, just moved back to D.C. and has asked me to have a child with her."

Dave raised his eyebrows. "That's a big commitment."

"I know. At first I thought her idea was completely ludicrous. I've always thought I would meet someone and we'd have children together. But we're both nearly 40 and neither of us have partners. Maybe it could work. I live in a cohousing community — it's a kind of intentional community — there are a lot of people who would help. Plus, both of our parents live in D.C."

Dave nodded, but looked skeptical. "Does she want you to be a sperm donor or a partner? I donated sperm to some lesbian friends of mine who live in Boston so I have made my contribution to the gene pool. But I don't think that's what Rita Jane had in mind when she asked you."

"No, I don't think so. I think she's looking for a co-parent. But she might be satisfied with a sperm donor. I'm not sure I'd feel comfortable in that role, however. Do you ever see the kid? What's it like?"

"I see him a few times a year. He knows I am the sperm donor, but he doesn't think of me as a father. It's like I'm a special uncle. I enjoy watching him develop. Sometimes I even feel a sense of pride. When he learned to read at age four I was sure it was because of my genes."

"I'm sure it was," Dan smiled. "You say it isn't strange when you see him, but wouldn't it be strange if you saw him every day."

Dave paused as if considering the question. "I'm not sure. It might be."

The wine and carob mousse were finished. All the other customers had left and Paul had already washed the floor. The awkward moment arrived when they had to decide whether to get together again. To his surprise, Dan wanted to.

"Listen," Dan said, "If you don't have other plans, why don't you come for Thanksgiving.

"I'd like that," Dave replied. "Can I bring anything?"

"We have a big community meal. There's plenty of food. But you can bring some wine if you'd like. There never seems to be enough of that.

"I'll do that."

"Good, then it's a date."

16. Thanksgiving

Instead of rushing to catch the early morning flight to Houston as she usually did on Thanksgiving, Claudia slept in, reveling in a day off from work. Lately she felt as if she couldn't sleep enough. She'd arrive at work exhausted from the Metro trip into the city. Instead of bounding up the steep escalators, she stood to the side and let the walkers pass her.

She felt a pang of guilt about not visiting her family, especially her mother, who would miss her, whereas her brothers, although she loved them, would not be upset if she didn't show up.

But she just wasn't up for a trip home this year. She had felt tired since October. Learning that her Uncle Earl was going to be there convinced her to stay in Washington. Even when they drove her crazy, she loved her family, with the exception of Earl, her dead father's brother, whom she despised. Earl put the "red" in redneck. He drove a white Ford pick-up truck with an extended cab, wore a ten-gallon hat, and smoked unfiltered cigarettes. He had a mean and mangy dog named Buddy, whom he allowed to run loose. Once Buddy bit a jogger, and Earl was pleased when he learned the victim was a Yankee.

She was still in bed when her mother called.

"Hi honey, I just wanted to call and say 'Happy Thanksgiving.' We miss you. Wish you were here."

"Hi Momma," Claudia said groggily. "What time is it?"

"It's 10 a.m. here. Were you sleeping? What's the matter? You never sleep this late. Are you sick? Are you working too much?"

"Would you stop talking long enough so I can answer your questions? I'm fine. I'm just tired. Everyone else sleeps in, why can't I?"

"Of course you can, sugar. I don't mean to be a pest. I just wanted you to know that we're all thinking of you today."

"I'm sorry to be grumpy. I'm thinking about you, too," she didn't add that she had been thinking about how glad she was not to be there.

"Donny wants to say hi." Donny was Claudia's oldest brother who had just separated from his wife and had moved back in with Audrey.

"Hey sis, good news about the election, huh? Glad the Republicans took back the Senate after that traitor Jeffords switched sides."

She didn't feel up to battling with her brother. Claudia was the only Democrat in the family and was used to constant harassment from the rest of them. While she was formulating a witty repartee, her mother said, "Don't get started on politics, it's Thanksgiving."

She heard someone else grab the phone, then heard Uncle Earl, who sounded like he was already well into his cups, despite the early hour. "What do you think of this here Sofer law, Claudia? I think it's a damn good thing. I don't want any queers coming to Texas to adopt our children."

"God knows why they'd want to, Earl — they might end up with a pint-size version of you."

Her cousin Diana came on the line next. "God I wish you were here. You and your mother are the only sane people in this family."

"I'm sorry. I'm just too beat. I've been working a lot. I seem to be tired all the time."

"You work too hard," Diana said. "I should go help Audrey with the turkey but let's talk soon when this riffraff is out of earshot. Love you."

"Love you, too," Claudia said, hanging up. Whatever slight feelings of homesickness she had were dispelled by the phone call with her family.

The Common House was filled with the welcoming aromas of a Thanksgiving feast. The smells of turkey, pumpkin pie and mulled cider welcomed the guests as did a cheerful fire burning in the gas fireplace.

Claudia was in charge of baking the tofurkey, a small turkey-shaped mound of tofu seasoned to taste like poultry. What it lacked in taste it made up for in convenience. It took less than an hour from the freezer to the table, and clean up was a cinch. Of course, Thanksgiving was one of those holidays when even some of the "vegetarians" ate poultry.

Rita Jane had told her that Dan had invited a date for dinner, so she wasn't surprised to see him enter the Common House with a man. But she was surprised when she saw a man who looked like a frumpy, absent-minded professor. Unlike his usual dates, who looked like they spent all their spare time working out, this man looked like he had never seen the inside of a gym.

Dan waved and walked toward her and she steeled herself for the introduction. She wasn't exactly jealous of Dave. She was glad, she told herself, that Dan had met someone. But she missed all the time they used to spend together, before Rita Jane moved to town and before they spent the night together. Claudia resolved to be friendly.

"Welcome," she said warmly. "You must be Dave. We're so glad you could join us for dinner." Dan's eyes expressed gratitude.

Dave had a surprisingly strong handshake for someone who appeared to be a nerd. When he smiled at her, she felt as if he were looking into the deepest part of her soul.

By 2 o'clock about sixty residents had gathered in the Common House. The boisterous commotion distracted her from her feelings of loneliness and fatigue. As was tradition, everyone stood in a large circle around the tables piled with food and held hands in a gratitude circle. Each person who was old enough to speak said something he or she was grateful for.

People were grateful for their jobs, their families, the TLC community, their health — the usual gamut of middle-class sentiments. Aimee, who had dressed for the occasion in a long woven Guatemalan skirt and had braided her hair said, "I'm grateful for Paul." Claudia's ears perked up as she realized that the two were an item. She wondered how long that had been going on.

When the circle got to her, Claudia said, "I'm grateful I'm not spending the day with my drunken red-necked Uncle Earl." She worried that she sounded too harsh, but several people laughed and others nodded in agreement. Dan said he was grateful for his new friend, Dave, who he introduced to the group. And Dave said he was grateful he wasn't at home alone eating a TV dinner.

Within minutes, everyone had helped themselves to large plates of turkey and gravy, stuffing, cranberry sauce, mashed potatoes, green peas with miniature onions, and sweet potatoes with vegan marshmallows — ones without gelatin in them — melted on top.

"How's Emad doing?" Frances asked.

"As well as he can be under the circumstances. It's his daughter I'm really worried about. Semya's four and doesn't understand what's going on."

Dan explained to Dave, "Claudia's representing Emad Khadonry. You've probably heard about the case."

Dave nodded, his mouth full of turkey. Claudia couldn't believe Dan would date someone who ate meat. "I read about it in the paper," Dave said. "It sounds like quite a case."

"Don't remind me about it. I feel so bad thinking about him in jail. I feel like I should go see him."

"I know how you feel," Dave said. "I work with kids at a juvenile detention center. I think about them a lot — especially on holidays."

"Are you a lawyer?" Frances asked.

"A psychiatrist," Dan said.

"You must be busy in this town," Frances said. "Just about everyone is on some kind of pill or another."

"Unfortunately there are a lot of troubled children in D.C.," Dave said. Turning to Claudia he asked, "How is Emad's daughter?"

"Her mother says she isn't sleeping well at night. She had been sleeping in her own room, but she's started sleeping with her mother again. She has bad dreams nearly every night. Sarah's not getting much sleep."

"I could talk with her," Dave offered. "If she'd like." Dan was looking at Claudia hopefully. She sensed that Dan really wanted her to like this guy, which made her want to dislike him. But he was so earnest and kind, it was hard to find anything wrong with him. "Thank you," she said, summoning up what graciousness she could find. "I'll mention it to Sarah."

Esme, who had been sitting at a nearby table, appeared looking like royalty, wearing a red tunic and her long gray hair held up in a large gold barrette and carrying a large glass of red wine. "Who's the new man?" she asked Dan. "Are you holding out on us?"

"I was just saving you for last, Esme. I wanted him to get his feet wet with everyone else before meeting you."

Esme said, "I'll take that as a compliment. I'm Esme Root," she said to Dave. "I'm very pleased to meet you."

"I'm familiar with your work," Dave said. "I read in the *City Paper* about a show that you are in. The article said you were one of the most renowned artists in the District. "I hope to get to your show this weekend."

Esme beamed at Dave. "I love this man," she said to Dan. "He obviously has exquisite taste."

Claudia saw Dan and Dave look longingly at each other. It made her feel lonely. Esme interrupted her thoughts.

"Claudia, I wanted you to know that plans for the event are coming along quite well. Rita Jane, Frances, Aimee and I have all gotten together three times and so far Frances and Aimee have only gotten into one really big row."

"I wouldn't call that a row," Frances said. "It was a slight difference of opinion."

Dan and Dave excused themselves to go to the living room to take part in the annual Scrabble tournament. Claudia went to the kitchen to help clean up and to get away from Dan and Dave. She methodically rinsed the dishes and carefully placed them in the dish rack as if by controlling them she could somehow control her emotions, too. The commercial dishwasher made a horrible grating noise, making conversation with the other members of the clean up crew impossible. Which was just as well. Claudia felt lonely, weepy and tired. She wasn't upset that Dan had met someone, she was happy for him she told herself, it was just that she was lonely without him as her primary friend. Being with Dan had taken away the bitter edge of being single, which only got worse at holiday time. Maybe she should have gone to Texas. Even though her family drove her crazy, she never felt lonely when she was with them.

Frances entered the kitchen with a platter of turkey remains and placed it on the counter next to Claudia. Claudia placed the leftovers in a plastic container and found to her amazement that she was craving it. She hadn't eaten turkey in over a decade. She looked around to see if anyone was watching and then hurriedly took a bite. The juicy, tender meat with crispy skin tasted marvelous. She ate the entire piece and was starting her second when Frances came into the kitchen.

Claudia quickly threw the remains in the trash looking away so that Frances couldn't see her guilty expression. Through the window she saw a bright red cardinal eating from a bird feeder.

"I need a walk," Claudia said to no one in particular. She grabbed the container of turkey and headed back to her house where no one could see her eat it.

17. Sneak and Peek

The Monday after Thanksgiving, Capitol Hill had the feel of a funeral parlor after all the guests had gone home. Members of Congress stayed in their districts, resting from their election battles. Most of Dan's co-workers at OutReach had not returned to work, either. Dan should have been at home, too. He had spent the weekend with his family — his four sisters, their spouses, and seven children — and returned home with a horrible head cold. He had gone to the office hoping to take advantage of the quiet as a chance to plan out his strategy for defeating SOFA, but after a morning of sneezing and coughing and not getting any work done, he called it quits and headed home.

He staggered to the nearly empty Metro train and leaned back against the wall with his legs stretched out on the seat next to him, enjoying the rare luxury of two unoccupied seats next to each other. Dozing, he would have missed his stop had the train not jerked, waking him from his slumber. Dan frequently missed his Metro stop either from falling asleep or because he was engrossed in reading or obsessing about his work.

Arriving home, he inserted his key into the deadbolt and realized that his door was already unlocked. Had he been in such a cold medicine-induced daze that he had forgotten to lock it? Maybe Rita Jane had unlocked it. She had an extra key, and sometimes came to his apartment during the day to borrow something or to play with his cats.

"RJ," he called out hoarsely. "If you're here, come make me a cup of tea. Please, I'm desperate."

He heard the scrape of a chair in his office, but no reply to his greeting. A white man dressed in a dark suit and carrying a brief case appeared in the kitchen. Dan wondered if the cold medicine was giving him hallucinations.

"Who are you and what the hell are you doing in my house?" Dan demanded, more angry than afraid.

The apparition reached into his jacket pocket, flipped open an identification badge, and barked, "Agent Warner. FBI. We're here to execute a search warrant."

Dan leaned against his kitchen counter for support. "A search warrant? For what? Why didn't you do it when I was home? I want to call my attorney."

"Don't get upset," Warner said, approaching him cautiously, as if Dan might be armed. "We're authorized to conduct a delayed notification search." Agent Warner smiled at him sardonically, "But as it turns out, you may consider this your notification." He handed Dan several sheets of paper stapled together. Dan tried to read them, but his brain was so foggy he could barely make out the small print that cited statutes he wasn't familiar with. He had the presence of mind to check the name and address on the warrant, and sure enough, they were his.

Another man walked into the kitchen. "Agent Turner," the man said, flipping open his badge, but Dan didn't bother to look at it.

"I'm really not feeling well. Do you mind if I sit down while you explain what's going on?"

Dan sat down on one of his sofas and the two FBI interlopers sat on the other. The idea crossed his mind that he should offer them something to drink, but he chastised himself. This wasn't a social visit — they were searching his house.

"We're looking for information about Claudia Connors, your former girlfriend. She's being investigated because of her connection to the terrorist Emad Khadonry."

"She's not my girlfriend. For Christ's sake, I'm gay." The exertion drained Dan. He felt lightheaded. "And Emad's not a terrorist," Dan said angrily. "This government is..." he stopped himself short, remembering from law school that anything you say can and will be used against you in a court of law. "This is ridiculous. Why on earth are you investigating Claudia? Don't you guys have any real terrorists to fight?"

The agents ignored his question. "Emad has been funneling money to terrorists through the front organization Widows and Orphans. We have reason to believe that others in your community have been helping him. We know that Claudia Connors has acted as a courier for him on more than one occasion, and we know that she used to spend a lot of time at your house."

Dan closed his eyes tightly and opened them slowly, hoping that the men would be gone. Nobody would believe that two FBI agents in dark suits were in his home office looking through his computer files.

"Listen, you guys are barking up the wrong tree. Why don't you go find some real terrorists, not people who are trying to help widows and orphans?"

The agents didn't say anything. One of them was looking at something on his coffee table. It was a copy of OutReach's monthly magazine. "I told you, I'm gay. Claudia Connors is not my girlfriend."

"Listen, buddy, what you do in bed is none of our concern, but we have witnesses who swore out affidavits to the effect that you and Ms. Connors used to spend a lot of time together and were seen more than once leaving each other's apartments early in the morning."

"We're friends," Dan snapped. "Who gave you that information?"

"Our sources are confidential, Mr. Canavan." Agent Warner stood up, "If you don't have any further questions today then we'll be on our way."

"Guess not," Dan said. He followed them wearily to his door.

"Wait a minute," he said, "I do have a question. Did you take anything?"

"No," Warner said. Dan felt relieved, but doubted he could trust them.

"Will you be coming back?"

"Not in the foreseeable future," Warner replied.

Dan shut the door and slid over the deadbolt, then rushed to the phone to call Claudia, abandoning all hope of a nap.

18. The Summons

When Claudia returned to work after the holiday, the climb up the broken escalator at Judiciary Square winded her. She had to stop twice, and by the time she got to the top, she was panting like a dog. She had been feeling nauseous since Thanksgiving and bone-weary for over a month. Her mother had been nagging her about going to a doctor, but she hated doctors whom she believed never did anything for you unless you had a broken bone or needed to be stitched up. By the time she got to her office, Claudia felt she needed a nap.

"An officer delivered this for you," Georgia, her paralegal, said, handing her a legal document.

Claudia skimmed the caption, assuming it was another filing in Emad's case, but then she realized that it was her name, not Emad's, at the top of the page.

"This is for me!" she said, grabbing the side of her desk. "I'm supposed to be in court on the 15th. I'm being charged with supplying material support to a terrorist!"

Her heart raced and she felt dizzy. "Are you alright?" Georgia asked. "You better sit down."

She sat down and someone handed her a cup of water. "You don't look so good."

"I've got to call Paul," Claudia croaked. "He knows the U.S. Attorney. He can tell me what to do." She dug her cellphone out of her briefcase and pulled up Paul's number on her speed dial. Rita Jane answered the phone. "Good morning, Paul's Place."

"They've charged me," she said, not believing the words. "I've got to talk to Paul."

"Charged you with what?" Rita Jane asked, alarmed.

"I don't feel so great. I feel lightheaded. I think I might...."

* * *

When Claudia came to, a sea of faces peered down on her. "Should we call an ambulance?" she heard someone ask. "I'll drive her there. It'll be faster," Georgia said.

It took Claudia a moment to realize they were talking about her. "I'm not going to the hospital," she declared emphatically. "I'm perfectly alright."

No one said anything for a few moments. "You fainted, Claudia," Georgia said firmly. "That's not normal."

Her cellphone rang. It was Rita Jane. "Paul found someone to cover for us. We're on our way down there now."

"Why?" she asked. Georgia grabbed the phone from her hands. Claudia started to protest but Georgia's expression told her not to bother.

"We're taking her to the Georgetown Emergency Room. She fainted. Meet us there."

With so many people telling her what to do, Claudia felt like a child, which was oddly comforting. A colleague walked with her down to the sidewalk and waited with her while Georgia went for her car. Claudia's mind was racing and she could barely concentrate. She noticed the scent of her own perspiration. *How could those bastards do this to me?* She cursed the prosecutors. She took a couple of deep breaths, reminding herself to stay calm. Once in the cramped car she felt faint again. She closed her eyes and leaned her head back, but that didn't help. She tried leaning forward instead, which seemed to make her feel a little better.

"We'll never get there at this rate," Georgia yelled. "Damn these busses. I hate all these tourists," she ranted, sounding her horn.

"That doesn't help anything," Claudia said. It was impossible to see down Eye Street because all three lanes were blocked with busses. "They're probably on their way to the White House. They'll turn down 16th Street."

The traffic light changed three times before they made it through, but Claudia's prediction was accurate. The traffic thinned once the busses turned off to view the White House.

By the time they got to the Emergency Room, Paul and Rita Jane were already there.

"Dan's on his way," Rita Jane said.

"I'm not dying. You guys didn't need to come down here," Claudia complained, although she was happy to see Rita Jane, and touched by her concern.

"We wanted to come," Rita Jane said. "We're worried about you. What happened? Are you in pain?"

"No. I just fainted. My stomach's a little upset. It's no big deal."

"It's better to check these things out. I mean, it could be something serious. My Dad is a cancer surgeon, and he's always telling me horror stories. I'm not going to tell them to you, but let's just say I think it's a good idea to get checked out."

Her cellphone rang. It was Dan saying that he was looking for a place to park. Rita Jane mouthed the words, "I'll be back soon," and left. Claudia leaned back in the hard plastic chair, trying to relax, but feeling anxious about all the work she should be doing back at the office.

Rita Jane returned with two cans of Coke, and two cans of ginger ale. "To help settle your stomach," she said, pouring the soda into a plastic cup. Paul was on the cellphone calling everyone he knew in Washington to find out all he could about the summons.

Rita Jane handed Paul a plastic cup, too. He smiled at her, and Claudia thought she saw something between them — sexual attraction perhaps? The idea disturbed her. Was she attracted to Rita Jane? It didn't matter, because Rita Jane was straight, and even if Rita Jane would consider a relationship with a woman, Claudia had sworn off having sex with straight girls. She had done that before, and it had ended badly.

Dan was pacing, talking on his cellphone, and Paul was at the other end of the room doing the same. A television blared with the noise of one of those live courtroom drama programs, where people volunteer to have their dispute resolved on television. Rita Jane took a seat next to Claudia, neither of them saying anything. Claudia was intensely aware of her presence, and wondered if she felt the same way.

Finally, a stout nurse, who was nearly as wide as she was tall, called her name.

Claudia said, "It's a good thing this wasn't a real emergency, I'd be dead by now."

"I'm sorry Mrs. Connors. My name is Anne. I'm going to take care of you today. Would you like your husband to come in with you?" she asked, looking at Dan.

"He's not my husband," Claudia said defiantly.

"I'll go with her," Rita Jane offered.

"Who are you?" Nurse Anne asked.

"Just a friend," Rita Jane said. Nurse Anne looked at Claudia. "It's up to you. Do you want her to come with you?"

Claudia nodded.

The nurse took them to a small cubicle with an uncomfortable cot and one hard plastic chair next to it. Claudia climbed on the cot and forced herself to sit upright, wanting desperately to lie down and close her eyes. The nurse took her blood pressure, temperature, and pulse. "Your blood pressure is a bit high, and you're running a slight fever. I'm going to get the doctor. You can wait here."

Claudia had succumbed to her exhaustion and nearly fallen asleep when a clammy hand on her forehead roused her. "I'm Dr. Cohen," said a young man who looked like he wasn't old enough to shave. "Tell me what happened?" he said. "What brings you in today?" he said.

"I'm perfectly fine," Claudia said defensively. "My friends overreacted."

"She fainted at work," Rita Jane said.

The doctor looked concerned. "Have you ever fainted before?"

"No. But there's a first time for everything, I suppose."

The doctor ignored her attempt at humor. "Did anything unusual happen?" he asked.

"She got some bad news," Rita Jane said.

"I can talk for myself," Claudia snapped, and immediately felt bad. "That's true," she said composing herself. "I went to work and learned that I've been charged with a serious crime."

Did she imagine it or did he pull away ever so slightly? "It's all bullshit, just trumped up charges," Claudia protested, realizing she sounded exactly like her clients did when they learned they'd been charged with a crime.

"I'm ordering some blood tests to make sure it's nothing more serious than stress," Dr. Cohen said.

He left before Claudia had a chance to protest. Nurse Ann returned with a needle attached to a vial. Claudia turned her head away. In seconds, the nurse had pulled up Claudia's sleeve, secured a rubber cord around her arm, and swabbed the inside of her elbow. Claudia barely felt the needle enter her vein, but she made the mistake of looking and the sight of her blood pumping into the tube made her nauseous.

"I think I'm going to puke," she said.

"We're almost done," the nurse said, taking out the needle and putting a bandage on the spot.

"It's too late," Claudia said as she turned her head and threw up on the floor. "I'm sorry," she apologized. "I'll clean it up."

"No worries," the nurse said cheerfully. "We'll clean it up lickety-split."

"Where's the bathroom?" Claudia moaned.

The nurse grabbed Claudia's arm and said, "Come along, dear." Then to Rita Jane, "Why don't you escort her to the bathroom?"

"I'm fine, really," Claudia insisted. "What I'd really like is another soda. Can you get me one, RJ?"

Alone for the first time in hours, Claudia sat on the toilet to catch her breath. Then she rinsed out her mouth and straightened her hair with her fingers. She walked back to her bed and lay down. I'll sleep for a few minutes, she told herself. When she woke, Rita Jane was there with a cup of warm ginger ale.

Dr. Cohen returned. "Your blood work is within the normal range, but we did find one thing of interest."

"What's that?" Claudia asked feeling relieved that there might be a simple explanation for her symptoms.

"Do you want me to tell you with your friend present?"

Claudia shrugged. She couldn't imagine that the doctor would tell her anything that she would want to keep private. "Sure."

"You're pregnant," Dr. Cohen pronounced. Seeing the look on Rita Jane's face, Claudia realized there were some things she didn't want others to know about.

19. Coming Clean

Dan slid into a corner booth waiting for Rita Jane's shift to end. In their many years of friendship they had many more rows than he cared to remember. Each had what Dan's mother called an "Irish temper." But each always made their relationship a priority, and took turns reaching out to mend rifts as they occurred. This time it was Dan's turn.

He had chosen a public place as the location for this meeting, lessening the likelihood of them getting into a heated argument.

He had brought along *The Nation*, the only source he trusted to provide him with accurate news, to read while he waited, but he was too preoccupied to comprehend what he was reading.

He had already eaten breakfast, but the smell of baking sticky buns, combined with his anxiety, was convincing him he was still hungry. While he was contemplating whether to order one, Paul arrived, placed a large iced bun and a latte in front of him and said, "I hope this cheers you up."

Rita Jane sat down across from Dan without greeting him with a kiss or a hug as she usually did. He hadn't seen her since the astonishing news of Claudia's pregnancy. Claudia had insisted that he tell Rita Jane about his role in that debacle, which he supposed was only fair.

"To what do I owe the pleasure?" Rita Jane asked, not bothering to hide her sarcasm.

This was going to be harder than he thought. "RJ, I've got some things I need to tell you. Do you want to do it here or go someplace else?"

"Here is fine." She sat with her hands folded and hostility oozing from her.

"You're not going to get upset are you?" Dan asked, fearing a scene.

"I'm not going to make a scene if that's what you mean. Jesus, Dan, you act like I'm still a teenager. I have matured somewhat in the last 20 years."

Dan refrained from reminding her about the last dinner with her parents. She may have matured, but Rita Jane could still be a drama queen. He hoped Paul's presence cleaning up in back would keep her in check.

"I've been meaning to tell you for a while, but I've been waiting for the right opportunity." She raised her eyebrows.

"Christ, RJ, this isn't easy for me. I slept with Claudia."

"I figured it was you," she said. "When?"

"Early October, right before you moved here."

"Why?"

"It was the night after Emad's arrest. We were both upset. She was drunk." His words sounded hollow. He looked in her eyes for some sign of forgiveness. "I honestly don't know why. It just happened."

"You're a little old for these things to 'just happen' to you. Whose idea was it anyway?"

"Mine." Dan said. His face reddened. His palms felt sweaty.

"But I thought you weren't attracted to women," Rita Jane said. She was twisting a strand of hair around a finger, one of her nervous habits.

"I'm not. It was an emotional need, not a physical one."

"It sounds to me like you were attracted to her."

"For that one night I suppose I was. But the next morning I left before she got up. We've never even talked about it."

"Why didn't you tell me? Did you think I wouldn't understand?"

"Believe it or not, I don't tell you about everyone I sleep with." Dan regretted the remark as soon as he said it. Maybe Claudia was right about him being an asshole.

"I'm sorry," Dan paused, choosing his words carefully. "I was embarrassed. You know I've always considered myself gay. I didn't know what this meant. I thought if I told people, like you, then people would question whether I was really gay. Hell, I started wondering myself if maybe I was bisexual. It was horribly confusing. I think I just wanted to forget the whole thing."

Dan was on the verge of tears. Telling the story had woken up the painful feelings of confusion and another emotion, guilt. "I certainly wasn't planning on having a child."

"Not consciously anyway," Rita Jane said.

"Christ, RJ, it's not about you. This had nothing to do with you. I had no idea you wanted to have a child with me."

She sat with her arms across her chest, hugging herself.

"When I asked you to have a child, why didn't you tell me about Claudia?"

"What was the point? It's not like I thought she was pregnant for God's sake."

"The point is that I'm your best friend and this was a really big thing going on in your life."

"I thought you would use it as a reason to talk me into having a kid with you."

Rita Jane laughed. "But I didn't want to have sex with you. I just wanted your sperm."

Dan felt embarrassed. "But you don't want it anymore."

"It's not relevant now."

Dan raised an eyebrow. "Giving up so soon? That's not the Rita Jane I know and love."

"I probably can't have kids," she said.

"What are you talking about? You didn't tell me this."

"I just found out a couple of days ago. I haven't told anyone yet."

"A few weeks ago I had horrible cramps, worse than I've ever had. I went to see Claudia's gynecologist and she told me that I have large fibroids that I should probably have removed."

"Did she say you wouldn't be able to have kids?"

"No. But she said the tumors are located in tricky areas that might make it difficult for me to conceive, and if I did they might grow and complicate the pregnancy."

"Can't you have them removed?"

"I can. She didn't say I absolutely couldn't have kids, just that I might not be able to."

"That's not so bad," Dan said. "Maybe it could still happen."

"Maybe."

Dan felt surprisingly disappointed. He hadn't wanted to have a child with Rita Jane, but he had hoped that she would have one.

"Life is so strange. You want to be pregnant and you can't get pregnant, and Claudia doesn't want to be and she is."

"When is she due?" Rita Jane asked.

"I think she's going to have an abortion," Dan said. "At least that's the direction she's leaning in."

Rita Jane looked horrified. "She can't do that. You've got to stop her. It's your baby, too."

"Get a grip. Don't go getting all Catholic on me."

"I support abortion rights, but not when it's your child. You've got to talk her out of it. Tell her to have the baby and we'll raise it."

"Now I know you're crazy," Dan said.

"No, I'm not. I want to have a baby with you and I probably can't have a baby. You want to have a baby, too. This may be your only chance. Please, Dan. Please don't let her get an abortion."

"I'm not going to try to talk her into doing something she doesn't want to do," Dan said.

"Just make her this offer. I'll talk to her. Will you let me?"

"I can't keep you from talking with her," Dan sighed. "Just try not to freak her out."

20. The Botanical Garden

The heat rushed at them as soon as they stepped out of the revolving doors into the Botanical Garden. The moist air made Claudia's glasses fog over. Tall palm trees reaching over fifty feet provided a tropical canopy. Dazzling pink bougainvillea and giant orchids draped from tree branches. The perfumed air smelled like lilacs. Streams of water gurgled in a pond with live fish. A brightly colored parrot perched on a nearby tree.

"This is the most amazing place," Rita Jane said. "Thanks for coming with me." She grabbed Claudia's hand impulsively and squeezed it, arousing Claudia. Claudia squeezed back. They walked with clasped hands for a few steps, and then Rita Jane let go. "I've got to take a picture of that tree. Isn't that bark amazing?"

They walked through the lush pathways ripe with tropical flora and fauna. Claudia wanted to return to handholding, but Rita Jane was too busy snapping pictures.

"It will be wonderful to have something colorful to paint," she said, her face more animated and beautiful, than Claudia had ever seen.

Claudia walked slowly, inhaling the air, pregnant with moisture, wondering what Rita Jane wanted to talk about. Was it possible that Rita Jane was attracted to her? Was it related to the pregnancy? Was it about Dan? She tried to focus on the moment, enjoying the beauty and warmth. Rita Jane would talk to her when she was ready.

After spending the morning basking in the lushness, the gray winter day seemed particularly dreary. They walked up Pennsylvania Avenue to

Le Bon Café for lunch. The restaurant's smell of coffee and fresh bread felt welcoming after the chilly walk. They chatted amiably drinking their warm coffees. This was Rita Jane's meeting and Claudia would wait until Rita Jane brought up whatever issue she wanted to talk about.

"Dan told me about what happened," Rita Jane said. "I suspected he was the father."

Claudia couldn't read Rita Jane's reaction. Since she moved to town, they had spent a lot of time together and were becoming close friends, but Claudia couldn't tell if Rita Jane was upset. Rita Jane didn't seem to be judging her, but how could she not judge them? People their age having unprotected sex. She wondered if Rita Jane was jealous. After all, she had wanted to have a baby with Dan.

"It wasn't planned," Claudia said looking into her coffee cup. "I want you to know that I'm not the kind of person who gets pregnant. I haven't had sex with a man since college, almost 20 years ago."

"Dan told me you were drunk. He said he started it."

"That's true," Claudia admitted. She looked directly at Rita Jane. "But I knew what I was doing. I was so upset I thought it would make me feel better. I did feel better for a few minutes. But now I feel worse."

Rita Jane took both her hands and looked her in the eyes. "It's understandable. Don't be so hard on yourself." They sat holding hands for an awkward minute. Claudia was relieved when the salads arrived and she could pull away.

Neither said anything for several bites. Finally, Rita Jane said tentatively, "I'd like to raise the child." Her eyes radiated hopefulness, like a child on Christmas Eve.

Of all the things that Claudia had imagined Rita Jane might say this was not one of them. "Would you do that?" she asked, surprised and repulsed. "Does Dan know about this?" Now it was her turn to feel jealous. Dan hadn't suggested that they raise the child together, but then again, Claudia had said she wanted an abortion.

"I suggested the idea to him. I asked him if I could talk to you about it. He told me not to freak you out."

Claudia laughed imagining Dan saying that. She wondered what he felt about the suggestion. "I don't think I want to have the child. I've been thinking about having an abortion."

Rita Jane grimaced. Claudia felt a pang of shame. Maybe Rita Jane was morally opposed to abortions. She knew that Rita Jane and Dan had gone to Catholic school together. Some of those teachings may have stuck.

"I wasn't sure if I was going to tell you or not, but I recently learned that it may be difficult for me to have children. I have a bad case of fibroids and may not be able to get pregnant."

"I'm sorry," Claudia said feeling embarrassed and guilty. She searched for the words to explain how she felt in a way that wouldn't make her sound so selfish. "This isn't a good time for me to have a child. I've got Emad's case and now my own case. I'm under so much stress

I can't imagine how I'll cope. I've already been feeling crappy — I'm exhausted all the time and nauseous, too."

"I suppose not," Rita Jane mumbled. She pushed the Salad Nicoise around on the plate, looking like she was going to cry.

Claudia reached across the table and grabbed her fingers, absorbing their strength. "I'll think about it. I promise. I know you wanted to have Dan's child. I know this wasn't what anyone had in mind."

"He wants to have a child, too," Rita Jane said.

"It's complicated," Claudia said. "If you hadn't been there when I found out, I'm not sure I would have told you."

"Would you really have had an abortion without telling Dan?"

Claudia winced at the judgmental tone. "I may have," Claudia admitted. "Look, it's hard for me to tell you this. I'm not proud of these feelings. I probably would have told him anyway, but in a way it just makes it harder for him to know."

Rita Jane was shaking her head in disbelief. Claudia tried another tactic. "I just wanted to try to figure out what I wanted before I mixed Dan or anyone else's desires in the mix. I wanted the choice to be mine."

Claudia was reminded of the anti-abortion bumper sticker that read, "It's not a choice — it's a child." Rita Jane nodded as though she understood, but Claudia wondered how much Catholic school had influenced Rita Jane's position on abortion.

"This could get very complicated. If I actually went through with the pregnancy I'd want to raise the child myself."

Rita Jane shrugged. "We can raise the child together. The more parents the better."

"Think of all the children who were screwed up by having two parents. Imagine what three parents could do," Claudia said.

"We'd be different," Rita Jane said.

Claudia couldn't tell whether she was serious or joking. "That's what everyone says," she said. "Every parent thinks they'll do better than their parents did, but we all just keep making the same mistakes again and again."

While Rita Jane got up to pay the check, Claudia contemplated her proposal. It was a crazy idea, but one worth considering. She tried to imagine what her life would be like with a baby. What she really wanted was a girlfriend. Rita Jane rejoined her carrying two mints. "Sweets for the sweet," she said, placing one in Claudia's hand.

"Thank you," Claudia said, smiling at her. As they walked outside, Claudia had an image of the two of them with a baby, an image that, to her surprise, did not freak her out.

21. The Arraignment

Claudia stepped into a blaze of cameras flashing outside the federal courthouse, glad she had heeded Rita Jane's advice to dress up. Claudia always dressed well, but Rita Jane had heightened Claudia's appearance by adding a scarf and makeup. "You look like an underfed ghost," Rita Jane had told her as she applied rouge, lipstick, and eyeshadow.

Paul had agreed to represent Claudia at the beginning of the case, but if it appeared the case would go to trial, he would help her find a trial attorney.

Claudia entered the formidable chambers of the D.C. Federal Court-house with her own wolf pack of friends surrounding her. Despite the large media presence, the hearing was quite uneventful. Paul entered a not-guilty plea on her behalf and the judge set a date for a pre-trial conference in three weeks.

As soon as it was over, the prosecutor approached Paul and said, "I'd like to talk about settling this."

"The only settlement my client is interested in is a complete dismissal," Paul declared as a few reporters listened in. "If that's what you have in mind, we'll talk," Paul said emphatically. Paul's forcefulness surprised her, but she realized it was a performance for the media. Besides, he was right, she wouldn't plead guilty to anything.

The prosecutor handed Paul his card. "Call me when you're ready to talk," and strode out of the room, probably on his way to make a press statement as they were about to do. In the foyer outside the courtroom, a small army of reporters attacked them with questions. On Paul's advice, Claudia said nothing. The sound of a dozen cameras clicked incessantly. Claudia felt dizzy. She fought the temptation to lean against Paul, who stood next to her reading a prepared statement:

> "My client entered a plea of not guilty today. Our position continues to be that this charge is unfounded and is an abuse of prosecutorial discretion. The government should be ashamed of itself for spending limited resources harassing an innocent attorney who is just trying to represent her client."

Claudia's legs ached. She desperately wanted to sit down. After his brief statement, Paul refused to take any questions and whisked her out of the building, walking the few blocks to Claudia's office.

Claudia excused herself and ran to the bathroom, barely making it to the toilet before she threw up. She had heard that morning sickness was more prevalent with women carrying boy babies, and wondered if there was any truth to that wives tale. She rinsed her mouth out with a travel bottle of Listermint that she had taken to carrying around with her everywhere, never knowing when the bouts of nausea would strike. She straightened the collar on her suit and ran a comb through her hair. On deciding that she looked presentable, she returned to the conference room, where her support team waited anxiously.

"I'm fine," she said, although it wasn't really true.

"I'm going to call the prosecutor to set up a meeting," Paul said.

"But…" Claudia began.

"I just said that in the courtroom in case anyone was listening. Of course I'm going to listen to what he has to say. I think I should meet with him without you being present. You'll only antagonize him."

"Fine," Claudia said defensively. "But I'm not pleading to anything." Paul nodded.

"But I guess it makes sense to hear what he has to say," she admitted.

"Glad you approve," Paul said with a hint of sarcasm.

"The nerve of these prosecutors," she felt herself getting angry. Rita Jane looked worriedly at her.

"I've been telling you all along you're not going to win this case in the courts," Dan said. "We need a PR campaign to get the public on your side. Now that the SOFA vote has been postponed a while, I have some time on my hands. Remember when I did all those PATRIOT Act gigs? I can go back to those groups and tell them about Emad's case, and now your prosecution. The material support statute was part of the PATRIOT Act, so it's all related. Paul and I can meet with organizations to drum up support. Start a petition campaign or something like that."

"I'll work evenings so Paul can go," Rita Jane offered. Claudia felt herself getting weepy again. She hated the fact that her hormones made her cry over everything. What possible evolutionary purpose did crying serve she wondered.

Paul had been on his cellphone during this discussion so he missed Rita Jane's offer. "I'm meeting him at Georgia Brown's at 1."

"You're having a lunch meeting with a prosecutor. I wouldn't be able to keep my food down," Claudia said derisively.

"That's not saying much," Rita Jane said. "I've hardly seen you keep anything down since I've been in D.C." Everyone waited for Claudia's reaction and when she laughed, they joined in.

"I appreciate what all of you are doing. I really do," she blubbered.

"Group hug," Dan said. Everyone linked arms and encircled her, surrounding her with love. And then they all left. Rita Jane went to cover the lunch shift at Paul's Place, Dan went back to work and Paul went to his lunch date. Claudia closed the door to her office, put her head on her desk, and fell asleep.

Just as Claudia was beginning to wake up, her paralegal, Georgia knocked on her door, opened it a crack, and peered inside.

"I hate to disturb you, Claudia, but I think you're going to want to read these." She handed Claudia two legal documents: a motion filed by the government to remove her as counsel for Emad Khadonry, and an order granting the government's motion.

"What is this bullshit!" she screamed. "Those bastards! I can't believe they did this! I bet this was their plan all along. They wanted me off the case so they brought the charge against me to force me off."

She slumped down on her chair and put her head back on her desk. It was only Monday morning. How would she ever make it through the week? She called Paul, who promised to call the judge's chambers to find out why she hadn't been given a chance to respond to the motion. "Claudia," he said before hanging up, "Don't call anyone else yet, okay? Wait until I get back to you."

She grudgingly agreed. As soon as she hung up the phone the other line rang, a call from Don Tucker, a crusty old *Post* reporter, wanting a comment on the judge's order. "I don't know anything," she lamented. "I just learned about it a few minutes ago." She sighed. "You probably know more than I." Don didn't reply. "Don," she said, her voice getting sterner. "Do you know something you aren't telling me?"

"I'm supposed to be asking the questions," he joked.

"Don, you've got to tell me. This isn't right and you know it."

"Listen, nothing's been verified yet, but the scoop is that there's been a leak at the U.S. Attorney's Office. That's all I'll say now until I can verify it."

"Leak? What kind of leak?

"I told you, I don't know," Don harrumphed. "Now if you learn anything you'll call me, right?"

"Same goes for you," she admonished him. She hung up the phone, which was already ringing again. This time it was Paul.

"I spoke with the judge's clerk. I told him I was representing you and wanted to know why you hadn't been given the opportunity to respond."

"And?" Claudia said impatiently.

"He said it was a clear-cut case of an ethical violation to allow a lawyer to represent a client when there were allegations of joint criminal conduct. I read the rule and he's right."

"But Emad did nothing wrong and neither did I," Claudia wailed. Her head was spinning and she felt the nausea return. Some days it never really went away, but was always hanging around on the edges of everything she did. She put her head on her desk, forgetting to hang up the phone. Georgia touched her on the shoulder and asked, "Can I get you anything?"

"A bucket," Claudia said, and Georgia handed her a wastebasket just in time for Claudia to throw up what remained of breakfast.

She made a valiant attempt at work but she felt too sick and depressed to concentrate. Georgia insisted that she go home and she reluctantly agreed, taking the documents with her. She left the office before noon, feeling so weak that she hailed a cab instead of taking the Metro. At home, she fixed herself a cup of chamomile tea and a bowl of soup to soothe her troubled stomach. All she wanted was a long nap, where she could temporarily escape from the nausea and emotional turmoil.

She had just lain down on her bed when her cellphone rang. She picked up the phone and saw that it was her mother calling. Her mother never called during the middle of the day. It must be some kind of family emergency. As she was trying to decide whether to answer, the phone thankfully stopped. She turned it off and curled up under an afghan blanket. The emergency could wait.

She put on a CD of nature sounds. She was drifting off to sleep with the restful gurgle of a babbling brook when the phone rang again. "Go away," she said. After seven rings it stopped, but before she could relax again, it started up again. She decided that it must be Georgia, so she reluctantly answered it.

"Hello," she said, straining to keep the irritation out of her voice.

"I'm so sorry to bother you," Georgia said hurriedly, "But your mother is trying to reach you. She said it's urgent. Something about FBI agents have been there asking questions."

The sudden movement of getting out of bed to answer the phone had made her dizzy. "I can't believe this day," Claudia said. "This is the worst day of my life."

"Do you want me to call her back?" Georgia said anxiously.

"No, I'll deal with it," Claudia sighed.

Tears of frustration were stuck in her throat. She absolutely didn't feel up to a phone conversation with her mother, but it couldn't be avoided. Might as well get it over with and reward myself with a nap afterwards. I could use a cup of coffee, Claudia thought, and then remembered she couldn't drink caffeine.

Audrey answered, half-hysterical, "Thank God it's you. I've been trying to reach you all morning."

"I'm not feeling well," Claudia said by way of explanation. Her mother wasn't listening.

"Two FBI agents came today asking questions about you. They said you're being investigated for suspected terrorism. Claudia, what is going on?" Her voice got high and squeaky when she was upset. "They were asking me for names and numbers of your friends and associates. Why would they ask something like that?"

Anger roiled inside Claudia. She wanted to scream or hit something.

"Mom, you have got to calm down," she said firmly. "I need you to calm down. I am not a terrorist. You know that. I am representing a client who is charged with terrorism. He's not a terrorist, either. But the FBI has been snooping around. They may be trying to drum up a case against me."

"That doesn't make any sense," her mother said. "Why would they want to do that?

"God mother, what rock have you been living under the last forty years."

"Do you need a lawyer, honey?" Her mother asked gently. I can help you hire one.

"Not yet. My friend Paul is representing me now. He's good friends with the U.S. Attorney handling the case. If it goes to trial I'll have to find someone else."

"Do you need money?"

Claudia's voice softened. "I'm okay now, but I might later. Thanks for the offer."

"Should I come out there? I can get on a plane tomorrow. Tonight even."

Claudia felt touched by her mother's concern. Maybe that was a good idea. But then she would have to tell her everything, which of course she would have to do anyway as she could hardly hide a baby from her family.

The anger melted into sadness and the tears she had been bottling up poured out. Blubbering she said, "Momma, I'd like it if you came to visit, but not right now. I need to figure some things out first."

"Are you sure, sweetheart?"

"Momma," Claudia sobbed.

"Yes, Claudia."

"There's something else I've got to tell you."

"What's that, sugar?"

She tried to form the words to tell her mother that she was pregnant, but she couldn't. How could she tell her mother in the same conversation that she was an accused terrorist and pregnant? She was a pregnant lesbian terrorist. The image made her laugh.

"Never mind," she said.

"Are you sure you're okay? You know I'm here for you honey."

"I'll be okay," Claudia said.

"I love you honey. You just say the word, and I'll drop everything I'm doing and get on the next plane to see you. You got that, baby?"

Claudia hung up the phone. She debated whether to get up or return to her nap. She was so tired that even thinking was an effort. She got under the covers, reveling in the soft comfort of her combed cotton sheets. She intended to rest for just a minute, to clear her head before deciding what to do next, but instead, fell into a deep sleep, comforted by the knowledge that her mother loved her no matter what and would come take care of her soon.

Part II – Dan and Rita Jane – Winter and Spring 2002-2003

22. Solstice Dinner

"It's a bit over the top, isn't it?" Rita Jane asked Dan as they finished decorating for the Solstice Party. Besides a large Christmas tree, a brightly colored menorah had been placed on a wooden table next to the tree, and several brightly painted African cloths and masks hung from the walls next to it.

"Of course it is, but that's the fun of it," Dan replied. "When we first moved in together, the community squabbled about such matters as whether to put a Christmas tree or a menorah in the Common House. We thought about alternating years, but that became too confusing, so we decided to celebrate everything — Christmas, Hanukkah, Kwanza and Solstice. But Solstice is, by far, the most popular event."

"You're all pagans at heart," Rita Jane said.

"I suspect you're right, but don't tell my mother who's convinced her only son is a good Catholic boy."

Rita Jane giggled, knowing full well Mrs. Canavan harbored no illusions about her son's Catholicism.

Rita Jane took out her notebook and reviewed the checklist. She had already made reminder calls to all of the people she had coaxed into cooking side dishes and desserts to augment her menu. She had decorated the tables with boughs of evergreens and white candles. To keep the children occupied, she had collected ribbons, cardboard and old photographs which they could use to make ornaments, and bought popcorn and cranberries to string together to make garlands. Everything appeared ready to go.

At Rita Jane's urging, Dan had invited Dave. Rita Jane had missed Dan's introduction to TLC. She knew Dave from waiting on him at Paul's Place, and she shared Paul's opinion that they were perfect for each other. Dan had a laundry list of reasons why he couldn't get involved with Dave. He wasn't a vegetarian, and Dan couldn't imagine being involved seriously with someone who ate animal flesh. Dave didn't follow politics, wasn't into the gym scene, and didn't go to bars. In short, Dave didn't do anything that Dan did.

Rita Jane had told him a dozen times that those were all reasons why they were perfect for each other. Opposites attract. Dan needed someone like Dave who was gentle and completely guileless. Dave was not impressed by what others looked like or what they did for a living. He liked people, whether they were poor or powerful. He particularly liked Dan.

Rita Jane left Dan in charge of stringing the lights on the Christmas tree and left to do her last-minute errands. She drove to the food co-op to load up on fresh organic vegetables, and stopped by Value Liquor for a case of wine. She bought white and red carnations at the florist. Then she returned to the Common House kitchen where she spent the afternoon cooking up a vegetarian storm — spinach turnovers, whole grain basmati rice, cabbage and mandarin orange salad, and chocolate tofu mousse for dessert (Paul's recipe). She was very pleased with herself for making such a delicious and healthy meal.

She finished her preparations by setting the tables. On each one she placed a small bouquet of carnations and a pair of hand-dipped tapers in candleholders. She tied red ribbons around the salt and peppershakers.

At five, Aimee and Esme arrived to help with last-minute set up, but most of the work had already been done. Esme opened some bottles of wine to let them air, and Aimee filled pitchers of water. At 5:30, Dan sauntered in dressed in a blue button-down shirt that accentuated the color of his eyes, his usual tight-fitting jeans, and loafers.

"Look at you," Rita Jane said, pecking him on the cheek. "You look great."

"Thanks," he said.

"I hear Dave's coming," Esme said. "How are things going with him?"

"It's not a date. We're just friends," Dan said.

Esme flicked her wrist in a dismissive gesture. "You don't have male friends. All your friends are women."

"That's not true," Dan protested. "Paul's my friend."

"Paul's friends with everyone," Aimee said.

"Thanks a lot," Dan said. "Look, he's a very nice man. But we're very different people. I don't know if anything could work out."

"I don't know about that," Aimee said. "I see how the two of you look at each other. You look like a couple to me."

"But he's not a vegetarian," Dan said. "I just can't imagine living with someone who has meat in the refrigerator."

"That could be a problem," Aimee agreed.

"Why don't you go on a few dates before you start worrying about moving in together?" Rita Jane suggested. Dan had always been a worrier and a pessimist and relied on Rita Jane to cheer him up. Although since she had moved back to D.C., they seemed to have switched roles.

At 6:15 people started arriving. Every time the door opened, Dan looked up to see who it was.

At 6:30, Dave finally arrived with rosy cheeks and bright eyes, smelling of fresh air. He hugged Dan and Rita Jane. Claudia arrived right behind him looking gaunt and tired. Rita Jane hugged her. "You look exhausted," she said, taking Claudia's coat and hanging it in the entryway. The pregnancy seemed to be draining the life out of Claudia. Rita Jane had always imagined that pregnancy would be a fertile, life-enhancing experience. Maybe a person's experience depends on their attitude. After all, Claudia hadn't wanted to be pregnant, whereas Rita Jane wanted it more than anything.

Three sets of tables had been pushed together, each piled with platters and bowls of food. For regular meals, the food was usually served buffet style, but on special occasions, like Solstice Dinner, they ate family style.

Some of the younger children were playing in the children's room, a small room adjacent to the main living room with a large glass window so that parents could see what was going on inside. Rita Jane watched them yearningly, wondering when Claudia would decide what to do about her pregnancy.

Dan poured everyone a glass of wine. He had insisted on buying the wine for the dinner, telling Rita Jane that he wanted quality over quantity for a change. When he reached Claudia, she declined the wine, which Rita Jane took as a good sign. Claudia was hungrily devouring her food, another good sign.

"The food's delicious," Dave said. "If I could cook like this I could happily be a vegetarian." She caught Dan's eye and they exchanged a smile. So far, so good, she thought.

Aimee and Paul were talking intimately to one another, sharing a private laugh. Frank and Esme looked stunning dressed in their fancy evening attire. Dan and Dave were talking together. RJ felt oddly alone, the way that single people feel when they are in a group of couples. She finished her glass of wine quickly, before anyone else was finished, and poured herself another. She was thinking of something to say to bring the group into a single conversation when Aimee beat her to it.

"Dave, Paul and I are having a dispute and we'd like your professional opinion. Some friends of ours, a lesbian couple, want to have a child and they are trying to decide whether to go with a sperm bank or a known donor. Does it make a difference later on for the child? Is it better for a child to have an anonymous biological father or a known one?"

Dan glared at Aimee, but Dave didn't seem to be the least bit bothered by the question.

"The most important thing is that the child is loved by his or her parents," Dave said. "There isn't any scientific research indicating whether one method is preferable to the other."

Aimee said, "I think it's better to go with a sperm bank. It's too risky to go with a known donor. What if he freaks out and decides he wants to be a dad and sues for custody?"

"That's always a risk, but known donors can work well. I donated sperm to friends who live on the West Coast and they have a healthy, happy 8-year-old boy."

"You were a sperm donor?" Rita Jane asked. "How did you feel when the baby was born?"

"As I said to Dan the other night, I certainly feel connected to the child, but I don't feel like a parent. I feel more like a special uncle. I think it's wonderful that I had the opportunity to help such great people become parents."

Rita Jane said, "Do you know of any cases where three parents raised a child together?"

Dan hadn't told Dave about Claudia's pregnancy as far as she knew. Dan scrutinized Dave's reaction. "I only know of one situation, and it didn't work well. It involved three women who each had relationships with the other two. But eventually it got too complicated and one of the women became very bitter and left."

Claudia paused from eating to look at Rita Jane. Rita Jane couldn't read Claudia's expression.

Dave continued, "I think it was easy for me to be a sperm donor because I'm very clear that I don't want children. I love children, that's why I chose to work with them. But after spending all day with them, I need a break when I get home. I'm afraid that if I had my own child I wouldn't be able to rejuvenate at night and I'd be a less effective therapist."

Rita Jane saw Dan's happy face turn sad. She was glad he and Dave were sitting next to each other so Dave couldn't see Dan's expression.

Dan stood up abruptly. "Can I clear away some of these dishes?"

"I'll help you," Rita Jane said.

When they were safely inside the kitchen Dan moaned, "I knew it was too good to be true. I never meet any men who want to have families. What is it with me?"

"I wouldn't give up on him yet," Rita Jane said. "People change their minds all the time."

"But why start something that you know is not what you want?"

"You can't always control whom you love," Rita Jane said.

"No, but you can choose whom you get involved with," Dan said, turning his back on her to load the dishwasher.

"I'm going to get ready for the ritual."

Rita Jane had already decorated the courtyard with pine boughs. She had made candleholders by cutting designs into white paper bags. When lit, the candles cast lovely shadows of winter themes. She placed the bags in a circle, around a metal fire pit that was stacked with kindling and ready to light. She lit the candles, lighting up the dark night, creating a warm glow. Josh arrived with his guitar. As people entered the courtyard, Esme and Aimee passed out mugs of mulled cider, and small white tapers. When everyone had gathered into a circle, Rita Jane lit the fire.

"Solstice is the shortest day of the year or the longest night. This ceremony is to bring light to the darkest night. I'll start by lighting my candle from the fire than I'll pass the flame to the person next to me and so on until everyone's candle is lit. These candles will give us light to make it through the longest night."

Josh softly strummed his guitar to the tune of "This Little Light of Mine." When everyone's candle was lit, Rita Jane said, "Now we will light the candles on the outside circle and whoever would like to can share a thought about the idea of bringing light into darkness."

Aimee said, "I'll start." She lit one of the tea lights and said, "May this light shine peace into the White House and direct our President away from war."

Frances lit a candle and said, "May this light guide us in how to help Emad and Claudia."

Dan said, "May this light guide Congress in the upcoming session."

Rita Jane lit her candle and looked at Claudia, "May this light guide all those who have difficult decisions to make." Claudia looked up at her and smiled.

Dave lit a candle and said, "May this light illuminate new love." He reached over and took Dan's hand. Happiness settled on Rita Jane like a well-worn blanket. She wondered what the new year would bring.

23. Sunday Brunch

Dan appeared at Rita Jane's door on Sunday morning, exhausted after being up most of the night opening presents with his family. Rita Jane answered the door wearing gray sweats and an oversized New York Yankees T-shirt. A pot of tea and the *Post* lay on her kitchen table next to a large stainless steel bowl of waffle batter. With no radio or television blaring, as there had been at his parents' home, Rita Jane's small home was a welcome oasis after the chaos of the holiday.

He handed her a bag of treats that his mother had put in his stocking: apricot and berry preserves, apple butter and real maple syrup. Dan wanted the treats out of his house because if they were around him, sooner or later he would eat them. He had been fat as a child, until he became an athlete in high school, and his biggest fear was that he would revert to his preadolescent body.

Rita Jane hugged him briefly as she took the bag. It had been three weeks since they had learned of Claudia's pregnancy. Dan's feelings vacillated between excitement, dread and terror. Work usually helped distract him from the emotional whirlwind, but now with Congress out on recess, the manic pace of his job had slowed, giving him time for daydreaming or day-nightmaring, depending on his mood.

"Thanks for these," Rita Jane said, unloading the bag. Dan poured himself a cup of tea and sat down at the table while Rita Jane began the cooking ritual. Rita Jane's waffle-making ritual had the flare of a Geisha serving tea. She had two different waffle irons — a Belgian waffle maker with large squares and a regular one. She had already laid out bowls of diced strawberries, fresh raspberries and blueberries, and fresh whipped cream. The vibrant colors of the berries contrasted with the pure white cream, resembling an artists' palate. Dan loved Rita Jane's waffles even though he suspected that the batter had egg in it. He didn't ask, she didn't tell. He had bought a container of tofu-whip, a vegan whipped-cream alternative, at the food co-op.

The batter sizzled when it hit the hot irons. Dan was calculating whether to go serious or keep it light when Rita Jane asked him, "Has she told you anything yet? The suspense is driving me crazy."

"No," Dan said simply. There's not much time left. Only about a week until the second trimester begins."

Rita Jane opened both irons and placed two steaming waffles onto plates. Dan took a bite and luxuriated in the warm, thick sweetness. He ate the two waffles quickly, temporarily escaping from the heavy issues weighing him down.

Rita Jane picked at her waffle. "She wouldn't have a second-trimester abortion would she?" Rita Jane asked.

Dan was lusting after her untouched waffle. "Don't get your hopes up," Dan said. "It's not a good time for her to become a mother. Or for me either. My career is crazy. And I haven't given up on the idea of meeting someone and having my own family, although that possibility is looking more doubtful every day."

"I've given up," Rita Jane said. "I'm never going to meet someone in time to have a child, even if my body would cooperate."

He wanted to tell her to stop being so self-absorbed, and he wanted her to make some more waffles. Instead he said kindly, "I don't think you've really given up on that dream. You're still grieving Sean. It takes a long time to heal from a break-up. Having a child now would be like having a rebound relationship."

"No it wouldn't." She stood up and turned her back on him, pouring more batter into the irons. "I've wanted to have a child my entire adult life. I'm just taking charge of my life instead of waiting for some man to make me happy."

Sometimes it was better to change the subject with Rita Jane instead of trying to talk her out of her morose moods. She was, in modern parlance, a drama queen, relishing her emotional pain. Dan's opinion, which he usually kept to himself, was that Rita Jane had lived such a life of privilege that she had never experienced any real deprivations, so she needed to make the most of her small dramas when they occurred.

She stood and walked to the waffle irons. She sighed tragically, and then brushed back her long hair from her face, with emphasis. "At least you've met Dave. He's perfect for you." She put two more steaming waffles on his plate.

"Perfect except for that small issue that he doesn't want to have kids," Dan said. He turned his attention back to the waffles, loading them up with apricot and berry preserves.

Rita Jane walked across the room and returned with a carved wooden box about the size of a shoebox. "Remember this?" she passed it to him. "It's my God box. I've had it since I was a kid. Whenever something is bothering me I put it in the God box, and it always gets resolved sooner or later."

"Yes, but everything gets resolved sooner or later if you just wait long enough," Dan said, rolling his eyes. "What religion did you get this from? It sounds like transubstantiation."

Rita Jane admired her box, then placed it carefully back on the shelf. "You know me. I've dabbled in a bit of everything. After I abandoned Catholicism, I tried the Methodists, Unitarians, Quakers, Buddhists, Hindus and Sufis. I take pieces of each one, never completely swallowing the whole bill of goods. I know you're a skeptic, but I'm telling you it works. Once I put it in the box, I can stop worrying about it. It's out of my hands and in God's hands. I put 'child' in the God box yesterday — once for you and once for me, so we should have resolution soon."

Before Dan had a chance to ask further, they were interrupted by a knock on the door.

"Were you expecting someone?" Dan asked.

"No," Rita Jane said. She opened the door to Claudia, who was wearing a green cloak and purple woolen scarf. Her cheeks were rosy from the cold.

"I thought you'd both be here," Claudia said.

"Come join us," Dan called out. "You'll be doing me a favor. Otherwise I'll end up eating all these waffles myself."

"I'd love some," Claudia said. "I actually feel hungry this morning. I didn't even throw up yet today."

"Well that's something," Dan said, unsure what to say. He moved his chair over, making space for her at the crowded table. "Any news about Emad?" he asked.

"He's doing okay. He's got a big firm taking his case, and two lawyers that seem to be doing a good job. It's just as well I'm not representing him now. I've been a bit distracted with this big decision hanging over my head."

Dan and Rita Jane exchanged glances, but neither said anything.

Claudia ate the two waffles greedily, barely pausing between bites. They both watched her eat, not saying anything. As soon as she had finished, Rita Jane plopped two more on her plate. "Mange, mange," she said. "It's good to see you eat."

Around her fourth waffle, she started slowing down. "Alright you two. I have a few questions for you. If I have this baby, how in hell are we going to raise it? How is this going to work?"

Rita Jane responded like a well-rehearsed actress, playing the most important role of her life. "I've got it all figured out. I can watch the baby during the day and the two of you can take turns caring for her, or him, at night."

"Right, so the two of us who have to get up and go to work will be the ones staying up all night with the kid?" Claudia asked.

"We could all live together and share the burden," Rita Jane said.

Dan and Claudia looked at each other. "I don't think so," Claudia said. "I'd want to stay at TLC and neither of our places is big enough to have all of us — plus a baby — living together."

"Do you even want to raise the child?" Dan asked Claudia. He tried to disguise the judgment he felt, but Claudia sensed it.

"I'm not going to lie to you," Claudia said. "I would not have chosen to be pregnant, but I know I couldn't have this child and then give it to someone else to raise. I know that's selfish, but I couldn't do it."

"I understand," Rita Jane, said touching her on the shoulder. "I couldn't either." She took one of Claudia's hands and said, "We don't have to work out all the logistics now, but you have our word that we'll be there for you. We want to be part of this child's life. I mean, I should speak for myself. I want to be."

Rita Jane looked at Dan who was scraping remnants of apricot preserves off his plate.

"What about you Dan?" Claudia asked.

"I just don't know," he said looking up from his plate. "I don't know if it could work. It might be too hard to raise a child with two people, neither of whom I have a committed relationship with."

Rita Jane looked at him as if he had just confessed to murder. "I'm just trying to be honest," he said, too defensively. "It's not how I want to live my life."

"Things don't always work out the way you want them to," Rita Jane said. "You do something and then you have to live with the consequences of your decision."

"Ouch," Dan said. "Raising a child is a big consequence for a one-night stand." Rita Jane started to say something and Dan interrupted her, "I know what you're going to say. You should have thought of that before you did it."

Claudia, who had remained quiet during their argument, finally spoke, "I appreciate your honesty, Dan. It's not what I wanted, either," she said. "But whether I want to or not, I have to deal with it."

"I'll support the child," Dan said. "I mean, financially, of course, I'll take responsibility." It sounded lame even to him, but he felt relief at being honest. He hadn't even realized until that moment how he had been feeling.

"Well that's good to know," Rita Jane said. "I'm glad we won't have to sue you for child support."

24. Meeting the Chairman

After tossing and turning and getting up to go to the bathroom four times, Dan finally gave up on the idea of getting any sleep. At 4:30 he was in the shower, rehearsing to himself what he would say to Congressman Weymouth. He had four hours until the meeting and wondered whatever would he do with himself for so long a time, besides get even more nervous? He took a long shower and dressed in the quintessential Washington outfit — a dark blue, almost black, suit with a pressed white button-down shirt and a red tie. He arrived at work before 6 a.m., the time Caribou Coffee opened. He felt both spacey and hyperalert, like a sleep-deprived person on speed.

Dan had been practicing for days what he would say — in the shower, at the gym, riding on the Metro. He imagined taking out the note, dramatically handing it to Weymouth, and demanding he explain why he permitted SOFA to go through. Dan fantasized Weymouth hanging his head in shame and agreeing to do whatever Dan asked.

The Rayburn Building, normally abuzz with activity, was eerily quiet, because most members were in their home districts for the holiday recess. Someone had decorated the security magnetometer with plastic evergreens that gave off a lovely smell. Perhaps someone had doused them with pine-scented air freshener, or maybe some primal smell was triggered by the sight of pine boughs. With no line to get through at the checkpoint, and no wait for an elevator, Dan arrived at Weymouth's office quite early.

No one greeted Dan as he entered the reception area. In a moment the congressman appeared, wearing a shirt and tie instead of the usual suit, to escort Dan into his office. Dan felt slightly overdressed. They shook hands and Dan felt a tingling sensation, like a centipede crawling up his spine. Dan caught a whiff of cologne — was it Brut? No two ways about it, Weymouth was hot. Dan had seen him, of course, many times at committee hearings, but had never stood so close to him. Against his will, Dan saw images of Weymouth and John in bed together. With terrific concentration, he forced those images out of his mind.

"Have a seat," Weymouth said, pointing to the leather couch. The congressman sat behind his large oak desk, putting a barrier between him and Dan. Dan thought he saw a touch of anxiety on Weymouth's handsome face and Dan felt sorry for him, wondering what his life must be like to be gay but living a double life.

"How can I help you?" Weymouth asked.

Dan had practiced this moment a dozen times, but his words failed him. He took out the note and walked over and placed it on the desk.

"I met a friend of yours named John Anderson. He gave me this note that you wrote to him." To his annoyance, Dan felt ashamed. Remember why you're here he reminded himself.

The congressman said nothing. His hands were folded together and he looked intently at Dan whose heart was pounding and sweat was dripping down the back of his neck. He couldn't believe that he was about to accuse Jim Weymouth of having had a homosexual affair. Weymouth was one of the most powerful men in Washington. He could ruin Dan's career. Finally, after an interminably long period of silence, it became clear that the congressman had no intention of responding. Dan would have to do all the talking.

When he first started as a lobbyist, Dan believed that if he could just find the right words, like a poet creating a perfect sonnet, he could convince anyone of the righteousness of his cause. Soon, reality exposed his naiveté. Politicians might start off their careers in Washington intending to do the "right thing," of standing up for what they believed in, but the reality of dealing with constituents and powerful interest groups, one's own party, and worst of all, the reality of raising millions of dollars for re-election campaigns, changed idealists into pragmatists. Politicians that rose to power in Washington did not do so by acting on their ideals.

Over time, Dan learned to lobby differently. Instead of merely arguing the merits of his cause, he looked for arguments to appeal to the member's self-interest. Lobbying someone was like putting together a puzzle with many pieces. You had to figure out how each person's interests fit together with those of the larger group.

But the visit to Weymouth was not the usual lobby visit. It was personal. Dan wanted to confront this powerful man with his own hypocrisy. He didn't harbor any illusions that he would be able to convince Weymouth to vote against SOFA, but he wanted Weymouth to know that he knew the truth about Weymouth. He had decided to be direct and to the point.

"I don't care about your sexual proclivities," he said, trying not to sound as self-righteous as he felt. "But I do care about SOFA. I don't understand how you could let this mean-spirited, hate-mongering piece of legislation move through your committee."

Weymouth chuckled. "Ah, c'mon Dan. You're a sophisticated Washington lobbyist." He pronounced each of the five syllables in sophisticated very slowly, drawing them out. "You know the way this game is played. I've been elected to represent my district and the interests of the people there." He unfolded and folded his hands again. Dan tried to read the expression in the placid smile. Was it — fear, need? Dan wasn't sure. "And the interests of my party, of course," he added.

"Why is it in your party's interests to promote hatred?" Dan demanded. "This isn't even a federal issue. Whether a state decides to give benefits to gay families should be a state issue. Congress should stay the hell out of it." Dan was losing control. He took a deep breath in an effort to calm himself down. "The Republican Party says it is for limited government but whenever it comes to private matters you can't wait to jump in and tell people how to live their lives. You're a bunch of hypocrites."

The congressman was amused by Dan's outburst. "Why don't you tell me how you really feel?" he said. "What do you think would happen if I killed this bill? I'd lose the next election and probably lose my chairmanship. Then you'd be stuck with someone worse than me."

"Why don't you frame the issue differently?" Dan suggested. "Make it a states' rights issue instead of a gay rights issue. Tell your party you support limited federal government and leave it at that."

The congressman looked like he was considering the suggestion.

"What do you intend to do with this information?" Weymouth asked.

As much as he wanted to scare Weymouth into doing the right thing, Dan realized he didn't have the heart to go public with the information.

"Nothing more than what I'm doing now. I'm not going to out you if that's what you're worried about."

Weymouth didn't say anything, but his demeanor seemed to relax. He had neither confirmed nor denied the allegation.

"I'll consider your request," Weymouth said. "Do you have anything written up about the federalism issue?"

Dan reached into his briefcase and pulled out a shiny folder with the OutReach logo on it, filled with position papers, letters, and talking points. "This is probably more than you'd ever want to know about the issue, but if there's anything else we can get for you, don't hesitate to call me anytime. My card's in there. It has my cellphone number on it."

It sounded like a suggestion for a date. The congressman was attractive and powerful. Dan could see why John had slept with him.

"Thank you for your time," Dan said as he got up to leave.

Weymouth nodded. "Thank you for your discretion."

Dan nodded in return, suppressing a giddy smile. As soon as he was safely out of the office he whooped in delight.

25. The Phone Call

One week later, at 8 p.m. Dan was still at work and swore when the phone rang again. It had been like that all day. As soon as he finished one task, the phone rang and someone asked him for something else — a staff person with a question about the gay composition of his district, or his communications director wanting information to put in the next issue of the newsletter, or his mother asking if he could come to dinner on Sunday. He considered not answering the phone, but he could tell from the prefix that it was from the Hill, probably a staffer seeking help. He decided he'd better pick it up. He answered, trying not to sound irritated.

"Dan Canavan, here."

"Dan. It's Jim Weymouth."

Trying to keep his cool, Dan asked, "How can I help you, sir?"

"I just wanted to let you know that I'm going to bring SOFA up at the committee hearing as soon as Congress resumes."

"I'd heard that rumor." Dan admitted.

"I've been thinking about this issue a lot since your visit and I've decided that I won't be voting for it."

It took a moment for Dan's brain to register the ramifications of what that meant. "That's great," Dan said, trying to rein in his enthusiasm.

"Don't get your hopes up. I'm not going to vote against it either. I'm going to take a pass."

Coward, Dan thought. Still, with one less "aye" vote to worry about that was one less "nay" vote Dan had to come up with. "I understand," Dan said. "Thank you for telling me. I was just doing a vote count and this information is very useful."

"How does it look?"

"With you sitting it out that brings it down to 18 ayes and 18 nays."

"Davidson is going to walk, too."

"You're kidding!" Davidson was a congressman from North Carolina who Dan had been certain would vote for the measure.

"You didn't hear it from me," Weymouth said.

"That means if we hold the Democrats we win."

"Do you think you can do that?" Weymouth asked.

"I don't know," Dan said. "But I'll sure as hell try."

"Keep me posted." Weymouth said. "Goodbye and good luck."

Dan hung up the phone. "Yes!" he screamed and raced out of his office in search of colleagues to share the news with.

Dan had about three weeks to secure his vote count. He needed all the Democratic votes, which was only going to happen if he could convince Reynolds to whip the Democrats, strong-arming them into voting as a caucus.

The last meeting with Parker, Reynolds' chief counsel, had been a disaster. Dan had to find someone else who could get to him. It occurred to him that Paul, Parker's predecessor, might have some ideas. He called Paul at the restaurant.

"You wouldn't believe what just happened. Weymouth's agreed not to vote on SOFA. I've got to line up the Democrats and I need you to come with me to see Parker," Dan said all in one breath.

Paul, who never lost his cool, said calmly, "You don't need me to get a meeting with Parker."

"I've got to convince him that Reynolds should whip the issue. I met with him in October and it was a total waste of time."

"It'll be a waste of time now, too," Paul said. "Parker won't go for it. He thinks "don't ask, don't tell" is too liberal. He isn't going to advise his southern members to vote against an issue like this."

"Can't you help?" Dan pleaded.

"I'd skip Parker and go straight to Reynolds."

"Parker will kill me if I go above his head."

"You want my advice, that's it. Skip Parker. I can get you in to see Reynolds. Just give me a few hours and I'll get back to you."

Dan called the offices of every Democratic member on the Judiciary Committee. He had the direct phone numbers of most staffers. Over the years he had made himself available whenever they needed help. He had answered their questions, researched issues and even written statements for their members to read on the floor. Now it was time for him to call in some chits. After three hours he had reached all remaining 15 offices and confirmed that there were still two Democratic members on the fence.

Paul called to tell him he had gotten a meeting for the following Thursday at 7:30 a.m. "I know it's early," he apologized. Dan assured him that he probably wouldn't be able to sleep anyway, so 7:30 was fine. "Are you eating?" Paul asked.

Dan couldn't remember the last time he had eaten anything resembling a sit-down meal.

"I've eaten Burritos three days in a row. The Burrito man is getting all my money."

Paul laughed. "There are certainly worse places you could go for sure, but you must be ready for a real meal. I'll bring you over some food tonight," he said.

"You don't have to, but I'd love it if you did," Dan said.

Dan left the office at 8 o'clock so tired his brain felt like it was moving in slow motion. He trudged home from the Metro wondering what wonderful foods Paul had prepared for him. He stopped at the Value Liquor Store and bought a bottle of Pinot Grigio. He was so lost in his own thoughts that he didn't see the figure on his porch until he practically ran into him.

"You look like a zombie," Dave said. "This might help revive you. Paul asked me to bring it to you."

"You're an angel," Dan said.

"I'd rather be a devil," Dave smiled seductively.

Dan hadn't spoken to Dave since the Solstice dinner. Dave had called several times, but between being sick, the crisis with Claudia and the SOFA vote, Dan had rationalized that he didn't have time to talk to Dave. In actuality, Dan had been deeply disappointed by Dave's pronouncement that he didn't want children. But since Dave had made the effort to deliver his dinner, the least he could do was ask him in.

Dave declined the offer to share Dan's meal of a field green salad, pesto fettuccini, and vegan carrot cake for dessert. He did, however, accept a glass of wine.

It was unnerving to have Dave sit at his table. He had been planning on eating his meal while watching mindless television. He wasn't up for any big conversations.

"Why haven't you returned my calls," Dave asked. "I thought you liked me."

"I do like you," Dan said contemplating how much he should tell Dave. "I've been busy. I was sick, and then I've been dealing with fallout from the FBI searching my place and now I'm crazy preparing for a big vote." He didn't mention the fact that he had accidentally impregnated his lesbian friend.

Dave nodded. "Are you sure there wasn't something else? It seemed like things were going so well until the dinner party, then you got really distant. Did I say or do something to offend you?"

"No," Dan said.

"Why do I get the sense you aren't telling me everything?" Dave asked.

Dan wished he were watching "Friends" on TV, alone with his dinner and wine. Maybe Rita Jane was right, maybe he was afraid of intimacy. He had always thought the problem was that he hadn't met the right person. It hadn't occurred to him that there might be more going on. Since things would never work out with Dave, there was no harm in telling him the truth.

"You didn't want to have kids," Dan said. "I do. So there's no point in going any further." There he had said it and Dave hadn't left the room.

"Oh," Dave said. "Were you going to tell me this or just leave me hanging?"

Dan flinched. He was the victim in this situation. He was protecting himself and Dave's words exposed him. "I hadn't decided," he admitted.

"If we're going to have a relationship — friendship or otherwise — you have to be honest with me." Dave's eyes pleaded with him. "Now I'm going to be completely honest with you. What I said about not wanting children is true. At this point in my life I don't want kids, but I haven't ruled out the idea altogether. My job is very intense right now, but that will likely change. I'm open to the idea later on."

Dan's mind raced with possibilities. He hesitated to tell Dave about Claudia, but Dave had asked for honesty so he might as well give it to him.

"There's more," Dan said. "I don't know any other way to say this but just to come right out with it. Claudia is pregnant with my child."

Dave reached for the bottle of wine. "I think I need more of this."

"It gets worse, or maybe better, I don't know what you'll think," Dan said. "It wasn't planned."

Dave's face registered confusion and then realization. "You had sex with Claudia?"

Dan nodded. "Before I met you," he added, as though that explained it. "It was a mistake. Rather, it wasn't planned. It just kind of happened."

Dave laughed. "You sound like my juvenile delinquent clients."

"It's so screwed up. I can't believe I did it. I had never had sex with a woman before and I can't believe she got pregnant." Regret encroached upon him as it did most days. He kept it at bay by working long hours and not talking about his feelings.

"It'll be okay," Dave said, so calmly that Dan believed him.

"It's such a mess. Claudia didn't want to be pregnant and was going to have an abortion, but Rita Jane wants a child, in fact she asked me to have a kid with her, and she asked Claudia to have the kid so that she, or we, or all of us, can raise it."

Dave laughed. "I'm sorry," he said between gulps of laughter. "I shouldn't be laughing. It's just such a bizarre situation I almost can't believe it's true. I can see why you would have been upset by what I said. You've got a lot going on."

Dan had spent two months convincing himself that a relationship with Dave could never work. Dave's declaration that he had not wanted to have children had cinched it. But talking to Dave had eased the anxiety he had been holding at bay. It was so comforting to talk with someone who really wanted to listen to you.

Dave touched his face gently. Dan leaned forward slightly and Dave cupped Dan's face with his hands and kissed him, deeply. Dave tasted like a summer morning, light and filled with hope. Dan let himself savor the kisses, willing his mind not to worry about all things that could go wrong and what the future might, or might not, hold. When at last they reluctantly broke away from each other, Dave said, "I've been wanting to do that for a very long time."

"Me, too," Dan admitted, "although I had convinced myself that I didn't want you."

"It sounds like I came over just in the nick of time," Dave said.

"Do you want to spend the night?" Dan asked, feeling shy as soon as he asked.

Dave nodded.

Dan kissed Dave again, this time with tongue. "Close your eyes," he whispered. When Dave complied, Dan cut a piece of carrot cake, then picked it up with his fingers and placed it in Dave's mouth. "Sweets for the sweet," he said.

"That was amazing," Dave said. He picked up a piece of the sticky moist cake and gently pushed it inside Dan's mouth, allowing Dan to suck his fingers as he withdrew them. Then they grabbed at each other, hungrily, greedily, kissing, sucking, and devouring each other with a ferocity that surprised them both.

26. Dinner with the Spencers

"You owe me big time, Spencer," Dan said to Rita Jane as they pulled into the driveway of the Spencers' Georgetown home. As much as he tried to get out of it, Rita Jane had finally convinced Dan to accompany her to dinner with her parents when she dropped the bombshell that she was going to be a mother.

Leigh threw open the door before they'd had a chance to knock. "Oh honey, it's so great to see you!" She kissed Rita Jane, then Dan, European-style, giving air pecks on both cheeks.

Dr. Spencer stepped forward and shook Dan's hand, "How are you, Dr. Spencer?" Dan asked. Even though he had known them for over 30 years, Dan still called Rita Jane's father, Dr. Spencer. He had called her mother Mrs. Spencer until she had finally insisted that he call her Leigh. Martin Spencer, however, had never suggested that Dan call him by his first name.

"We're well, Dan. How's life on the Hill?

Dan desperately wanted to avoid a conversation about politics. Dr. Spencer was Chief of Surgery at Georgetown Hospital and a conservative

Republican. Leigh, active in Democratic Party politics, disagreed with her husband on most important issues. Dan had never understood how their marriage had lasted 43 years.

The Spencer home was like an Ethan Allen showcase, lovely but unlived in. As kids, Rita Jane and Dan had usually played at Dan's house where you could put your feet up on the coffee table and not worry about spilling soda on the sofa. Dan's parents had been public school teachers — his father had taught science and his mother had taught social studies. Their home swarmed at any given time with cats, dogs, birds, hamsters, and one time they had even had a tarantula. The Spencers had never had a tarantula in their home.

Aesthetically, it was a lovely home, a renovated townhouse from the turn of the 20th century located in a desirable section of Georgetown, tastefully decorated with art from around the world. A Persian carpet with an intricate floral design adorned the hallway that led to the living room, which had a large overstuffed chartreuse-colored sofa decorated with Chinese silk pillows, also in floral designs. Leigh changed pillow covers depending on the season.

Rita Jane plopped down on the couch next to her mother. Dan wandered over to the wet bar where Dr. Spencer was mixing drinks. The Spencers drank Manhattans every night before dinner. Rita Jane, who rarely drank anything beyond an occasional beer or glass of wine, requested a gin and tonic. Dan stuck to Diet Coke.

Rita Jane and her mother were sitting on the couch holding hands as Rita Jane caught her mother up on her life.

"It's been so great living at TLC, mom, you've got to visit. My apartment is great, small but great. Everyone is really nice and socially conscious."

"Does this community have a shared mission or philosophy?" Dr. Spencer asked skeptically.

Rita Jane shrugged her shoulders and looked to Dan for an answer. "Not really. We make all our decisions by consensus. We try to keep certain principles in mind like sustainable development and equality. We operate a day care center out of the Common House."

"It takes a village to raise a child," Leigh said. "That's what Hillary Clinton says and I think she's right."

"Anything Hillary Clinton says should be ignored at all costs," Dr. Spencer said.

Rita Jane ignored them both. "The Common House is beautiful. There's a large living room and dining area, a kitchen, a children's play area, an office, a workout room, and a huge shop where I paint."

"You were born under a lucky star," Leigh beamed. "It's not easy to find good housing in the District."

Rita Jane smiled. "Are you going to get a real job?" her father asked.

"Martin, don't start." Leigh interrupted.

"I'm just asking questions, Leigh. Like any concerned parent would."

Her face burning with frustration and her fists clenched in anger,

Rita Jane tensed. Ever since she had graduated from college, and after traveling through Europe, Rita Jane and her father had fought about her "career." Dr. Spencer didn't like to lose, and had been known to have a temper tantrum on the golf course after playing a bad round. But he was losing the battle with his daughter. To have a conventional profession that paid a healthy salary and had health insurance and a retirement plan, was what Dr. Spencer considered appropriate employment. Rita Jane's idea of a job was something one did to get money to buy art supplies.

Rita Jane contemplated whether to argue with her father. "I do have a job, dad, as you know. I'm waitressing at Paul's Place. And I told you I'm having a show there next month."

"I have a colleague who is on the advisory board of the Smithsonian Institute. I'm sure he can put in a good word for you."

Rita Jane was spared from answering the question by the arrival of Tillie, the housekeeper and cook, who announced dinner. She escorted the group to the formal dining room, the showplace of the Spencer home. A glass wall with a southern exposure overlooked a large forested lot. An outside light illuminated the woods, where Rita Jane and Dan had shared their first kiss. Rita Jane had asked Dan to help her practice kissing before she went to the eighth grade prom with Bill Parker.

They took their places at high-backed chairs with tastefully embroidered cushions in a Southwest motif. Dan sat across from Rita Jane at the large mahogany table that could easily seat 16. Light from the chandelier reflected off the gold-rimmed white china, the Waterford crystal wine glasses, and the silver engraved with an "S."

Tillie served the meal: a mixed green salad with walnuts and blue cheese, Gazpacho, broiled salmon (a veggie burger for Dan), and steamed broccoli. "We're trying to eat low-fat," Leigh explained apologetically.

"It looks divine," Dan said.

Tillie poured white wine into the tall glasses and left the room. "Will you say grace, Martin?" Leigh asked.

Dr. Spencer mumbled, "Bless us, Oh Lord, and these Thy gifts, which we are about to receive from Thy bounty, through Christ, Our Lord, Amen."

"Mention our guests, Martin," Leigh chided.

"And thank you for bringing Rita Jane and Dan to visit us this evening."

"Amen," Leigh proclaimed. "Here's to a healthy and happy new year for all."

They lifted their glasses for a toast, but they were seated too far away from each other to clink glasses.

The wine warmed and relaxed Rita Jane giving her confidence to go forward with her mission.

"So what are your plans, Rita Jane?" Dr. Spencer asked. "Is the situation at Paul's Place temporary?"

Rita Jane stopped herself from saying that everything in life is temporary. She said a little prayer for strength under her breath. There was no easy way to say what she had to say. "I'm going to be a mother."

"What?" Leigh choked on her drink. "Are you pregnant? Is Sean the father?"

She looked at Dan for reassurance. He shrugged his shoulders. "No, Mom. I told you, Sean and I broke up because he doesn't want to have kids. I'm not actually pregnant. I've wanted to be a parent for a long time. You know that."

"How do you propose becoming pregnant?" Dr. Spencer asked suspiciously.

"I'm going to adopt," Rita Jane said, wondering how many of the circumstances she had to tell them. Talking to her father was like removing a Band-Aid. It was better to get it all over with in one pull.

"That can take years," Dr. Spencer said.

"The mother is pregnant now. She's just starting the second trimester. The baby is due in July."

The Spencers were, not surprisingly, confused. Both blurted out questions at the same time, "Who's the mother?" Leigh asked. "Why is she giving the baby up for adoption?" Dr. Spencer asked.

"Her name is Claudia Connors. She may not give it up for adoption. We're going to raise it together."

"Are you a lesbian?" Dr. Spencer said the L word with such disdain that Rita Jane wanted to yell out "yes" just to spite him.

"I'm not a lesbian," Rita Jane said. "We're just friends."

"You're going to raise a child with a friend? I don't know which is worse. What about the father? Where does he fit into the picture? Are you friends with him, too?"

Rita Jane hated her father's sarcasm, which he used like a weapon, to threaten anyone who disagreed with him.

"Yes," she whispered.

Nobody said anything for what seemed like a long time. The Spencers were clearly waiting for more information.

"I'm the father," Dan said.

"You?" Leigh asked, "I thought Dan was gay," she said as though Dan weren't in the room.

"He is," Rita Jane said. "Lots of gay people have kids. We're going to raise the child together. TLC is a perfect place to do that."

"It sounds like some hippie commune," Dr. Spencer said, "raising children together without being married. It's a sin."

Leigh tried to mollify the tension between father and daughter, as was her usual role. "Now Martin, calm down."

She turned to Rita Jane. "Honey, I'm afraid I have to agree with your father on this one. Raising a child is a very big commitment. I mean nothing against Dan but — this is all kind of a shock. You moving back so unexpectedly, and now this, eh, baby idea."

"But it's not a new idea, really. I've been talking about having a child for years. You know that."

"We didn't know you were a lesbian," Dr. Spencer said. "We never dreamed you'd raise a child out of wedlock, and raise it with a total stranger," Dr. Spencer said.

Dan, who had been silent throughout the unfolding drama, said, "We're hardly strangers. We've been best friends for 30 years."

"This is your fault," Dr. Spencer said. "You and your influence."

"Stop it," Rita Jane yelled at her father. "It's not Dan's fault."

"It sure sounds like it's his fault if he's impregnating a woman he's not married to. Hell, he's not even straight."

"It's my idea." Rita Jane said. "I probably won't be able to have children," she blurted out, struggling to hold back the tears that were choking her throat. "I wanted to get married. I was engaged." The words trailed off as the tears, angry and bitter, ran down her face.

"Don't cry. It will be alright," Leigh said. "You're still young. You'll meet someone else." Leigh said.

"Of course you will," her father added. "What's this nonsense about you not being able to get pregnant? Who told you that?"

"It doesn't matter," Rita Jane said, feeling very tired. "Even if I can have a child, I'm almost 40. It'll be too late soon. By the time I meet someone and we get to know each other well enough to get married, I'll be in menopause."

"Women are having babies later and later," Dr. Spencer said. "There's new reproductive technology coming on line every day. In fact, I have a colleague who runs the best fertility clinic in the area."

"But what if I meet someone and he turns out to be like Sean," Rita Jane said. "He told me he wanted to have children. I waited for years and then the bastard changed his mind."

Tears were helpful with Leigh but not so helpful with her father, who hated female emotional outbursts. Rita Jane hated crying in front of him, but she couldn't stop herself.

"It's just as well that he changed his mind," Rita Jane said between sobs. "He was a jer, jer, jer, jerk." Tears were flowing in earnest now. "He's way too selfish to be a good father. That's why I want to raise a child with Dan. He's my best friend and he will be a great dad." Rita Jane avoided looking at Dan, hoping that she wasn't stretching the truth too much.

Leigh got up from her place and walked over to her daughter, stroking her hair. "I'm sure he would be a good father." She sighed. "It's just very complicated."

* * *

After dinner they retired to the living room for coffee and Girl Scout cookies. Leigh loved Thin Mints. She bought several cases every fall and froze them so she could serve them throughout the year. Tillie offered Rita Jane decaf from a heavy silver coffee urn. Rita Jane declined and requested a port instead. Her father went to the wet bar and returned with a bottle of Tawny's. "What about you Dan? Will you join us?"

"I've got to drive home," Dan said.

She was into her second glass of port when her father asked Dan, "I suppose you were disappointed by the elections."

Dr. Spencer was itching for an argument. Wanting to spare Dan a partisan argument with her father, she brought up another issue that was sure to infuriate him.

"Isn't all this talk of war horrible? It's bad enough we invaded one country, two is outrageous." She dangled the bait in front of her father, provoking him to turn his anger toward her.

"Oh honey, let's not talk about depressing things," Leigh said.

"I agree." Dan said.

"But, it's not going to go away if we ignore it," Rita Jane persisted.

"It's not going to go away if we talk about it, either," Dr. Spencer said. "Besides, we'd be better off without that bloody dictator anyway."

"But what about all the innocent people who will be killed if we go to war?"

"There are plenty of innocent people being killed already."

Leigh started smoothing the pillows on the couch. Dan couldn't take too much more Spencer drama. He looked at his watch, and then stood up. "I've got a big meeting tomorrow. We should be going. Thank you for dinner."

"You're welcome," Leigh said.

They were nearly at the door when Dr. Spencer said, "Rita Jane."

Rita Jane turned around slowly. "Yes, Daddy?"

"Do you need any money? All you have to do is ask."

"Thanks, Daddy," she said. "I'm okay now."

"Yes honey, let us know if you need anything," Leigh added. "And come again soon."

Once they were safely inside the car, Rita Jane said, "That went well, don't you think?"

"Considering that you told them you are planning on raising a child with two gay people, neither of whom you are married to, I'd say it went pretty well."

The idea was so preposterous, they had to laugh.

"Usually all my Dad wants to know is what I'm doing for work. Now he has something else to worry about."

"Yes, I'd say you succeeded in giving them both something else to think about," Dan said.

27. Coming Out

After the visit with her parents, Rita Jane needed to take a walk to clear her head. Dan said good night, and Rita Jane walked around the neighborhood in the chilly February night. The weather forecast had predicted snow, and the air felt thick with moisture. Rita Jane hoped it would snow. She loved the way it coated the city and made everything clean and pretty. Life slowed down when it snowed.

When she returned from her walk, she saw the lights on at Claudia's and decided spontaneously to knock on the door.

Claudia answered the door dressed in a T-shirt and boxer shorts that exposed her long, strong legs. Her unkempt hair made her look younger and less serious than she usually did.

"Well, hello," Claudia said with a mixture of surprise and pleasure.

"Sorry to come by so late," Rita Jane said, realizing that it was past 10 o'clock on a Sunday night and Claudia would likely be going to bed soon. "I just had dinner with my parents and I'm too wired to sleep."

"It's fine, come in," Claudia said. "Would you like some tea?"

"Yes, that would be great." Rita Jane plopped onto the soft couch. Legal documents covered the coffee table. She glanced at them surreptitiously, wondering if she was violating some confidentiality rules by reading it. When she heard Claudia come in from the kitchen, she quickly looked away.

"Sorry for the mess," Claudia said, clearing off a space on the table. "What's up? You seem upset?"

"I told my parents about the baby," Rita Jane said. "Dan came, too, although I kind of wish he hadn't. He's never going to let me forget it."

"Oh," Claudia said. "Maybe you need something stronger than tea."

She walked over to a cabinet and retrieved a bottle of whiskey. Rita Jane thought to protest but didn't bother. The drink burned going down, making her shudder and wince, but warming her up. After a few sips, she relaxed, letting the stress of the evening dissolve, like water on a hot surface.

"I guess it didn't go too well?"

"You could say that," Rita Jane replied. "They think I'm insane, but I suppose it is a crazy idea. I feel like this is my fault. I practically forced you into having the baby. You probably would have had an abortion."

Claudia's reached over and squeezed Rita Jane's hand. Her hair smelled like ginger.

"I wouldn't say you forced me into having a kid. Dan and I did that on our own. We're just trying to make the best of a challenging situation. And you will be a good parent. We'll all be good parents."

Claudia leaned over to hug her, and Rita Jane hugged back and turned her head in so that Claudia was holding her. Claudia stroked her hair like her mother had when she was a little girl. Rita Jane felt intensely aware of the touch. A little shiver went down her spine. The tea warmed her from the inside out and Claudia's soft touch calmed her.

Rita Jane had a habit of taking mental pictures, using her memory like a camera, to record happy moments — the sights, the smells, the sensations. She stored the happy memories until later when she needed to be cheered up. Rita Jane recorded this memory of Claudia.

Rita Jane swore it was Claudia who made the first move, although afterwards they would debate the point endlessly. She felt Claudia move and then she moved, too, melting into the softness of Claudia — her lips, her skin, her hair. Their mouths connected and soon they were tearing at each other's clothes, searching for each other with an intensity that surprised them both. Rita Jane let Claudia lead since she was a novice at loving women. Claudia's moans of pleasure reassured her that she was doing something right. Afterward, they lay entwined on the couch, covered by an afghan blanket, in that state of afterglow where everything in the world seems wonderful.

"That was a–ma–zing," Rita Jane said, slowly, as if she were in a trance. "I've never come with a woman before. Except myself, of course."

"I've been thinking about doing that for a while," Claudia said.

"Really?" Rita Jane asked. "I had no idea."

"You're joking," Claudia said. "I thought it was obvious. I've been attracted to you since I first met you, but I thought you were straight…" She let the thought trail off unfinished.

"I am," Rita Jane said. "Or at least I was. If I have sex with a woman, does that make me a lesbian?"

"No, Claudia said. It's not only about sex, it's about love. You're a lesbian if your emotional and sexual attachment is to women. It's the attachment that makes a person gay."

Rita Jane pondered that thought. She had always had close women friends and men friends. Dan was her best friend in the world. Sex had never been an issue with them, or at least not one they had ever discussed openly. There had been times in the thirty years of their friendship that she had fantasized about what it would be like to be with Dan, but that had been a while ago. Now sex with Dan would have felt incestuous. It was ironic that she and Dan had been lovers with the same woman. In an odd way that she couldn't explain, it made her feel closer to him.

"It's funny," Rita Jane said. "My father asked me tonight if I was a lesbian. I said no, of course."

"Perhaps you'll change your mind about that?" Claudia said.

"Perhaps," Rita Jane said and they kissed until Rita Jane forgot about her parents and Dan and motherhood and everything, lost in a fleeting sensation of perfect connection.

28. Meeting with Reynolds

Dan practically skipped to the Takoma Metro Station at 6:30 in the morning to meet Paul for his meeting with the Democrats. He felt like Maria from the "Sound of Music" when Von Trapp finally declares his love for her. Nothing that happened with the Democrats could spoil his mood. Once they were seated on the train, he told Paul, "I've got news."

"Finally," Paul said, before Dan had a chance to tell him the news. "I thought you guys would never hook up."

"I haven't even told you what my news is yet."

"I can tell from your Cheshire-Cat smile that you got laid. I'm assuming it was Dave."

"Your plan of sending him over with the food worked," Dan said. "Thank you.

"I had to do something. I've never seen you hold out this long before. You guys have been dating for three months."

"I'm growing up," Dan said. "No more one night stands. I've been looking for love, and I think I found it."

On the short ride to Union Station, Paul gave Dan pointers for dealing with Reynolds. "Laugh at his jokes. Don't interrupt him no matter how long he drones on. And believe me, the guy can talk. He loves name-dropping, especially telling stories from his glory days in the civil rights movement. Some of them are interesting, it's just that he can lose track of time and if you don't get to business right away he sometimes has to run off to a meeting and he leaves before you ever have a chance to discuss why you came. Also, bring him a mocha. He loves them, but he's too cheap to buy them for himself. His staff is always buying them for him. You'll score major brownie points with a mocha."

"Should I bring one for Parker, too?" Dan asked.

"Parker drinks straight shots of espresso. I've seen him order triples. Since we're bringing coffee you should definitely bring one for him, too."

"What do you think of Parker?" Dan asked.

"I think he's an asshole, but he's our asshole. You've got to learn to deal with him. He'll only pay attention if you have power over him or if you have something he wants. Going to Reynolds over Parker's head will piss him off, but he'll also respect you for it."

Dan hated Starbucks and would have preferred to patronize the independent coffee shop on Independence Avenue, but that would have required walking three blocks out of their way and then getting through security with four cups of coffee. He grudgingly paid for the coffee, reassuring himself with the fact that he could claim it as a business expense on his taxes. He decided against ordering the chocolate croissant in the pastry counter. Now that he had someone in his life who would see him naked, he was especially worried about his weight.

Reynolds's receptionist had not yet arrived, so there was no one in the outer office to greet them. Hearing voices from the congressman's private office Paul walked in without waiting for an invitation.

"Paul, my friend. It's so good to see you," the congressman said, rising and giving Paul an amiable hug. Dan stayed a little behind.

Paul said, "You know my good friend, Dan Canavan?" Dan shook the congressman's hand.

"Of course I know Dan. Nice to see you again." The congressman's pinstriped suit was immaculately pressed with his Member of Congress insignia pinned onto his right lapel. His thinning black hair was slicked back with oil, covering a bald spot. His moustache appeared to be a little crooked, but maybe Dan just imagined that.

While Paul and Reynolds caught each other up, Dan looked around the room. The walls documented the history of the civil rights movement, with photographs of the congressman with such luminaries as Rosa Parks, Medgar Evers, Martin Luther King, Jr. and Jesse Jackson when he was a very young man. A photograph of Reynolds with a much younger woman and a small child rested on a large oak desk.

Parker arrived looking like he had stepped out of *Gentleman's Quarterly*. Paul gave him a warm handshake. An outside observer would never have guessed that Paul disliked him. Paul handed him a coffee. "Dan brought you a triple shot."

"Just had one," Parker said, declining the overture.

"You better have another one," the congressman teased him. "It's going to be another long day." He spoke to Dan. "We were here until 2 a.m. this morning working on the bankruptcy bill."

"I'll save it for later." Parker said, reluctantly taking the cup. "Thank you," he added as an afterthought.

They had planned for Paul to do the talking and he wasted no time launching into the details of Dan's conversation with Weymouth. The congressman appeared to be listening, as he nodded occasionally, in between examining his cuticles and gulping the mocha. Parker sat to the right of the congressman's imposing desk, crossing and uncrossing his legs, gazing off into space. Paul finished his remarks and turned to Dan.

"Sir, the Democrats can kill this bill in committee if you hold firm and vote against it as a caucus." Reynolds did not ask Dan how he had convinced the congressman to abstain from taking the vote. Dan thought it odd that the congressman didn't ask him how he had gotten to the congressman.

Reynolds surprised Dan with his reply. "We definitely should whip this. Gay rights are the major civil rights issues of our day." Reynolds noticed Parker shaking his head and said, "But I better ask my advisor what he thinks." He looked at Paul, then Dan, "I tend to go out on a limb, and this guy here," he pointed to Parker, "his job is to make sure the limb doesn't break on me."

Parker kept shaking his head back and forth robotically. "Congressman, with all due respect to our friends here, we simply can't ask our Bible-belt members to vote against this. We've got several vulnerable seats. A vote against this bill could lose those seats to the Republicans." He looked at Paul and Dan. "We've got to look at the big picture. We've got to take back the House." He gestured towards Reynolds, "We've got to make this man chairman so we can make progress on these issues."

Dan had heard the argument so many times he knew it by heart. The Democrats moved to the right to keep their seats in an elusive bid to take back power. It seemed to Dan that the further to the right they moved, the more power they lost.

"You've got a point," Reynolds said. "Bartlett and Perry are both in tough districts."

"Sir," Dan said, trying to keep a lid on his temper. "How can we ever make progress on these issues if people like you don't take a stand and do the right thing? If the Democrats of today had been around in the fifties, we'd still have Jim Crow laws in most states."

Reynolds nodded and scrunched up his face. "You're probably right," he admitted.

It was obvious that Reynolds would not make a decision contrary to Parker's advice. Dan decided that the meeting had been a waste of time. Parker leaned back in his seat, preparing to launch into another of his diatribes. "It's one thing to take a principled position when you're in a safe district, it's another thing all together if you're going to lose your reelection bid and lose the seat for your party. That's downright irresponsible," Parker declared, flicking his hair back with his hand.

Reynolds stood up and put his hands on his desk. "Look, it's all academic anyway. I can whip this issue all I want but people are still going to vote how they're going to vote."

Dan couldn't help himself. Trying his best to remain respectful, he said, "With all due respect, Congressman, you know the score. You know how to make them pay if you want to. You can refuse to bring up their bills for the rest of the session. The question is whether you're going to pull out all the stops on this issue or not."

Parker opened his mouth to say something, but the congressman said. "I could ask them to take a walk. Would that help?"

"We need them to vote 'no' just to get a tie," Dan said. "With Weymouth walking and Davidson voting against it we need all the Democrats to vote against it for it to tie. If they walk, it passes 18-16."

Parker piped in, "They can't walk. Too many people will be watching the vote. The Christian right will score it. Anyone who doesn't vote for the measure will get a black mark on their report card."

"OutReach will score it, too," Dan said.

Parker rolled his eyes. "Somehow I don't think they're too worried about that."

"Maybe they should be," Dan tried to sound threatening, but his words rang hollow.

Dan looked at Paul who stepped in to help him, "Congressman, as a matter of principle you should whip this vote. Let the chips fall where they may, but at least you'll know that you did the right thing."

Reynolds nodded again. "That sounds right."

Dan stood up, anxious to leave the office before he said something he regretted.

"We've taken enough of your time," he said, extending his hand to the congressman. "Thank you so much." He gritted his teeth and reluctantly offered his hand to Parker. "Thank you for your time," he said insincerely. Washington lobbyists, like members of Congress, learned the art of saying one thing while meaning another.

Dan and Paul left the office and didn't say anything until they were safely on the elevator. "That was a waste of time," Dan said. "I'd rather deal with Weymouth than Parker. Reynolds is okay, but Parker is a pompous SOB."

Paul sighed. "Nothing is a waste of time. You never know what effect you've had."

Dan impulsively pushed the second-floor button, "Let's go see Weymouth. Maybe he knows some other Republicans that could take a walk."

"I should get going to the restaurant," Paul said.

"It'll just take a few minutes, come on," Dan pleaded. Dan knew Paul missed the excitement of the Hill, if not the frustrations and disappointments. He wouldn't miss an opportunity to meet with the chairman of the Judiciary Committee.

"Maybe it would be better if I didn't go. He might feel uncomfortable with someone else around." Dan considered that, but discounted it. "He knows you from before, right? He probably misses you and would like to see you again."

"Do you really think you can drop in on him without an appointment?" Paul asked.

"If he won't see me, what's the big deal?" Dan said philosophically. "We're already here. It's not like it's out of the way or anything."

It was not quite 8:30 when they walked into Weymouth's office. Dan's adrenaline was pumping and the caffeine was kicking in. He thought about the night before and a wave of happiness washed over him. Love made him optimistic, and perhaps a bit reckless.

No one was at the receptionist desk, so he strode confidently to the open door of the congressman's office and knocked. Weymouth looked up from his reading. He looked taken aback, not expecting anyone to disrupt his few minutes of morning solitude.

"You're back," he said simply, making no effort to rise or shake their hands.

"Yes, Congressman, like a bad penny. You remember Paul Petrovich?"

"Hello, Paul," the congressman said formally, continuing to stay seated. "It's nice to see you again," he said, without warmth.

Dan was beginning to think he had made a big mistake, but decided there was nothing to do but plunge ahead. "Can we have one minute of your time? I promise we'll be brief," Dan asked.

Before waiting for Weymouth to say no, Dan sat down on the couch where he had been just a week earlier, surprised at how easily he was making himself at home.

"Please, have a seat," Weymouth said, motioning to Paul. "Your friend has."

Dan's face reddened slightly, but he didn't acknowledge the remark. "We just came from a meeting with Reynolds and his lackey, Parker." Weymouth raised his eyebrows at this. "I don't think they're going to whip it. At least Reynolds isn't going to put pressure on his members to oppose it."

"I'm not surprised," Weymouth said, "It's a tough vote for southerners to take."

"There are only two Democrats likely to vote for the bill. Reynolds thought he might be able to talk them into taking a walk. That still leaves us with an 18-to-16 vote and we lose. I got to thinking, maybe there are some other Republicans who would take a walk. Especially if you tell them you're going to walk. What do you think? Is there anyone else you could talk into not voting?"

Weymouth sighed deeply. "You're expecting me to muscle my caucus when you can't get Reynolds to pressure the Democrats?" He shook his head. "You're crazy."

Paul interrupted. "Surely you can convince some of the 'limited federal government' types that they should stay out of these family issues." Weymouth drummed his fingers on his desk. Dan couldn't tell if he was concentrating deeply or just irritated. He pushed back his seat.

"You're asking a lot. You know the Christian-right groups will score this, and whoever takes a walk will be considered equivalent to a no vote.

Dan was feeling antsy. "But the voters don't think of it the same way. If the member has a good reason why he wasn't at the hearing, the voters won't hold it against him."

Weymouth looked down at the stack of papers on his desk. "I need to get back to work." Softening slightly, he said to Dan, "I'll think about it."

"Thank you, Congressman," Dan said, reluctantly reaching across the desk to shake his hand. Dan noticed a trace of a smile on Weymouth's handsome face. Dan had a fleeting moment wondering what Weymouth would be like in bed, but then reminded himself that he was in love with Dave.

Once again they waited until they were safely on the elevator to debrief. "You were ballsy," Paul said. Dan couldn't tell if Paul was impressed or appalled. He decided to take it as a compliment.

"Thank you," Dan said. "I feel fueled by moral outrage." Paul didn't say anything.

"I'd say your next step is to try to get to the Democrats. I'd meet with your two no votes and tell them that Reynolds told you it was a very important caucus issue, which is true. Give them the impression that Reynolds is going to whip the issue and ask them to either vote against the bill or to take a walk."

"But they'll call Parker," Dan said, "who will tell them that Reynolds is not going to whip the issue."

"Maybe, maybe not. Those two don't like Parker anymore than you do, and would not be likely to seek his opinion."

"It's worth a shot. Maybe I'll drop by their offices now."

"I definitely can't stick around. I gotta go cook lunch," Paul said.

"Thanks," Dan said. "I owe you one."

"By my count you owe me more than one," Paul said walking toward the exit.

29. The Vote

Dan arrived at the spacious Judiciary Committee hearing room an hour before the hearing was to begin, in order to make sure that he got a good seat. Adorning the walls of the enormous room were portraits of men who had served as chairman of the committee. The most recent portrait was of Weymouth standing up with his hand on a table next to a book that looked like a Bible. There were no pictures of women or people of color.

Dan felt a rush of adrenaline, like he used to feel before a big game, or before having sex with someone for the first time. Being alone in the grand room always humbled him. Most of the time he took for granted the fact that he walked the halls of Congress as if he owned them, shaking hands with some of the most powerful people in the world. Every once in a while, during a quiet moment, he thought about that fact and felt awe and gratitude for his job where he could make a meaningful difference.

The room started to fill with reporters and lobbyists, the usual players, and with tourists who just happened to be on the Hill for the day. The opposition arrived with large lapel buttons that said, "Adam and Eve, not Adam and Steve." After about a dozen button people arrived, Dan went in search of better company. He left his newspaper and umbrella on a seat in the front row to save his place and went into the Democratic caucus room to do some last-minute lobbying.

Staffers were huddled around an enormous box of pastries and dough-nuts and two large coffeemakers, the fuel that lawmakers ate before making decisions of major importance. Remembering that he hadn't eaten breakfast, Dan skipped the sugar and went to the cafeteria in search of a bagel. Waiting in line to pay for it, he ran into one of his favorite staffers, Brian Walker. They greeted each other fondly. "Ready for the big day?" Brian asked. "Have the Bible thumpers arrived yet?"

"Just starting to. I thought I'd take a little refuge down here until more of my people arrive."

Brian laughed, "They won't hurt you, they'll just try to convert you. Show you the error of your ways and all that."

"Then I'll have to give them a lecture about population control and how the breeders of the world are destroying the environment. It wouldn't be pretty."

They walked up the hall, skipping the elevator in favor of the stairs. "What do you think will happen?" Dan asked.

"Just what you think will happen. Everyone will vote against it except for Bartlett and Perry," Brian replied.

"But do you think they'll vote for it or walk?" Dan persisted.

"Dunno," Brian said.

They parted in the big room. Dan joined some other lobbyists from his side who were milling around and sharing intelligence. The button people sat on the left-hand side of the room near the Republicans, and the gay rights' lobbyists sat on the right side. Representatives from various religious organizations arrived, some liberal, some not, each taking a seat in whichever section their beliefs lay.

The members started arriving, carrying cups of coffee with eager staff trailing behind, desperately trying to brief them.

Weymouth entered the room and walked to the middle seat in the highest row. He sat down regally and banged the gavel. "This meeting will come to order." The room quieted. There were several items on the agenda, and as Dan expected, Weymouth took up the minor ones first. Dan figured he had at least an hour to do last-minute lobbying. He left the committee room and took up a post in the Democratic caucus room, next to the donuts, knowing that was his best chance of catching members and staff at the last minute. Parker was in his office, adjacent to the caucus room, wearing his most dapper suit, Dan suspected, in anticipation of post-vote television appearances. Reynolds walked in, joking with the receptionist about something he had read in the paper. He greeted Dan and motioned him to a corner of the room.

He lowered his voice conspiratorially and said, "I spoke with Bartlett and Perry and asked them to take a walk."

Dan looked at him expectantly, waiting for him to elaborate.

"They wouldn't commit either way." Reynolds shrugged. "I wish I had better news."

Dan wasn't surprised, but he was disappointed. "I appreciate the effort, sir. Thank you very much."

Reynolds grabbed a jelly donut. "Would you like one?" he asked Dan.

Dan declined. It was 23 years since his days as a fat kid, but the memories still haunted him.

"You've got willpower, my boy. That's good. Wish I did." Reynolds took a large bite, and a glob of bright red jelly oozed out. "Messy thing. He took another bite, managing to avoid having the jelly fall on either the floor or his shirt. Members of Congress become adept at the art of eating while standing up. Then he strode into the committee room.

With no one left to lobby in the anteroom, Dan headed toward the door that led to the hall and back into the room. He could use the door that led directly to the committee room, but did not want to attract attention to himself. As he was leaving, Parker called after him.

Mustering all the politeness he could, Dan stood outside his doorway, "What's up?"

"Come in and sit down," Parker said like a lion inviting prey into his den. "Close the door."

Dan reluctantly sat on the edge of a hard chair.

"They're not going to walk," Parker said smugly. "They'll lose their seats. I'm sure you understand. We can't lose any more seats to the Republicans." Parker smiled victoriously.

Dan suspected that Parker had gone behind his boss's back, but decided not to press the issue. He'd figure out a way to get even. Smiling pleasantly, though he was seething inside, Dan said, "Thanks for the information," and quickly left the room before saying something he'd later regret.

He returned to the committee room, which by now was packed with buttoned people of all stripes. On his side of the room, members of PFLAG — Parents, Family and Friends of Lesbians and Gays — wore buttons that said: "My child is gay and I'm proud." A gaggle of ministers and priests sat on both sides of the room. One priest wearing a black shirt and starched white collar had a button that said, "Catholics for Free Choice." Dan smiled, pleased to see his old church making some progress on the issue. The guy's probably gay, Dan thought.

He returned to his front-row seat, nodding at a number of staffers he knew standing next to their bosses or sitting at a table in the front of the room taking notes. He sat down and felt a searing pain in his lower back, from an old football injury that tended to act up at the most inopportune times. He leaned over, trying to stretch out the muscles in his back and shoulders. He moved his head from side to side, stretching out his neck. When those tricks failed to give him any relief, he got up and stood in the back of the room, leaning against the wall.

Weymouth finished with the last of the noncontroversial bills and then called up SOFA. "This bill has been previously marked up in subcommittee. Are there any additional amendments?"

"I have an amendment at the table," said a right-wing Republican from Nebraska who introduced bills every year to allow posting the Ten Commandments in the hearing room.

"God only knows what he's up to," Dan said to the priest next to him, then felt sacrilegious for invoking God's name.

"A funding measure," the priest said. "He wants to cut off all federal funding to states that allow gay people to marry or adopt."

"You've got to be kidding me," Dan said. "He's outdone himself."

The chairman called on the sponsor of the amendment, who began: "This country was founded as a Christian nation. Our founding fathers respected the teachings of Christ, and they would never have permitted the blasphemy of having members of the same sex marry. The family is the basic unit of our society, and if that basic building block is corrupted, the whole structure will be undermined." He paused, pulled out a handkerchief from his breast pocket and dabbed his forehead. "I don't have anything against gay people. I want to help them. I helped found Safe Souls, an organization that helps homosexuals find peace through Jesus Christ."

Dan didn't know whether to laugh or cry. Sometimes when he sat in this room listening to this kind of nonsense he wanted to stand up and scream like they did in the British House of Commons on Questioning Day. He wanted to denounce the member as a bigot, but knew that would only fuel the opposition to brand him as hysterical.

"Will the gentleman from Nebraska yield?" Reynolds asked.

"I'll yield to my friend from Georgia."

"Thank you," Reynolds said.

Reynolds started out in his deep Southern preacher voice, "I have no doubt that my good friend has the best of intentions, but I urge all of you to vote against this amendment. Our founding fathers, and mothers," he added with a little laugh, pleased with himself for being so politically correct, "understood the importance of separating the church from the state, which is why they would be horrified by this amendment. They believed that everyone had the right to choose their own religion, and that government funding should not be connected with a person's religious beliefs." Dan watched the audience, which had gotten quiet under Reynolds' spell. "Not only do I plan to vote against this amendment, but I am introducing an amendment to call for an investigation of Safe Souls to ensure that as a nonprofit tax-exempt organization it is not involved with funding candidates for office."

Cries of protest were heard from the audience, as well as bursts of laughter.

"Order," Weymouth said, banging his gavel three times, "The committee will come to order."

"May I have a minute?" the sponsor asked the chairman, who nodded gruffly. Parker and his chief Republican counterpart gathered in a huddle.

"Making a deal, no doubt," Dan said to the priest. The Republican staffer walked up to Weymouth and whispered something in his ear. Weymouth nodded and announced, "We'll stand in recess for 10 minutes."

Other staff gathered around the chief counsels, trying to get their pictures on C-Span. Parker entered the committee room and took charge of the conversation. Dan ducked outside to take some ibuprofen and walked up and down the great hallway, stretching out his back. One thing about this job, it was never boring.

Weymouth called the committee back to order. "Does the gentleman from Nebraska wish to continue?"

"During the break my good friend and I came to an agreement, and with the chair's permission I will withdraw my amendment on the condition that the gentleman from Georgia will not introduce his."

Weymouth turned to Reynolds, "Is that your understanding?" Reynolds nodded. Dan smiled, his faith in the Democratic Party temporarily restored.

"If there are no other amendments, we will proceed to debate on the bill."

Clark did not open, even though he was the primary sponsor of the bill. The Republicans had wisely chosen their token woman committee member to open the debate. Morales, an attractive Latina from California who had inherited her seat after her husband died in a skiing accident, spoke in a sweet voice, "This is a bill about states' rights. We believe every state should have the right to decide whether or not gay people should be allowed to marry or adopt children. No state should force its agenda on another state. A few liberal judges from Massachusetts should not have the power to force another state to accept that radical view."

Dan rolled his eyes and leaned over to the lobbyist next to him. "I can't believe they had the token woman start the debate."

"Will the gentlewoman yield?" Another member of the California delegation piped up, a feisty woman from Northern California. "I'm afraid I'm going to have to disagree with my good friend and colleague. This is a bill about discrimination, plain and simple. Gay people are being discriminated against and we need to end it. We should be passing laws to promote tolerance, not bigotry." A small group in the audience burst into applause. "Quiet in the chamber," Weymouth thundered, slamming down his gavel, a little too angrily, Dan thought. The applause stopped immediately.

"Will the gentle lady yield?" interrupted Pierce, a tall bookish Republican, one of the two who were voting against the measure. "I'll gladly yield," she answered coquettishly, "to my friend on the other side of the aisle."

"I thank the gentle lady," Pierce said. "We are focusing on the wrong issue." Pierce looked directly into the camera. "This is an issue about federalism. As a conservative, I support limited government. That means if it is not a power specifically enumerated under our Constitution to the federal government, then the power is reserved to the states. I am not aware of any references in our founding document to marriage. Please, correct me if I'm wrong," Pierce paused. He waited for someone to speak, and after an uncomfortably long pause he said, "I rest my case."

The debate proceeded for nearly an hour, ranging from the sublime to the ridiculous. Dan had written the statements for many of the members who were opposing the bill, and felt quite pleased to hear them become part of the Congressional Record.

After an hour, Weymouth pronounced, "The time has expired." Dan thought he looked uncomfortable. The clerk called the roll, and after each name the member announced aye or nay. The clerk called Bartlett's name and there was no response. She called it again — still no response. Dan looked up and realized Bartlett had left the room. That meant that if the other undecided Democrat didn't vote it would be a tie, and would not pass out of Committee.

The clerk called Weymouth's name. There was a long pause. Dan held his breath. He was one of the few people in the room that knew Weymouth's plan. "Pass," Weymouth said. An audible gasp came from the audience. "I'll be darned," the priest said. "Did you know about that?" Dan nodded. The priest looked admiringly at Dan whose heart was dancing with glee.

"Perry," the clerk called the name of the other undecided Democrat. He paused, and then mumbled, "Aye."

"Damn," Dan muttered. He'd been silently praying for a miracle.

"The clerk will report the vote," Weymouth said. There was a long, silent pause while everyone waited for the clerk to announce.

"There are 18 ayes and 17 nays."

"Are there any members wishing to change their vote?" Weymouth asked. All eyes turned to Perry. No one said anything, and then a voice piped up. "I'd like to change my vote," said a very young Republican from Pennsylvania, Derek Smuckers. "I'd like to pass, sir."

Dan couldn't believe the miracle he was witnessing. The measure that had been a shoo-in for passage was going down in committee, and the Republicans were killing it. "Does any other member wish to change their vote?" Weymouth asked. Dan was sweating profusely. He desperately wanted Weymouth to close the vote before someone changed their vote in favor of the bill. His heart was pounding loudly when Weymouth slammed down his gavel. "The measure fails."

Parker looked astounded. Dan suppressed his urge to give a victory yell. The only thing worse than a bad loser was an arrogant winner. He was so happy he didn't even get upset when the fundamentalists responded by bowing their heads and praying.

30. Victory

Dan hadn't been so excited since his high school football team had won the division championship after he scored the winning touchdown. Dan had never succeeded in defeating such a significant piece of legislation. When it came to gay rights issues, "don't ask, don't tell" was about as good as he could expect to achieve, and God knows, that policy was a fiasco.

Back at his office, his colleagues whooped and yelled, slapping him on the back and hugging him. He could get used to winning.

Hannah handed him a press release. "Thank God you're here. Five newspapers and two television stations have called already. Take a look at this and let me know if this is what we want to say." Hannah was OutReach's media guru. Towering over six feet, the former football-player-turned woman was wearing a short-sleeved red suit with matching pumps that accentuated her muscular calves and biceps. The combination of feminine wiles and brute strength seemed to help her with reporters as she usually succeeded in getting good coverage for OutReach.

Dan skimmed the release while darting to his office to check his messages. He had mastered the art of walking and reading at the same time and only occasionally ran into furniture or co-workers. The voice mail voice told him that he had 12 messages. As he pondered whom to call first, his phone rang.

"You did it," Claudia screamed into the receiver. "I can't believe you pulled it off. You're a political genius. Every K-Street firm is going to be knocking at your door trying to steal you away from OutReach."

"Yeah, I know," Dan said, not bothering to feign modesty.

"We saw you on C-Span. Did you know the camera caught you whooping? Very cute!"

"What're you doing watching C-Span in the middle of the day?"

"I wasn't feeling great so I'm staying home incubating. I dragged Rita Jane out of her studio to watch it with me. She was very impressed. She wants to say congratulations."

"You were great," Rita Jane said. "I'm so proud of you. What are we going to do to celebrate?"

"I was thinking of dinner at Nora's," Dan said.

Claudia picked up the other phone, "Nora's would be great. How'd you get Smuckers to change his mind?'

"I can't really take credit for that," Dan admitted. "God alone can explain that one. It was nothing short of a miracle. I guess he must have been swayed by Weymouth. Figured if the chairman could take a pass so could he. Who knows, maybe he's in the closet, too."

Hannah poked her head into his office, "Get off the phone pretty boy. Fox is on the phone. They want to know if you can do a live show at 2?"

"Gotta go, girls," Dan said to Claudia and Rita Jane. "Do we want to do Fox?" Dan asked. "They're usually so homophobic. Tell them to call Weymouth for a comment."

"I already said that," Hannah replied rolling her eyes at him. "They already spoke to Weymouth. He's going to be there and he wants you there, too."

"In that case, I'll be there."

"You've got calls from the *Post*, the *Times*, and the BBC waiting on the line."

"Put the first one through and take messages for the others."

* * *

At 1:32 Dan ran out of his office and was fortunate enough to hail a cab on the first try. At 1:52, he pushed open the heavy glass door to the ornate hallway of the Fox Network office. A receptionist took his name and asked him to take a seat. "I'm supposed to be on the air at 2," Dan said trying not to sound too impatient. Almost immediately a very thin

woman with long painted nails and arched eyebrows greeted him and
escorted him to the green room, where Weymouth was already waiting.

Dan wanted to hug him and boast about their victory, but he found
himself feeling shy. He didn't really know if Weymouth was happy with
the vote or if Weymouth wanted to be acknowledged for his role in the outcome. He decided to play it cool and take his cues from the congressman.

"Thank you for coming," Weymouth said. "When I had seven calls
for interviews before I got back to my office, I realized this was going
to be a big story. I wanted your advice on developing a message for the
media."

Dan nodded. "Did you know Smuckers was going to switch?"

"No." Weymouth smiled, exposing his perfectly even, bright teeth that
must have been whitened. "But I went to see him as you asked me to."

"You did?" Dan said.

"Sure. You know we actually listen to you lobbyists sometimes. I
went the day you barged in on me after your meeting with Reynolds."
Dan's expression must have betrayed his surprise. "Listen, don't give
yourself too much credit. I realized it would be in my best interest if
there were other Republicans not supporting this thing, too. Make me
look a little less out of the mainstream, you know?"

Dan considered whether he felt comfortable making a joke and decided against it.

"Did you expect that the bill would be defeated?"

"Honestly, I wasn't sure. I knew there was a chance." Weymouth
paused. "Between you and me, a lot of Republicans don't like this
bill either. Most everyone knows someone who is gay. Even Cheney's
daughter is gay. We don't like to promote homophobia, but we are constantly getting pressured from the Christian right."

The makeup people arrived and took them into a small room with two
barbershop stools and a large mirror surrounded by bright light bulbs. The
makeup artist chatted with Dan as she spread thick pancake make up on him,
combed the hair out of his face, and sprayed it in place with Aqua Net.

In the studio, the sound woman clipped a small black microphone
onto Dan's lapel. "I need to test this, baby," the large, friendly woman,
told Dan. "Say something. Tell me what you ate for breakfast."

"I didn't eat breakfast," Dan said.

"Tell me who you slept with last night," she chuckled.

Dan blushed. "I usually eat dry toast and a double espresso."

"So that's how you keep your figure," she teased.

Before she had a chance to ask him, the congressman said, "I had
scrambled eggs and grits. And coffee, of course. But I don't spend all
that money on the espresso, just drink the old-fashioned stuff."

The two hosts – conservative Steve Schultz, a forty-something black
man, and liberal Doug Wagner, a forty-something white man – arrived
on the set and quickly shook hands with both men. With hardly any
warning they heard the announcer proclaim, "You're watching the

Schultz and Wagner Hour. We keep you current about what's happening on both sides of the aisle here in the nation's capital."

"So, let's start with you, Congressman," Schultz asked. "Tell the audience why you didn't support SOFA, which the Republicans have been claiming to be one of their top priorities?"

"Thank you Paul for giving me the opportunity to talk about this important issue," Weymouth smiled into the camera, clearly comfortable being on television. "As you know, I am a strict constructionist, and there is no mention in our founding documents of the federal government having any say over family matters. Any powers not given to the federal government by our founding fathers are strictly reserved for the states. I think this is an issue best left to the states."

"What about abortion?" Wagner asked. "The Constitution sure as heck doesn't mention abortion, but you Republicans are always ready, willing and able to get involved in that issue, too."

Not missing a beat, Weymouth said, "The Constitution is very clear that every person has the right to life, liberty and the pursuit of happiness. I believe that includes the unborn, too."

Wagner motioned to Dan, "How does it feel to be aligned with the top Republican leadership?"

Dan forced himself to smile. He felt like a deer in headlights. "Out-Reach works with both sides of the aisle. Gay rights is not a partisan issue, there are gay Republicans and Democrats," he said.

"Let's be honest here Dan. Isn't it fair to say that your organization works a lot more with Democrats than it does with Republicans?"

"That's true," Dan said. "But I'll take my allies wherever I can find them, especially if he happens to be the Chairman of the Judiciary Committee." Everybody laughed. Dan smiled. The hot lights were making him sweat. He hoped the thick pancake makeup would keep the sweat from shining through.

"Were you surprised by the vote?" Schultz asked. "Congressman, you answer first."

"No," Weymouth said. "I was pretty sure what the vote count would be."

"Dan," Schultz repeated the question, "Were you surprised by the vote?"

"Yes, pleasantly surprised."

"That's all we have time for today, thank you, gentleman," Wagner said. "Coming up next, discussion of the bankruptcy bill and how it will change your life."

The sound lady unhooked them from their microphones. Dan and the congressman walked out together. Dan's stomach growled reminding him that he had missed lunch. He thought about asking Weymouth to a late lunch, but felt strangely shy. Besides, the congressman would almost certainly have other things he had to do. The two shook hands before climbing into separate cabs to head back to the Hill. Dan felt strangely melancholy as he said goodbye to his nemesis, wondering if they would ever be on the same side of any issue again.

31. Spring Cleaning

Rita Jane sat on her porch drinking coffee, soaking up the sun and daydreaming about Claudia. Her first thoughts each morning were of Claudia. She loved everything about her: her intelligence, her beauty, her charm, her grace, her kindness — and the fact that Claudia did things to her in bed that made her blush didn't hurt either.

Rita Jane loved springtime in Washington when the entire city came to life with beautiful cherry trees in bloom. From her deck she could see some pink cherry blossoms, purple crocuses, and yellow daffodils, too. Being in love made her optimistic. The fact that it was springtime only increased her happiness.

They had been carrying on their furtive love affair for several weeks, sneaking in and out of each other's units and stealing glances at Common House events. Claudia didn't want to tell the community about their relationship until she was sure of it. She feared that Rita Jane's interest in lesbianism might be short lived. Rita Jane assured her repeatedly that she wasn't going to leave her and that she wanted to be with her and only her, but Claudia didn't want to go public yet.

As new lovers tend to do, Rita Jane imagined that she would be with Claudia forever. She couldn't imagine that she had ever felt this strongly about anyone or that she ever would again, but she was old enough, and cynical enough, to know that things might change.

She was desperate to tell Dan. More than anything, she wanted him to be happy for her. She thought he would, but she also suspected that he, like Claudia, would wonder if the relationship was only a temporary affair. She wanted to convince them both that she was serious, but she supposed that only time would do that.

It was a community workday, and she and Dan would be spending the morning together doing yard work. She was planning on using their time together to tell him about Claudia. Dan was in charge of landscaping. Rita Jane knew nothing about landscaping, but liked the idea of growing things, and had volunteered for the unpopular job of tilling the compost heap. They had arranged to meet early, before the workday started, so that Dan could explain to her the intricacies of composting.

Rita Jane reluctantly tore herself away from daydreaming in the sun and walked to the back of the TLC property where the community had erected a composting area. There was a large plastic box with a removable lid. All winter, residents deposited table scraps, yard cuttings, and paper products and with the aid of worms, these melded into rich soil just in time for spring gardening. Dan told her that one time he found a purple bra and panties in the composting box.

When she arrived at 8, he was already at work in the compost heap, dressed in shorts and a tank top, which showed off his muscles as he shoveled the piles of the earthy-smelling, composted material onto the dirt pile. Rita Jane half-listened as Dan explained the composting process, absorbed in thinking about Claudia and the best way to tell Dan about her new love.

"Claudia's really sick today," she started off, not sure why she had started the conversation in that manner.

"That's too bad," Dan said perfunctorily.

"She's been throwing up almost every morning."

"Mm-hm," Dan said. "Do you see these worms here? They eat the material and then…"

"Dan, I don't care about how garbage gets to be worm shit. I'm trying to talk to you about Claudia."

"What do you want me to say?" He put down the shovel and glared at her. "She didn't have to have the baby. For Christ's sake, she wanted an abortion. This baby was your idea."

"My idea! I'm not the one who had sex with her and got her pregnant. She's the one that had to make the choice about what to do. It's not an easy choice to make."

"Choice!" Dan yelled. "What choice did I have? It's not like she cared what I had to say about the situation."

"You had a choice," Rita Jane screamed back, "You didn't have to have sex with her in the first place!" She picked up a handful of disintegrating garbage and threw it at him. "I can't believe what an asshole you are."

He turned towards her and tightened his fist as if to punch her, then put his arm down and hung his head like a cowering dog trying to decide whether to bite or beg to be petted. "I wish I had never slept with her. It's the biggest regret of my life."

Complicated thoughts and emotions melded together. She was at a loss for words. His despair was her happiness. She had found love and a baby, but at a big cost to him.

"We're lovers," she said softly, deciding to skip over the preamble, all the "I- have-something-I-have-to-tell-you" introductory clauses.

She couldn't tell if he had heard her or not.

He picked up a rotting orange covered with brown muck and threw it at her chest. "As far as I can tell, you're the only one who's getting what she wants!"

In their 30-year friendship, the two had had a long history of fighting. Rita Jane was tall and strong and could hold her own. She charged at him with both of her hands in front of her and knocked him into the box.

"You bastard!" Rita Jane jumped on his chest and pushed his head into a pile of coffee grounds and grapefruit rinds. He grabbed her wrists and pulled her over into the box and smeared another handful of muck into her hair. Something that looked like a beet green tangled in her curly hair.

She slipped one wrist free and managed to grab another handful of muck and smear it in his face before he grabbed her wrists again.

"What the hell?" Aimee stood above the box with a large plastic container filled with vegetable peelings from the Common House. "What are you two doing in there? That is the most disgusting food fight I have ever seen."

"She started it," Dan whined.

"You deserved it," Rita Jane retorted.

Aimee helped them out of the bin. A crowd was assembling on the piazza waiting for their working orders. Laughter broke out when they saw Rita Jane and Dan, looking like creatures from a horror movie. Dan rummaged in his back pocket and pulled out a list of chores he had already compiled. He handed it to Aimee. "Will you assign tasks while I go clean up?"

By the time Rita Jane returned from her shower, the workday was well underway. Several people were clipping hedges and digging up annuals, children were walking the perimeter of the property picking up trash, and another group was draining the hot tub. Dan was nowhere to be found.

She was clipping dried morning glories off the perimeter fence when she had the uncanny feeling she was being watched. Several cars were parked in front of the fence but they appeared to be empty. Beads of sweat appeared on her forehead and stained her shirt. She walked back to Tulip Lane for a drink of water and noticed a black Ford Explorer with tinted windows. The car was strangely out of place with the assortment of Toyotas, Hyundais, and Hondas in various conditions that lined the street. She thought she saw two men wearing suits sitting in the car. Why would someone sit in a car wearing a suit on a day like today?

"Come take a look at this car," she called out to Aimee who was weeding on the other side of the fence. "Does it look strange to you?"

"Drug dealers or the government," Aimee said. "Or maybe both," she laughed at her own joke. "I'll go find out," she said, putting down her trash bag.

"You shouldn't go alone," Rita Jane said, but it was too late. Aimee was already rapping at the window.

In a few seconds she called back, "It's Dan's friends, Agent Warner and Agent Turner. They want to know if we've been hanging out with any terrorists lately."

Rita Jane ran over and joined her. "Why are you here?" she asked angrily. She wanted to yell at them to leave Claudia alone, but didn't want them to have the satisfaction of knowing they had upset her.

"Relax," Agent Warner said, "we're just doing routine surveillance."

"You've already charged Claudia. What more do you want from her?" Aimee said.

"We're still investigating the case," Warner replied. "We've spoken to many of Connors' associates."

"Associates?" Aimee said sarcastically. "What are you talking about?"

"People who know Ms. Connors," Warner said, unperturbed. Aimee rolled her eyes, "Why didn't you say that in the first place."

"Is this some kind of a commune?" Warner asked.

"It's a cohousing community," Aimee said.

Turner said, "Do any Republicans live here?"

"I don't know," Aimee answered seriously. "I'm not sure if any Democrats live here. We don't consider a person's political affiliation as a condition for membership. Personally, I'm a member of the Green Party, which is also the D.C. Statehood Party. The Democrats are a bit too conservative for my taste." Warner nodded as she spoke, but looked like he had no idea what she was talking about.

"But I better not give you any names or you'll go investigate them, too, won't you?" Aimee was having fun with the agents, clearly not intimidated by them. Her bravado inspired Rita Jane to ask, "Do you really think Claudia Connors is a terrorist?"

Now it was Warner's turn to be serious, "You can't really be sure what terrorists look like. After 9-11, we've learned to be suspicious of everyone. All I know is that Emad Khadonry is a terrorist and Claudia Connors helped him."

"Emad is no terrorist. Why can't you guys find Osama bin Laden? It's been what, a year and a half and you still haven't found him. Maybe if you'd stop picking on Emad Khadonry and Claudia Connors you could find yourself a real terrorist. But I know you won't answer that question so here's another one for you, do you guys know that female FBI agent whose been reporting all the security breaches since 9-11?"

"She's a whacko," Turner said.

"A real nutcase," Warner agreed. "She didn't get a promotion and she's bitter. She's itching for a lawsuit."

"Why didn't she get a promotion?" Aimee asked. "Because she's a woman?"

"No, because she's a nutcase," Warner repeated. "She's just got a grudge, that's all. She's probably going to sue under the whistleblower laws and get a lot of money."

"Are you suggesting that she made all that up just to get attention?" Rita Jane asked.

The two men nodded.

"I'd say you guys are the nutcases," Aimee said. "Anyway, you'll have to excuse us because we have a lot of yard work to do. Good day, gentlemen." She gave them a small bow. Rita Jane wanted to yell something clever but all she could think of was, "Leave my girl friend alone," and she decided not to say that.

The women returned to their work and after a few minutes, the black Suburban drove away. As it passed by, Rita Jane gave the agents the finger.

32. Metamorphoses

Having spent all day Saturday doing work around the community, on Sunday, Rita Jane gave herself the gift of a day in her studio. For two decades, Rita Jane had created a life where she pretty much did whatever she wanted to do and what she usually wanted to do was paint. She had minimized her outside responsibilities, taking only jobs that she did not care about, conserving her energy and time for her art. If a job got to be too much of a hassle, she simply quit, without worrying about it.

Although she had fantasized for a long time about being a parent, she didn't have a realistic picture about what it would mean to have to care for another person. Now she had lots of people in her life who needed her. She had a pregnant girlfriend who was accused of providing support to a terrorist, was sick a lot of the time, and stressed out the rest of the time. She lived in a community that demanded time and attention and had a job where the owner relied on her to run the business while he worked to keep her girlfriend out of jail.

She still tried to paint everyday, but often there just wasn't time. She wandered through her life in a mostly pleasant daze like a cross between being in love and having a bad head cold. The days blended into one another. Mornings she spent in the shop-turned-studio painting dark and hazy images in gray and violet, subsisting on green tea. She broke at 11 to work the lunch shift at Paul's Place, and depending on Paul's schedule she might stay until dinner. When Claudia got home at 7, Rita Jane turned her full attention to caring for her: cooking her meals, doing her laundry, rubbing her tired feet, listening to her talk about her case or just sitting on the couch with her watching television. The happiness she felt at the thought of the coming child was sometimes overcome by a panicky feeling, like she was swimming in deep water and couldn't touch the bottom.

She was vaguely aware that other people were trying to reach her. There were four messages on her answering machine from her parents. She listened to her mother urging her to call, but the idea of talking seemed to take too much effort. Sooner or later she would have to call them, but she wasn't ready for their judgment.

She was deep in the middle of a painting when Dan appeared at her studio.

"I brought you a present," he said, handing her a stuffed panda. "It's the Washington mascot. I thought you could use some company."

"She's beautiful. Thank you very much."

"How are you?" he asked.

"I'm great," she said, trying to sound cheerier than she felt. "And a bit overwhelmed."

Dan sat down on a red love seat. "I don't know which is more diffi-cult, taking care of Claudia or taking care of a newborn. I guess it's good practice, either way."

Rita Jane joined him on the couch, letting the comforting softness envelop her. "It's not that bad. I love spending time with her. It's just that so much is happening so soon. Most people know each other for years before they decide to have a child together."

Dan cocked his eyebrow. "I suppose that's true in the ideal case, but I think unplanned pregnancies are pretty common." Dan said.

"Not with lesbians," Rita Jane said.

Dan laughed. "True enough."

"How are things with Dave?" she asked changing the subject.

"Fantastic," he smiled copiously. "I'm in love."

"That's great," Rita Jane said, trying to muster up an appropriate tone of enthusiasm. "He's a wonderful person. You two are perfect for each other."

"I told him about the pregnancy," Dan said.

"Really? How did he react?"

"He's been very supportive."

Rita Jane wondered exactly what Dan had told Dave. They hadn't discussed what role Dan would play in raising the child. There was time enough to figure out those details later.

"I'm worried about how my parents will react to the news that I'm involved with Claudia. I've been avoiding them."

"It's not any weirder than you planning on raising a child with a woman you weren't involved with."

"That's true." Tears stuck in her throat. The pent-up frustration she had been suppressing was catching up with her.

"They'll come around, eventually," Dan said.

"It feels different. What am I going to tell them? 'Mom, Dad, guess what? You were right? Come to find out I am a lesbian.'"

"When you put it like that, it does sound a bit strange. But this was your choice, remember?"

"I remember," Rita Jane said. "I still think I'm doing the right thing. Some days I feel excited and some days I'm overwhelmed."

Dan nodded.

"I think I'd feel better if I told them," she said. "Would you come with me?"

"Are you crazy? I'm not repeating another dinner like the last one. I'm the last person they'll want to see. Your father will blame me, again."

Rita Jane giggled. "It is kind of your fault, I suppose."

"If it works out, I'll take credit."

"It'll work out," Rita Jane said. "It has to."

33. Another Birthday

Brightly colored helium-filled balloons wafted up to the high ceiling in the Common House. Twisted crepe paper hung from the rafters and cutout flowers made from construction paper and felt adorned the walls. Every month, the community celebrated the birthdays of all the people born in that month. The March birthday babies included three-year-old twins Simon and Sydney, 90-year-old Dick and soon-to-be-39-year-old Rita Jane. Her actual birthday wasn't until the following weekend, the same night her show opened.

Normally, Rita Jane loved celebrating birthdays. She always remembered her friends' birthdays and sent cards that she spent hours making. She wondered if she would still feel that way next year when she turned the big 40.

Claudia placed a pointed paper hat decorated with stars on her head and kissed her on the lips. Startled by the public display of affection, Rita Jane pulled away, then felt guilty and kissed her back.

"What was that about?" Claudia asked.

"Nothing. I'm sorry. I've just been in a funk lately." She didn't feel like talking about it, in part because she wasn't sure what "it" was. "Look at the cakes," she said, changing the subject.

Two gigantic cakes – one chocolate, one vanilla, each with thick, gooey layers of frosting – rested on a table covered with a plastic birthday table cloth.

"They're vegan," Dan announced proudly. "And there's plenty of Soy Delicious ice cream for everyone. No animals were harmed in the preparation of this birthday celebration."

Once a sufficient crowd had assembled, Dan declared it was time to light the candles, and then the crowd broke into a rousing chorus of "Happy Birthday." When it was over, the four birthday people blew them out collectively.

"That is so unhygienic," Dan remarked. "No one ever says so, but really shouldn't we end this tradition of having people spit all over the cake?"

"You're such a wet blanket," Claudia said. "What do you think, Dave, is it okay to blow out birthday candles?"

"Dan's right. It's not a hygienic tradition."

"You'd just agree with anything he said because you're so in love," she said. She turned her attention back to Rita Jane. "You have to make a wish," she said, handing her a piece of paper. "It's a tradition. We collect the birthday wishes and read them on New Year's Eve."

Rita Jane wavered between wishing for a healthy baby and wishing that the U.S. didn't go to war. She decided to wish for both.

She took a bite of the chocolate cake, suspicious of a cake made without eggs, butter, or milk, but was surprised at how delicious and moist it was. She was on her second piece when Aimee announced it was time to put the wishes in the time capsule. Rita Jane handed her slip of paper to Aimee.

Simon had a piece of chocolate cake in one hand and a handful of chocolate soy ice cream in the other, and chocolate covered his face, hair, and clothes. Rita Jane reached over with a napkin and attempted to clean him up before he joined the other toddlers who were already running around the room. "Come play me," he said to Rita Jane, grabbing her hand and leading her into the children's room.

Simon sat her next to a play kitchen set. He handed her a plastic plate with a piece of plastic food. "Hamburger," he said. "Chicken," he said, handing her another one. Rita Jane wondered how a young vegetarian could identify these meat products that were barely identifiable to a carnivore.

"Thank you," she said, picking up the hamburger and pretending to take a bite. Simon smiled and ran after his sister who was throwing a ball and chasing after it. Three-year-old Adrian was drawing on a blackboard with a thick piece of pink chalk. She grabbed a piece of yellow chalk and sketched out a scene of a little boy holding a piece of chalk. "That's me," he said, pointing to the picture.

"That's right," Rita Jane said. "Good job."

Simon saw the picture and yelled, "Do me, do a picture of me," and soon, a half dozen children were sitting at her feet, begging Rita Jane to draw pictures of them.

She noticed that the wall next to the blackboard was completely bare. The idea occurred to her that she should paint a mural with the kids. She'd have to ask Claudia what committee that would go through. It would probably involve many meetings and discussions, which she had no interest in doing. She imagined sneaking into the children's room in the middle of the night and painting it and imagined peoples' reactions. She couldn't imagine that anyone would make her paint over it once the project was actually done.

Through the glass window that separated the children's room from the main room of the Common House, Rita Jane saw Claudia and Dan talking together, gesturing in her direction. She was glad to see them getting along better now. She wondered what they were talking about, but not enough to go find out.

When she had drawn all the kids, they lost interest in the blackboard and turned to other games. Simon poured her a cup of tea from his plastic teapot into a pink plastic mug and she pretended to drink it. "Delicious. It needs sugar. Could I have some sugar, please?"

"We don't eat sugar," Simon said. "You can have honey." He handed her a small plastic container, whose purpose was unclear. Sydney grabbed it out of his hand and clutched it tightly. Simon wailed, "Give it me. Mine."

"That wasn't nice," Rita Jane said to Sydney, unsure how much she should discipline a three-year-old. One of the twins' mothers intervened making Sydney give the fake honey container back to Simon.

It was hard to believe that she would soon be a parent herself. Would she know how to handle squabbles then? How did parents learn to do things like referee disputes with children? In her family, it had been simple. Her father had been the disciplinarian, which wasn't much of an issue because Rita Jane rarely got into trouble. How would she and Claudia sort through these roles? Would Dan be involved? If so, how? There were so many details to figure out. Would they live together, and if so, where? Rita Jane made herself a mental note to put those questions in her God box.

She smelled her wild patchouli and lavender before she felt her hand. "A penny for your thoughts," Claudia asked her.

Rita Jane smiled. "I'm thinking about the future. A dangerous thing to do, I know."

"Birthdays do that to you. They always put me in a reflective mood. Have I done what I wanted to this past year, what are my goals for the coming year, that kind of thing," Claudia let the thought trail off.

"I can't wait to see what your baby will look like," Rita Jane said. "It's going to be gorgeous, of course, with you and Dan for parents."

Claudia took Rita Jane's hand and placed it on her belly. "It's not my baby, it's our baby. Can you feel it kicking?" Claudia moved her hand. "There it is, feel it? This kid is going to be a soccer player."

Claudia placed her hand over Rita Jane's hand. "It's our baby," she repeated.

"Our baby," Rita Jane repeated softly, wishing she felt that it were true.

34. Opening Night

"RJ there's another delivery for you," Esme called out. "Aren't you popular?" Earlier, a florist had delivered two dozen roses — pink, yellow and white — from Claudia with a card that said, "All my love."

Rita Jane looked up from arranging pieces of pottery. She opened the card and read out loud, "Happy Birthday to our special daughter. We're proud of you, Mom and Dad.

She transferred the flowers — a bouquet of orange gladiolas, bright yellow daffodils and purple irises — from the plain glass vase to a large blue ceramic vase with splotches of color painted on that looked like flowers blowing in the wind. The flowers improved the appearance of the vase, like putting furniture into a room improves the appearance of a room. Objects looked their best when used for their proper purposes, she mused.

The flowers brightened Rita Jane's mood, especially the bouquet from her parents. Always in the back of her mind was the little voice that told her that her parents would have preferred her to be a lawyer, a diplomat or something more respectable and dependable than a painter.

Paul had gone all out for the big event, buying several cases of wine and preparing dozens of dishes with fancy finger foods like: Swedish meatballs in mushroom sauce and artichoke tofu spread. A crystal bowl filled with bright red strawberries stood next to a fondue pot bubbling with melting chocolate along with green and red grapes adorning a tray of assorted cheeses.

Esme had solicited donations for the auction from all of her many artist friends. Two long tables covered with a white lace tablecloth, a bequest from Grandma Jane, held various donations from other artists who had contributed to the cause of Emad's defense. A potter had donated a set of earthenware dishes, bowls, and mugs brightly painted with abstract floral patterns. A bead artist had created several sets of necklaces and matching earrings. A photographer contributed a dozen shots of Washington at various times of the year, including several of the Capitol Building surrounded by magnificent pink cherry blossoms. Another sculptor had donated two small statues of heads — a man and a woman — with African features.

Rita Jane turned her attention to a last-minute inspection of her paintings. She walked around the room, taking in the images as if she were an observer and not the creator. She moved the corners of the frames up or down, trying to line them up evenly. She stopped in front of her favorite: a mottled gray background in which you could see a faint outline of the Capitol. Two squares were imposed on the foreground. One contained a barren tree branch and the other was empty.

At 5 o'clock, there was nothing left to do but wait. Rita Jane took a brisk walk around the block without her coat on, letting the cold air wake her. By the time she returned to Paul's Place, Dan was there, holding a bunch of mixed flowers, the kind you could buy at the Metro stops for $3 a bunch. "I didn't have time to go to a proper flower shop," he said apologetically.

"They're lovely," Rita Jane said, adding them to her collection.

"Are you nervous?" Dan asked.

"Yes," she admitted.

"It'll be great. You're stuff looks great," Dan said reassuringly.

"Not about the show. About Claudia and my parents being in the same room together."

"Oh, that. They're both well mannered. It will be fine. Nobody's going to cause a scene."

"What gave you the idea that my father is well mannered?" she said. "Here, help me pick out some items to put into the silent auction."

Rita Jane busied herself arranging the silent auction items and practiced her deep breathing exercises. As people began to arrive, her anxiety increased, and with each arrival she turned to see who it was. Punctual as always, her parents arrived just before 6. Her father wore the standard Washington outfit — a blue suit, white shirt and red tie — and her mother wore a blue linen pants suit with a white silk blouse. Rita Jane hugged them both. "Thank you so much for coming."

"Of course we'd come," her mother said with a trace of irritation.
"Wouldn't miss it for the world," her father agreed.

Soon after, Claudia arrived. Rita Jane prayed Claudia wouldn't kiss her in front of her parents, and was relieved when she gave her a quick hug, the kind you'd give a good friend, instead of their usual slurpy kiss.

"Mom, Dad, this is Claudia. The one I've told you about," Rita Jane said.

"Nice to meet you," Leigh said politely, but not warmly. Before they had a chance to continue, Paul interrupted the crowd by clanging a glass with a knife.

"Thank you all for coming this evening. All the proceeds from this evening will go toward Emad Khadorny's defense. Emad was charged back in October with providing material support to a terrorist group. Claudia Connors from the federal defender's office was representing him until the government charged her with the same crime. Both of these charges are unfounded. They are an indication of the ridiculous lengths our government will go to make it look like it is doing something about terrorism.

"Because of the charge against her, Claudia was forced off the case. Presson and Dunn, who have taken the case pro bono, are now representing Emad but they need help paying expenses. So please, be generous. Bid early and often."

Rita Jane anxiously awaited her turn to speak. Esme had insisted that she say something to the crowd since she had donated so many of her paintings to the cause. While she normally enjoyed speaking to a crowd, anxiety about her parents interacting with Claudia was distracting her. She decided to keep it simple. Short and sweet. People liked that.

"Thank you all for coming. The paintings on the walls are a series I am calling 'The Color of Fear.' I am trying to put into color and shape the mood in our country since September 11. I am donating all of the proceeds from tonight's event to a public campaign to raise awareness about Emad's case."

Claudia clapped loudly, and the crowd joined in.

When she finished, Esme came and stood next to Rita Jane and lifted her glass. "I'd like to propose a toast to Rita Jane. She's been working on these pieces for several months, and as you'll see, they are quite exceptional. I'd also like to toast all the other artists who have donated work for tonight's event."

The din of the crowd made small talk impossible, which was just as well, as it would mean there was less chance that her parents and Claudia would actually speak to each other. Rita Jane walked around the room, craning to hear remarks about her work. No matter how many shows she had, each one felt like she was opening her soul, waiting for people to accept or reject it. She fought the urge to hide under a table or go outside and wait until it was over. She overheard snatches of conversation, "Nice," and "Interesting," which she always interpreted to mean the person couldn't find anything truly complimentary to say about her work.

Dan handed her a plastic cup of red wine. After two sips she felt lightheaded and remembered that she hadn't eaten all day. Emad's wife Sarah, wearing a black veil and plain black dress, embraced her warmly and said, "Thank you so much for organizing this party. Your work is brilliant."

"Thank you," Rita Jane said. Brilliant was a word she liked.

She felt a hand on her shoulder, "Very nice, sweetheart," Leigh said.

"Yes, congratulations," her father said, making an effort to be warm.

"I'm Sarah Khadonry," Sarah said warmly, extending her hand to first Leigh, then Dr. Spencer. "You must be so proud of your daughter. She's so talented."

"We think so," Leigh agreed.

Rita Jane worried that her dad would make some comment about the case, but thankfully he did not. She was dying to know what Claudia thought, so she excused herself and walked over to where Claudia was looking intensely at a picture of a woman sitting on a porch swing. In the background was the image of a prison and a disembodied face staring out at the viewer. Rita Jane wondered if Claudia realized it was a picture of her.

Rita Jane stood like a statue holding her breath, waiting for Claudia's reaction. Finally she couldn't wait any longer and she said anxiously, "What do you think?"

Claudia turned around, "I'm overwhelmed. There are so many of them and they are all so different."

Rita Jane smiled. "Do you recognize this one?"

"Is it me?" Claudia asked tentatively.

"Yes."

"I like it. How much are you asking for it?"

"Eight hundred, but you don't have to buy it. I'll give it to you, or paint you another one."

"Are you kidding? It's a bargain," Claudia said. "Plus it's a good cause."

Rita Jane walked Claudia over to the cashier. She was gratified to see that several of her paintings had already sold. The hard part was over. Even one sale was enough to reassure her. Selling several so soon was unusual. She attributed it to the fact that it was a fundraiser, but still, her work was selling.

Rita Jane watched her parents and Sarah walk over to where she and Claudia were standing together. As the various pieces of her life joined together, she hoped they would fit, although more likely her father would not want to be part of this puzzle.

Sarah grabbed Claudia and Rita Jane's hands. "We are eternally grateful to these two women," she said proudly. "The lawyer and the artist. What a team."

"Indeed," Leigh said looking suspiciously at Rita Jane. She knows, Rita Jane thought.

"Sarah's been telling us about her husband's case," Martin said. "I didn't realize how weak the charges were."

"I told you, Daddy," Rita Jane admonished him.

"I'd like to make a donation. How much is the sculpture over there?"
He pointed to one of Esme's sculptures, a birdbath in the form of a tree,
its thick trunk and lush branches formed the basin.

"For you, a mere $10,000," Esme joked.

"I'll take it," Dr. Martin said. Sarah burst into tears and threw her
arms around the doctor's neck. He flushed with embarrassment and
quickly pulled away from the embrace. Claudia squeezed Rita Jane's
hand, furtively, but Rita Jane saw that her mother noticed.

35. Meeting Audrey

Rita Jane dashed around her apartment, frantically trying to find
something to wear to meet Claudia's mother, Audrey. She was expected
at 7. At quarter to, she still had not decided what to wear. Southern
women tended to dress up, so she couldn't wear jeans. She tried on an
Indian print cotton dress that her mother had bought her, but that made
her look like a hippie. Finally she settled on a nice pair of black pants
and a multicolored tank top with matching sweater. Perfume? Lipstick?
She decided yes to both, putting on a light pink shade and a subtle scent
called Cotton Wind.

She had met Sean's parents, and the parents of other significant others,
but she couldn't remember feeling this nervous before. She hadn't seen
Claudia since Audrey had arrived in Washington two long days ago. Her
body ached from missing Claudia. She had spent the 48 hours of their
separation willing the time to pass quicker so she could see her again.

Before she left she sat in front of her alter where she kept her God
box, some candles, and statutes of the Virgin Mary and Buddha
— and prayed that the meeting would go well. Then she wrote the
word "Audrey" on a slip of paper and tucked it into her God box.

She felt excited like she had before junior high dances — the anticipation of hoping for some meeting that would transform her pedestrian life
into something extraordinary.

The bubble burst when Claudia opened the door and gave her a quick
kiss, more like the kind you'd give your friend than your lover. Not to be
deterred, Rita Jane grabbed her and squeezed her. "I've missed you," she
whispered in Claudia's ear. Claudia looked good. Her cheeks had some
color and she looked less gaunt. Maybe a visit from her mother had been
just what she needed.

Audrey got up from the couch and walked over to greet Rita Jane.
Rita Jane stuck out her hand, but Audrey ignored it and wrapped her into
a Texas-sized hug.

"It's very nice to meet you, Mrs. Connors," Rita Jane said, after she
pulled away from the embrace.

"My mother was Mrs. Connors. Please, call me Audrey."

"Nice to meet you, Audrey," Rita Jane repeated. "I brought some wine and juice," she said to Claudia. "Shall I open them?"

"That would be lovely," Audrey answered. Rita Jane looked at Claudia, who nodded.

Rita Jane went into the kitchen, searching for the corkscrew. Claudia followed behind her. "I'm so nervous," Rita Jane said. "I can't remember the last time I met someone's parents. I want her to like me."

"She'll like you," Claudia said brightly. "How can she help it?"

Claudia took three sea-green-colored Mexican glass goblets into the living room. Rita Jane followed behind with the two bottles.

Claudia sat next to her mother on the couch and Rita Jane sat in an adjoining seat. Did she imagine it, or was Claudia trying to put distance between them? She suspected she'd do the same thing if it were her parents.

Rita Jane poured the drinks and raised her glass. "A toast, to meeting the mother of the most amazing woman I have ever met." Rita Jane noticed Audrey stiffen but she recovered quickly.

"What a charming thing to say," Audrey said tersely, raising her glass.

Rita Jane didn't know whether to believe her or not. She decided to steer the conversation to more neutral territory. "Are you having a nice visit?" she asked.

"Oh my yes, it's been lovely. We saw the cherry blossoms. I've always wanted to see them and they were as spectacular as everyone says."

"Mom was kind enough to drive to and from the Tidal Basin, which was more than my nerves could handle. I threw up on Route 66," Claudia said.

"You poor thing," Rita Jane said, sounding sympathetic, but thinking, as she had, many times before, that her body would have handled pregnancy much better than Claudia's. She had broad hips and a more earthly shape than Claudia, who looked like a starving person whose belly was distended from hunger.

"Have you gotten to see any of the museums yet?" Rita Jane asked, changing the subject.

"Yes, we went to the Asian art museum. What's it called, Claudia?"

"The Freer."

"That's right. That was lovely, too."

"And we're going to a performance of the Alvin Ailey Dance Company at the Kennedy Center."

"Sounds wonderful," Rita Jane said, feeling hurt that she hadn't been included. There was a pause in the conversation. Rita Jane studied her glass for what felt like a long time. Finally, Audrey broke the silence.

"Claudia tells me you're an artist."

Rita Jane nodded, trying to gauge from Audrey's tone if she could sense any judgment. People were usually fascinated by or judgmental of her career choice. Rita Jane couldn't tell with Audrey.

"Yes, I'm a painter," she said.

"What do you paint?" Audrey asked. Rita Jane smiled to herself, thinking about the piece she was working on now, a nude of Claudia.

Claudia interrupted. "She paints all kinds of things, Momma. She just did a show not too long ago called 'The Color of Fear' based on the terrorism color-coded alerts that the administration is always putting out."

"Oh," Audrey said, as though unsure what more to say. "That sounds very interesting."

"I bought one," Claudia said, getting up from the couch and walking over to the stairs. She walked up to the landing of the staircase where the painting was hanging and brought it over to her mother.

Rita Jane tensed as she waited for Audrey's reaction. She probably wouldn't like it. It was too abstract. Audrey studied it closely, as though she were really trying to understand it. Rita Jane waited with her breath held. Finally Audrey said, "That's really good. You're obviously very talented."

Rita Jane blushed and let out her breath. "Thank you."

"Mom was an art history major," Claudia explained.

"Really?" Rita Jane asked, surprised.

"Yes, but there's not much call for art history majors in Texas, I'm afraid. I haven't really done anything with my degree."

Audrey took a long sip of her wine and put down her glass. She didn't protest when Rita Jane refilled it.

"Girls, I know this is a bit awkward, but I think we have to discuss a few things like how are the two of you going to raise this child?"

Rita Jane hadn't been expecting Audrey to bring up the subject so frankly or so soon. She wasn't sure what to say. Before she had a chance to say anything, Audrey asked, "Do your parents know? Are they supportive?"

Rita Jane flinched. "Well, they know Claudia is pregnant and they know I'm planning on raising the child with her." She took a large sip of wine gauging how to continue.

Audrey sensed her hesitation. "What is it sugar?"

"They don't know that we're, together. I've never been with a woman before. Romantically, I mean."

Audrey laughed so hard she had to put her glass down. "Sweetheart, I think that if you've told them about the baby, the other piece will pale in comparison. How did they react? Are they excited about being grandparents?"

"I don't know. I don't think so. I think they're embarrassed. They don't know how they'll explain it to their friends. Or to the priest. They're Catholic."

"Yes, I see. Well, I'm sure it is a bit of a shock," Audrey said. "I can vouch for that." She took a large swig of wine then looked Rita Jane straight in the eye. "When exactly are you planning on telling them?"

Rita Jane felt idiotic. "I don't know."

Audrey nodded. "What about Dan? What role is he going to play?"

Rita Jane and Claudia looked at each other. "We haven't totally figured that out yet," Claudia admitted.

Audrey raised an eyebrow. Rita Jane looked away and drained her glass of wine and poured herself another.

"Honestly, Momma I wasn't trying to get pregnant," Claudia said. "We used a condom." Rita Jane shot her a glance, trying to catch her attention. She knew they had not used a condom.

Audrey burst out laughing. "You sound like a teenager. You know the women in our family are very fertile. Why we only need a man to look at us and we become pregnant. We drop babies like there was no tomorrow."

Claudia and Rita Jane sat quietly feeling like children being scolded. Audrey finished her second glass of wine. "I hate to say this, but it doesn't seem like you've thought this thing out very well."

Without planning what she was going to say, Rita Jane blurted out, "It's not her fault. I talked her into having the baby. I was the one who wanted to get pregnant. I've wanted to be pregnant for at least the last five years. When my fiancé broke up with me I decided to ask Dan, who's my best friend, to be a sperm donor." The words flew out of her. Why was she telling her all of this? "Then I found out that I probably can't have children so I was going to adopt. That's when Claudia told me she was pregnant and we decided to raise the child together."

"I'd hardly say it is your fault, Rita Jane. You didn't force Claudia to get pregnant. It sounds to me like you're helping out the two of them who are too wrapped up in their careers to think about anyone besides themselves."

Rita Jane hadn't looked at the situation that way before. It made her feel comforted, like she was doing a good thing instead of being selfish.

"Do you think your relationship is ready for the stress of raising a child?" Audrey asked. Claudia looked on the verge of tears.

"I think we'll do okay," Rita Jane said, trying not to sound too defensive. "We'll probably do as well as most people."

"I'm not so sure," Claudia said. "I think I'm going to be a horrible mother." Claudia burst into tears. Rita Jane put her arm around her.

"Nonsense," Audrey said, "Once you make up your mind to do something, you always do a good job. I'm sure you'll both be competent parents." Rita Jane wondered if she really meant it.

"People don't tell you this, but parenting puts a big strain on relationships. It sure did with your daddy anyway. Lord knows it might be easier when you have two women doing it together. Your father was not very helpful when you children were born. I think the whole thing freaked him out."

"We're going to need your help Momma," Claudia said.

Audrey reached over across the couch and held her daughter. "You've got it, baby girl. You too," she said to Rita Jane, patting the seat on the couch next to her, inviting her to join in as she wrapped her arms around both of them.

36. The Offer

"Listen to me," Paul said, his tone on the edge of impatience. "It's not going to get any better than this. What do you want, anyway?"

"A complete dismissal and an apology," Claudia said. "And dismissal of the charges against Emad."

Paul slammed his hands on the table. "Dammit Claudia, be reasonable. I can only represent you, as you bloody well know."

Dan watched his friends, the public defender and former Hill staffer, with amusement wondering which of the stubborn lawyers would win the day. He was biding his time to interrupt and play mediator, but held off, enjoying the spectacle unfold.

"It does seem like a good deal, sugar," Audrey drawled. "Just get this case over with. Put it behind you."

"Can you explain it one more time?" Rita Jane asked.

"He'll dismiss the charges on a couple of conditions," Paul said.

"I can't stand the smell of that fish," Claudia said, referring to the lox that Paul had brought, along with a dozen bagels. "I'm going to puke." She walked away from the table and opened the kitchen window, letting a frigid breeze blow through the kitchen.

"Are you okay?" Rita Jane said, walking over and putting her arm around Claudia. "We can discuss this later if you're not up to it."

"She's pregnant, she's not an invalid for Christ sake," Paul said. "You need to deal with this now Claudia."

Audrey laughed. "Spoken like a man. I wish men could get pregnant, even just for a month or so, and experience what it's like to feel like you have a bad case of the flu for nine months, and that's the easiest part of it."

Dan decided he couldn't wait any longer to intervene. "Let's go over this one more time," he said. "As I understand it, the government will dismiss the case against you on two conditions: you agree to stop representing Emad and sign an affidavit that admits that you engaged in improper conduct, but hadn't realized it at the time."

"No way," Claudia said. "It's not true. I can't sign an affidavit to something that's not true."

Paul reached into a backpack and pulled out a stack of photocopied cases.

"I knew you'd say that," he said handing it to her. "I did a little research. It appears that it is true. Those letters you mailed were written to the organization Emad donated money to. He was under a court order not to contact them. By mailing the letters you assisted him in violating a court order."

"Bullshit," Claudia said sullenly.

"And then there was the phone call," Paul continued, unfazed by her reaction. "You placed a call to the Widows and Orphans Office in Saudi Arabia. They have the phone bill to prove it. Again, acting as his lawyer, you facilitated your client in breaking a court order."

"I didn't help my client — I made a call on behalf of his wife."

"Who was acting on behalf of her husband," Paul insisted.

"Where's the proof?" Claudia yelled. "I can't believe you would have me sell out on this, Paul. Besides the whole charge is trumped up. Emad hasn't done anything wrong. The court order isn't valid. How can I provide material support to a terrorist who isn't a terrorist?"

"Not true," Paul said. "I researched that point, too. Even if a person is being held wrongfully on a charge for which they are innocent, it is still illegal to disobey a court order related to that charge."

"Christ," Claudia said angrily. "This is such bullshit. How can you even deal with these people!" she yelled at Paul.

Rita Jane patted her on her thigh. "It's okay," she mouthed silently. "Don't get upset."

Paul said, "Listen Claudia. Will you stop acting like a client and start acting like a lawyer? You did, technically, break the law. Why won't you sign an affidavit admitting it?"

"Because it's a bullshit technicality. I didn't do anything wrong. I can't believe you guys are telling me to agree to this." Hot, angry tears of pain and rage burst out and she sobbed uncontrollably. "If you're sick of representing me, I understand. I can find someone else."

She got up and left the room, with Rita Jane and Audrey following after her. Dan couldn't remember ever seeing Claudia cry in front of people. She prided herself on her ability to control her emotions. He looked at Paul, but neither knew what to do.

Claudia walked into the kitchen and sat down heavily. Dan felt sorry for her. "I'm sorry Paul. It's these damn hormones. Is there anything else I need to know?"

"They want you to go public with your admission of wrongdoing."

Claudia shook her head. "Never."

"If you sign the affidavit it will be public record anyway. Reporters will find it and make it public. You might as well be the one who goes public so you can control the story."

She shook her head again but didn't say anything. It was a lost cause. No agreements would be made today. Dan would have to think of something else to do to get the case resolved. He had an idea, but didn't want to discuss it with this crowd.

"Please tell me that you'll at least think about it?" Paul whined.

Claudia nodded, too drained to argue any longer. "Thank you for everything you've done for me. I do appreciate it, even if it doesn't seem like that."

"My pleasure," Paul said, but it didn't sound like he meant it.

After Paul left, Rita Jane said, "It sounds like a good deal to me. I don't understand why you won't take it."

"You wouldn't," Claudia practically spat at her. "It's a matter of principle — something you don't understand. Locked in your studio you have no idea what is happening in the world."

"You apologize right this instant, Claudia Jean," Audrey said. "What is wrong with you anyway?"

Rita Jane stood up and headed for the door, shouting, "I might not understand everything that's going on in the world, but I do know what it takes to raise a child. Unlike you, who thinks only about yourself. You don't care about anything except you, yourself and you."

She was at the door when Dan grabbed her. "Don't go, RJ. Stay and work it out."

But Rita Jane wrestled herself free and ran out the door. Women, Dan thought, but knew better than to say it out loud.

37. Dan's Plan

While Paul had been negotiating with the U.S. Attorney, Dan had been secretly organizing a public campaign to draw attention to Claudia and Emad's cases. Dan knew that Claudia was unlikely to agree to any kind of offer, short of an outright dismissal, and he knew that the U.S. Attorney would only dismiss the case if there were sufficient public pressure to do so. Dan believed the case could, and indeed would, be won in the court of public opinion.

In three months, Dan had met with a couple of dozen community organizations discussing Emad's case, and then Claudia's case. He had traveled to neighborhoods in the city where he had never gone before. Church groups were particularly sympathetic. He'd go wherever he was invited and had spoken in small storefront churches, and in large stone ones. People in Southeast identified with Emad, knowing what it was like to be the target of a criminal investigation based on one's race. People in Northwest identified with Claudia. While they did not approve of prosecuting a man because of his religion or ethnicity, they were horrified by the idea of going after his lawyer.

Letters started appearing in the local *Takoma Voice*, *City Paper* and even the *Washington Post*, calling Emad and Claudia victims in the "war on terror." Dan had, of course, drafted the letters himself and asked people to send them to the editor, but still, there were lots of people willing to sign their names to the cause. He was working on his right-wing friends to try to get something in the *Times*, but so far he hadn't been successful.

On a Sunday afternoon in April, twenty activists crowded into the living room at TLC to listen to Dan outline his strategy. His plan was simple: daily protests in front of the U.S. Attorney's office demanding that the cases be dropped. A daylong vigil would not be possible most days, but even a pair of respectable looking people outside the office at the start or end of the workday or over the noon hour would attract attention. With twenty people committed, if they each agreed to two shifts a month they'd have the weekdays covered for an entire month.

The meeting went smoothly and finished in less than an hour, probably as much a function of the nice weather and the longing to be outside than anything else. Dan passed around a sign-up sheet and filled up all but two week days during the month of May, which was only a couple of weeks away. They scheduled another meeting in two weeks and everyone made a commitment to bring at least one other person to the meeting, thereby doubling the number of hours they could cover.

Dan hadn't told Paul, Rita Jane or Claudia about the daily vigils, assuming, correctly, that he'd get better media coverage if the plan were not being organized by the defense lawyers.

"You were brilliant," Dave said after the crowd left. "I knew you were good in bed, but I had no idea you were such a good public speaker."

"Lots of practice, I guess," Dan grinned. "I've been an organizer since high school. The first demonstration I organized was a protest against the school administration for violating Title IX by spending more money on boy's sports than girl's sports."

Dave laughed, "That must have gone over well."

"The girls loved me," Dan said. "Of course, they weren't the ones I was interested in."

He reached over and touched Dave's hand. He felt content. It was a feeling he hadn't experienced in a long time and he knew it was because of Dave. The day was warm so they sat on the front porch of Dan's unit drinking cold beers and talking about everything and nothing. Neighbors had come by curious to meet Dave. He had introduced him as "my friend Dave." It was such a euphemism. But what should he say, "This is my lover Dave" or "This is my boyfriend Dave?" It was much too early to say partner. He thought boyfriend would be okay, but they hadn't talked about it yet. After mulling over the issue Dave realized he could just ask Dave what he thought instead of worrying about it. He couldn't remember if he had ever felt this comfortable in a relationship before.

"Hey, what should I call you? Are you my boyfriend?"

Dave reached over and took his hand. "I hope so."

And it was that easy. They were boyfriends. The next time a neighbor came by Dan said, "This is my boyfriend Dave." He wondered if everything would be so easy with Dave.

38. Game Night

Empty pizza boxes and soda bottles scattered across the kitchen counter alongside bowls of popcorn and veggie chips. The Common House air smelled like a gymnasium after a high school basketball game, musky with sweat from bodies crowded together. Groups of residents hovered around folding tables, some deep in concentration, others hooting with laughter. The monopoly crowd was heavily dominated by the pre-teen set. A gaggle of grade school children, supervised by Frances, were playing "Go Fish the President" with a deck of cards that contained all the U.S. Presidents. Paul and Dave, along with some of the other men, were deep in concentration over a poker game drinking cheap beer and munching on popcorn. Rita Jane, Audrey, Dan, Claudia and Aimee were engaged in a cut-throat game of Scrabble, acting as though winning at Scrabble were a sign of higher intelligence and none of them wanted to be proven dumb.

Audrey had dressed for Games Night as though she were going to a formal dinner party. She wore a tailored silk suit with a matching chartreuse colored lightweight sweater and a string of pearls.

"You're way overdressed," Claudia and Rita Jane had warned her, but Audrey could no more wear jeans to a social event than a Texan could eat grilled meat without barbecue sauce.

Halfway through the game, Audrey had half as many points as the rest of them. It might have been due to the fact she and Rita Jane had drunk a bottle of Merlot between the two of them. Audrey showed Rita Jane her letters and they burst out laughing.

"Those are the saddest bunch of letters I have ever seen," Rita Jane said. "Throw them back and play with me."

Rita Jane tried to ignore Claudia, who was pouting over something. The two had each apologized for their outbursts on the day of Paul's visit, but the light-hearted feeling of perfect love had definitely gone. A week ago she would have rushed over to see how she was doing, but she didn't. She needed a break from worrying. She normally didn't drink wine around Claudia, since Claudia wasn't drinking, but she enjoyed feeling tipsy. She had earned the right to relax after several weeks of working double shifts at Paul's Place and in between times taking care of Claudia and entertaining Audrey.

"I'm adding to the 'OR' to make 'EXCELSIOR'!" Rita Jane declared triumphantly. "And the 'X' falls on a double letter space. You guys don't stand a chance now."

"It's far from over yet," Dan said. "Besides, I don't care if you win, nothing can break me of my good mood," he said glancing over at Dave who was sitting at the poker table. "I've got a hot date after the game. I might even let you win I'm in such a good mood."

"Let me win," Rita Jane scoffed. "You couldn't beat me if you tried. You've been this way since you were seven years old. You can't admit it when you've been beat fair and square."

Claudia stood up to stretch her legs and back. "I'm going to walk around," she announced to no one in particular.

Rita Jane marshaled her forces and kept herself from running after Claudia, wishing that she could be a bit more like her mother.

Rita Jane had taken to Audrey, or rather, the two of them had taken to each other. Audrey's visit had been going well, much better than Rita Jane had imagined possible. They both loved art and had spent hours roaming Washington's museums: the East and West Wings of the National Gallery of Art, the Asian and African art museums, and an exhibit of early women painters at the National Museum of Women in the Arts.

Audrey adored D.C. and seemed to be getting along with everyone at TLC — even wacky Aimee who was constantly talking to whomever would listen about the war. Audrey didn't really have an opinion on the war but she listened politely and nodded while Aimee ranted.

Claudia returned holding a brown glass bottle. "Look what I found. I was walking along the backyard where the soil was tilled the other day and I found this. It must have gotten dredged up by the tiller. It looks like it has something inside."

She tried unscrewing the lid, but after several unsuccessful attempts to loosen it, reluctantly handed it over to Dan.

Dan wiped his palms on his jeans, gritted his teeth together and squeezed as hard as he could. Just then, Billy Frank ran around the corner being chased by the twins and slid into Dan causing the bottle to fly through the air and land in a shattered mess.

"Billy, you should be more careful," Claudia snapped. "You're not supposed to run in the Common House."

"That's one way to open it," Rita Jane laughed, retrieving the message. Dan went for a broom shooing the children away from the pile of broken glass.

"Let's read it," Rita Jane said, grabbing Claudia and leading her over to a floor lamp that gave off more light.

Rita Jane unfolded a thick piece of faded yellow paper, smelling of musty whisky. Much of the ink had faded, but some of the words were still legible.

"It's a love letter," Rita Jane said, "to a woman named Millicent. It's dated December 1944. It says, 'We must stop meeting. Franklin will be very upset if he finds out. He'll ruin you. I think he suspects something. I will send you a message when it is safe to resume contact. Until then. All my love, Eleanor.'"

"How wild," Claudia said. "I wonder if this is how they communicated with each other before the days of cellphones and e-mail. I'll ask my friend, who works at the Library of Congress, to see if she can find out anything about them."

Rita Jane, who believed in messages and signs from above, wondered what it meant that Claudia should have found this message at this time. A sign that they should be together, she wondered.

"How're you doing?" she asked Claudia softly.

"I'm miserable. I've been feeling sick all day and resenting this creature," she pointed to her stomach. "All in all, I find pregnancy to be a bit of a drag." She rubbed her belly, "Sorry little one, don't take it personally."

The wine had given Rita Jane a slight headache. She stopped herself from getting irritated by Claudia's complaints about her pregnancy. Why couldn't she be grateful for the fact that she could be pregnant? Instead of saying anything, she rubbed Claudia's shoulders, working her fingers through her tight shoulder muscles.

"That feels so good," Claudia relaxed under her touch. "I'm sorry I'm in such a foul mood. I have so much to be grateful for. Like you," she said turning to face Rita Jane. "We could have been born Millicent and Eleanor and been reduced to hiding our love in a glass bottle."

"Instead we're Millicent, Eleanor, and Franklin," Rita Jane said, to which they both laughed, and returned to the game, walking arm in arm.

39. Dan's Public Opinion Campaign Begins

On May Day, the first protesters, a Quaker couple in their 70s, arrived at noon at the U.S. Attorney's office. They carried handmade signs that read, "Claudia Connors is a Victim of the War on Terror" and "Arrest Osama bin Laden, not Emad Khadonry." The couple stood silently outside the door while lawyers dressed in conservative suits left for their lunch hours, taking a break from the tedious job of prosecuting criminals.

Dan sat down on the steps across from the entrance to the office, eating the black bean burrito he purchased from the Burrito Man who worked the corner of K and 15th Streets in a trailer converted into a one-person kitchen. After finishing his burrito, Dan walked over to them and thanked them for coming then quickly left to avoid being associated with the protesters.

The next day, he repeated the lunchtime scenario, this time ordering a black and tan burrito with guacamole, a little splurge that he allowed himself once a week. As expected, a group from the Catholic Worker's House had shown up carrying signs. One man was very tall and thin with a long beard and ponytail. Dan recognized him from other demonstrations. Once again, Dan thanked them and left.

On the third day, a group from the Committee against Political Repression arrived. As Dan approached, he saw a reporter from the *Post* talking to a woman he recognized. He was glad the reporter had come on that particular day, as the woman she was talking with was extremely articulate. "We're here because we oppose the prosecution of Claudia Connors," she said to the reporter.

"But she broke the law. Shouldn't she be punished?" the reporter asked.

"It's not clear that she violated any law. Her so-called 'crime' was mailing a package for her client and making a phone call for her client's wife. These are not acts of terrorism."

The reporter interrupted. "But she could have been sending information to terrorists. She's a lawyer, shouldn't she know better?"

"But there's no proof that the letters contained any secret communications. In the name of fighting an enemy, the government passes laws making it a crime to do innocent things. Our organization was founded during World War II to protest the internment of Japanese Americans. That was another horrible example of overreaching. Our government acted legally when it interned Japanese Americans, but what it did was morally wrong. It's the same situation here. What is happening to Claudia Connors may be legal, but it's wrong."

Dan was cheering to himself. This was exactly the message he wanted to get out to the press.

"Of course, what's happening to Claudia is not an isolated act. We represent dozens of people, mostly Arab Americans, who have been detained without any charge. Some have been held for hours, some for days, without being permitted to contact their families or an attorney. Do you understand the kind of terror this creates in people? There are people in this country who live in fear, not of another September 11 attack, but of what their own government may do to them or their loved ones."

The woman paused for a moment and her companion, a younger woman who Dan didn't know, piped in, "And the poor woman is pregnant. They're causing her so much stress I'm surprised she hasn't miscarried."

Dan grimaced. Claudia was not the kind of woman that liked people knowing her business. Of course anyone who had seen Claudia recently could probably figure out that she was pregnant, but Claudia would not want it advertised to the entire D.C. Metro area.

"She's pregnant?" the reporter asked. The young woman looked at Dan for confirmation. Dan approached. "She is, but I'm not sure that's really newsworthy, is it?" He didn't want to ask the reporter not to report the fact of Claudia's pregnancy figuring that would certainly encourage her to do so.

"It's certainly an interesting fact," the reporter said. "I suppose it's going to come out sooner or later. People will notice that she's pregnant."

"Yes," Dan said. "But Claudia would hate the idea that someone felt sorry for her because she was pregnant. It distracts from the real issue, what the government is doing to her."

"I'm sorry," the young woman said. "I thought everybody knew."

"Do you have a phone number for her?" the reporter asked. "I want to confirm this information."

Dan jumped in, "She doesn't know about this protest."

"She doesn't know?" the reporter asked, surprised. "I thought this was part of her defense strategy.

"No," Dan said, "We're concerned Washingtonians who believe our government has better things to do than harass attorneys who are trying to defend their clients."

The reporter took down everything Dan said, including Claudia's phone number, while Dan watched, grinning.

40. The Memorial Day Parade

"Are you almost ready to go?" Rita Jane called to Claudia, who at seven months pregnant rarely moved quickly anymore, and rarely dressed in anything besides sweat pants and Rita Jane's oversized T-shirts.

Claudia walked down the stairs wearing a navy blue maternity dress that Audrey had brought from Texas. Rita Jane looked up from reading the latest editorial about Claudia's case and had to stifle a giggle.

"How do I look?" she asked.

"You look great," Rita Jane lied.

"No, really, how do I look? I feel like an oversized blueberry."

"Honestly, you look very, how should I say, straight."

"Is that bad?"

"No, that's good. Blue is the perfect color to wear to a Memorial Day Parade. It's very patriotic." She gulped down the rest of her coffee. "Did you read this morning's editorial? Listen to this: 'Doesn't this administration have better things to do than harass pregnant women?' Isn't that great?"

Initially Claudia had been horrified to learn about the daily protests at the U.S. Attorney's office and had been mortified when news of her pregnancy made national news. But Dan had convinced her that she would only win her case if she had public opinion on her side. Since the daily demonstrations had begun almost a month ago, all the D.C. daily and weekly newspapers had editorialized against the Department of Justice's decision to prosecute Claudia. Claudia was Washington's cause célèbre of the moment.

Since the story had broken about Claudia's pregnancy people were naturally curious to learn who the "father" was. After several heated discussions among the four of them — Claudia, Rita Jane, Dan and Dave — Claudia had decided to say that there was a sperm donor who wished to remain anonymous, which also happened to be true.

They took the Metro to Union Station. The heat descended upon them as soon as they left the air-conditioned station. By the time they reached the starting point of the parade at Third and Pennsylvania Claudia's hair was plastered to her forehead and she looked gray, but at least she had managed not to throw up.

The Quakers had suggested that Claudia walk in the parade. Ten years ago they had successfully sued the city to march in the parade arguing that war protestors should be honored as well as veterans. Since Claudia and Emad were victims of the "war on terror" it was fitting, according to Dan and the Quakers, that she participate in the Memorial Day Parade.

Dan was lecturing the assembled marchers, many of whom had been taking part in the daily protests, on the way to handle questions from reporters. Signs read, "Free Emad," "Seven months is long enough — bring Emad home." Sarah's sign was a blown-up picture of Emad and Semya that said, "Bring my Papa home." Dave handed out bunches of glossy brochures to distribute to people along the parade route.

"Our message is simple, Dan said, expounding with his hands as he spoke, "We want law enforcement, not harassment. Emad and Claudia are not terrorists. Bush and his buddies should go find some real terrorists. And stay away from the pregnancy issue. If anyone asks, say it's not relevant."

Rita Jane thought that Claudia's pregnancy and impending parenthood with a lesbian partner was the issue for a lot of people, but she agreed with Dan that it was best to try to stay away from that issue. Claudia had become a poster child for both the right and left: the right thought she was committing a horrible sin and the left thought she was a hero.

Dan left the others to look for a parade organizer and she and Claudia found a spare bench in the shade. They didn't hold hands like they normally would have, aware that others might be watching. Dan returned with a map of the parade route and a handsome man who looked familiar.

"We're behind the peaceniks," he said, "towards the end. Everyone, I'd like you to meet Congressman Weymouth, Chairman of the Judiciary Committee." Dan recited everyone's name and Weymouth made the effort to shake everyone's hand. Dan introduced Claudia, "This is my friend who's being persecuted. I mean, prosecuted," and this is my good friend, Rita Jane."

When he shook her hand, he looked right into her eyes, managing to convey warmth and concern. Of course, he was a politician, Rita Jane reminded herself. He was much better looking in person than on television. No wonder the Republicans loved him.

"Can I talk to you guys for a second?" Dan asked, pulling them away from the rest of the group and forming a huddle with the congressman. Dan was grinning from ear to ear and practically jumping up and down with excitement. "The congressman wants to learn more about Claudia's case. He's thinking about calling for a Congressional Oversight hearing into this prosecution."

Claudia's mouth dropped open. Rita Jane couldn't read her reaction to the news. "I'm flattered," she said.

"I'm very concerned," Weymouth said seriously. "We should meet soon." Looking at Dan he said, "Call my scheduler next week to arrange it." He shook hands again. "I'm sorry I have to run off. I need to get in place before the parade starts. Very nice to meet you both."

"Thank you, sir," Claudia said. Once Weymouth was safely out of earshot she and Dan hugged each other, squealing with delight. "You're amazing," Claudia said.

"I know," he smiled.

By mid morning the pleasant temperatures had turned oppressive. It was 90 degrees with nearly 100% humidity. The parade route afforded no shade and the air was thick and unmoving. Rita Jane hovered near Claudia, making sure that she drank fluids regularly. Along the way people occasionally asked Claudia questions or offered her a cool drink. Rita Jane accepted the drinks and made sure they were caffeine-free before she turned them over to Claudia.

They felt the first hint of a storm at around noon. At first it was just a few sprinkles that didn't warrant an umbrella. The hair on the back of Rita Jane's neck prickled from the electricity. Suddenly an enormous crash startled the crowd and a flash appeared that seemed to be right next to them. The sky opened up and rain dumped out, drenching them instantly. The parade was almost over and without waiting for direction from the organizers the friends took off running to the nearest shelter, the Ronald Reagan Building at Pennsylvania and 12th Street. It was a beautiful modern building used for offices and public events, especially business-related ones.

"Finally, Reagan was good for something," Dan said after they passed through the metal detector and had shown their IDs to the guards.

"You know he gets a bad rap but a lot of decent things happened under his administration," Aimee said.

Rita Jane was wet and tired and the last thing she wanted was to hear a protracted argument between Dan and Aimee about the merits and evils of the Reagan administration. She and Claudia dashed into the women's room attempting to dry themselves with the electric hand dryer.

Claudia's dress clung to her wet skin, forming an outline of her swollen belly and protruding naval. Rita Jane felt the familiar twin emotions of regret and jealousy, chalking them up to being tired, hungry and soaking wet. She missed her mom and wished she could talk about the pregnancy with her. Her parents were trying to be supportive, but no matter what they said or did, Rita Jane knew the pregnancy didn't make them happy. She had invited them for the Memorial Day barbecue that afternoon, but doubted they would come.

The rain was over almost as soon as it had begun. The parade had broken up from the shower and crowds were heading to the Mall to feed the ducks in the reflecting pond or eat picnic lunches near the Lincoln Memorial. The TLC crowd headed back home for the annual Memorial Day Kick-Off-the-Summer barbecue, which, like the Columbus Day event, was filled with food, drinks, games and political speeches.

By the time they returned, the party was in full swing and the air, thick with the smell of grilled meat. Rita Jane led Claudia to a plastic lawn chair to get her off her feet. She handed Claudia a chilled bottle of sparkling water and asked, "Can I fix you a plate?"

"I want chicken," Claudia said, to Rita Jane's surprise. "No, make that ribs. I want ribs. No, I want chicken and ribs," she laughed at herself. "I shouldn't but that's what I feel like eating so I'm going to declare this a guilt-free day. There must be a rule that allows pregnant vegans who have been suffering from morning sickness for months to eat meat if they want to."

Audrey said, "Baby girl, you've got to give in to those cravings. It's your body telling you that you need to eat something. When I was pregnant with you I used to crave beets." She laughed and put her hands on Claudia's shoulders. "I hate beets. You couldn't get me to eat a beet if it was the only food and I was starving. But with you I ate beets. As soon as you were born, I was back to hating beets."

Rita Jane laughed. "I for one am glad to see you crave anything. You don't eat enough as it is. If you want to eat ribs, I'll eat them, too. Paul will be thrilled."

Rita Jane was surveying the buffet table for the healthiest options when Audrey tapped her shoulder. "Are those your parents over there?" Without waiting for an answer, Audrey ran over and hugged them both. "You must be the Spencers," she said in her thick Texas drawl. "It's mighty nice to meet you. You have such a charming daughter and I am so happy to meet you." She pumped Martin's hand several times and embraced Leigh again. "We have so much to talk about. We're going to be grandparents. Is this your first time?" She didn't wait for an answer, knowing the answer already. "Me too. I can hardly wait."

Rita Jane was grateful for Audrey's enthusiasm, which balanced her parents' despair. But she appreciated that her parents had made the effort to come to the picnic, which couldn't have been easy for them. She wondered if Audrey and her parents would find something to talk about.

"Audrey Connors this is Martin and Leigh Spencer. Mom, Dad, this is Claudia's mom, Audrey."

"It's nice to meet you," Leigh said stiffly.

"I'll check in with Paul to see if there's anything I can do," Dr. Spencer said, leaving the women alone.

The atmosphere relaxed with the doctor's departure. Even Leigh seemed happy to see her husband go.

"How are you?" Leigh asked Claudia as if she wanted to know the answer, not just as a way to make conversation. "Rita Jane tells me you've been awfully sick."

Claudia nodded. "I haven't taken well to being pregnant."

Audrey interrupted, "Who would with all the stress you've been under." Leigh nodded agreement. Claudia shrugged.

"I think she's going to have a boy," Audrey announced. "I was hardly sick at all with Claudia but her two brothers made me wish I was dead most of the time." She laughed. No one said anything. Rita Jane racked her brain for something to say, but Claudia beat her to it.

"Leigh what was your pregnancy like?" she asked. "If you don't mind me asking."

Leigh's face lit, happy with the memory. "Of course I don't mind. I was a little sick at first, although nothing like you, and then I felt great and then I got to the point where I couldn't wait for the baby to get out." She smiled. "We wanted to have more, but I never got pregnant again," she said wistfully. "I wanted to adopt, but Martin didn't. But we were so lucky to have Rita Jane. She was healthy and happy and has been such a joy to us." Leigh looked embarrassed. "Now I sound like a boasting mother."

"You should be proud, she's a lovely girl. I mean woman," Audrey corrected herself.

Martin returned with a tray of drinks and Paul carried a large platter of grilled chicken and ribs. Claudia took a piece of each and devoured them as though she hadn't eaten in weeks.

They ate without serious conversation enjoying the food and the warm evening. The doctor didn't say much. Audrey and Leigh kept the conversation going with Leigh telling Audrey all the Washington sights that she "had to see." Rita Jane ate her meal, steadfastly trying to ignore her father's stony silence, urging herself not to say anything to make the situation worse. Just when she thought she couldn't take another minute of his judgment, he picked up his drink and said, "I'd like to toast the chefs. Thank you for the excellent meal."

Everyone joined in agreement. He paused as though deciding whether to say anything further then added, "And a toast to the new baby and its mother. Here's to a healthy pregnancy."

As everyone raised their glasses, Rita Jane saw tears roll down Claudia's cheeks. Leigh smiled at her and she felt her loneliness dissipate, like fog lifting off the water as the sun rises.

41. Meeting with Weymouth, Again

Dan's heart beat rapidly as he, Paul and Claudia waited for the Rayburn elevator. Too hot to talk, the three waited silently, each lost in private thoughts. By 9 o'clock the day promised to be a scorcher. The heat, humidity and anxiety had already created large sweat stains under his arms. He made a mental note to keep his jacket on during the meeting. He ran through his argument mentally for what must have been the millionth time. To prepare for the meeting, he had spent all day Sunday reading the entire files from Emad and Claudia's cases.

The congressman was waiting for them with the door to his personal office open, the smell of power emanated from it.

"Hello, Dan," he said, getting up from his desk and walking to the front of it to greet them. Instead of sitting behind his ominous desk as he had at prior meetings, he sat on an easy chair and directed the three of them to sit on the leather couch.

Dan systematically laid out Emad's case, arguing all the ways that the prosecution was overreaching, while a very young-looking woman frantically took notes. Weymouth interrupted with questions, which Dan or Paul answered deftly. Then they laid out the case against Claudia, detailing her acts of mailing packages for her client and making the phone call to Saudi Arabia.

Claudia sat quietly on the couch, sipping a glass of water. She excused herself to go to the restroom and when she returned the congressman said to her, "I'm sorry we've been doing all the talking. I want to hear what you have to say. What do you think of the idea of holding an oversight hearing?"

"Honestly, the idea of it makes me tired." She sighed deeply, looking like she might cry. "I don't want my life to be the center of attention." She paused again. "But I don't want to agree to their deal just to make my life easier and to make this case go away." Dan looked at her approvingly. "I do believe the U.S. Attorneys are abusing their power. If you think there are grounds for oversight, then you should do it. I'll cooperate with the investigation."

Dan and Weymouth both nodded. She continued, "The most important case to investigate is Emad's. He's been in prison for four months. His wife and child are frantic with worry. At least I'm out on bond."

"I'm very disturbed by this information," Weymouth said, pulling on his chin, a nervous habit that Dan found endearing. "I thought the charges against him seemed trumped up, but this..." His voice trailed off. "I like your attitude. You're not in this to be a media star. You'll make a good witness."

"There's one problem," Claudia said. She patted her belly. "You must have heard I'm a pregnant lesbian terrorist? Don't you think this will detract from Emad's case?"

"It's not relevant," Weymouth said sternly. "I'll not allow any discussion of it while I'm running the hearing. Although frankly, whether you're a lesbian or not, people feel sympathetic toward pregnant women."

Weymouth stood up abruptly, "I'm sorry, but I have to run to another meeting. I'll get back to you soon," he said to Dan. "Thank you for coming in."

"Thank you," the three echoed together.

They walked out of the office not saying anything. Once the gold ornate elevator doors closed behind them Dan made a fist and brought his arm down, "Yes!" he shouted. "That was great!"

They high-fived each other and Claudia looked on in amusement. "You were great," Dan said, taking her hand. "So poised. The perfect Southern woman."

"I didn't do anything," Claudia said. "I just told the truth."

Paul shook his head, "Dan's right, you were perfect. You clearly didn't have an ax to grind. You didn't want to make this a political issue. You just wanted to do the right thing."

Paul laughed, "Who would have thought? A Republican from Mississippi holding an oversight hearing on the U.S. Attorney. Maybe there is hope for this country yet."

"There's queers everywhere," Dan laughed.

"I think he has a crush on you," Claudia said, punching Dan in the arm.

"He's hot alright," Dan said. "But I'm in love. Plus, he's a little old for me. And I don't do married men."

* * *

When the congressman called Dan the following Tuesday to inform him that he had already contacted the Department of Justice and the U.S. Attorney's Office, Dan wondered if maybe Claudia's theory about Weymouth's crush was correct.

"They want me to review some documents before deciding to hold the hearings. They said the documents would allay my concerns and explain why they are pursuing the case."

"Yea, right," Dan said sarcastically, and then wished he hadn't said that. He tried a more formal approach, "It makes sense to wait until you see what they have." God I want to see those documents, Dan thought. But he didn't say anything else.

"I told them they had 72 hours to have the documents on my desk," Weymouth said. "I should be able to make a decision by next week."

Dan immediately called Paul with the news. Paul said he would call his contact at the Justice Department to see how they were reacting to Weymouth's threat of an oversight hearing. He called Dan back right away with the surprising news that his friend didn't know about Weymouth's interest in the case, suggesting that the higher ups were trying to keep Weymouth's interest in the case secret.

How was he going to wait a whole week for Weymouth to make up his mind? He felt antsy. None of his issues were moving. Nothing much was happening at all in Congress, as most members hadn't yet returned to Washington from the Memorial Day recess. There were no interesting hearings scheduled, no demonstrations scheduled, no meetings to attend. Sure there was work he could do. There was always work to do, but like most lobbyists, he was an adrenaline junkie and it was hard for him to get anything done unless he had a huge deadline looming.

He thought about the meeting with Weymouth. Weymouth's attention and concern dazzled Dan. Whenever he thought of all that Weymouth had done for him — or rather for the issues Dan cared about — he felt elated. He had arrived. No one could doubt his credentials as a true Washington power broker. He had the ear of the Chairman of the Judiciary Committee. He was hot stuff. His mind wandered to thoughts of Weymouth without his clothes on. This would not do. No good could come out of such a liaison. He called Dave and made a date for later that night, vowing to remain faithful to his boyfriend.

Part III – Claudia and Rita Jane – Summer 2003

42. Another Offer

Paul kissed Claudia on the cheek. "How are you?" he asked looking at her with a worried expression on his face.

"I feel like I'm in prison. I never leave the house except to go to work or doctor's appointments. Otherwise, I stay home and watch television, knit and sleep."

Audrey arrived in the living room carrying a tray with two large glasses of ice tea.

"You'll have to excuse my daughter," she said to Paul. "She's not much of a hostess these days. I brought you some ice tea. Here's sweet tea for you, Paul, and the herbal kind for Claudia."

"Thank you, ma'am," Paul said.

"Thanks momma." Claudia ignored Audrey's jab, refusing to let her mother irritate her.

Paul took a large sip then placed the glass on a coaster on the coffee table. He leaned forward and put his hands on his knees. Claudia had been waiting anxiously since his call an hour earlier telling her that he had another offer from the government. He sighed deeply then pulled out a piece of paper from a file in his briefcase. She couldn't tell from his body language if the news was good or bad. Just get on with it. A naturally impatient person, she hated to wait and it seemed like that's about all she did these days.

"I've got good news," Paul said finally. Claudia relaxed. "At least I think it's good news." He paused and took another sip. Claudia stiffened again. "But I thought the last offer was good news, too, and you didn't agree with me."

"Yes," Claudia said trying to keep the impatience out of her voice.

"They're willing to dismiss the case. Outright. You don't need to sign any affidavits."

Claudia felt a huge weight lift off her shoulders, but knowing prosecutors as she did she asked, "What's the catch?"

"I'm getting to that," Paul said. "The only condition is that you agree that you will not have any more contact with Emad until this case is resolved."

Claudia started to say something but Paul stopped her. "I know what you're likely to say. You're going to say that this is outrageous and you didn't do anything wrong and he didn't do anything wrong, and that you should be able to return to representing him, blah, blah, blah. But Emad is in good hands with his new lawyers and you'll be busy with your baby soon. You won't have much time to work on his case or see him."

"But he's my friend." Claudia protested.

"Before you say no, I want you to promise me you'll do one thing."

"What's that?" she asked suspiciously.

"Talk to Emad."

"Of course he'll tell me to take the deal," Claudia said. "That's not fair to him. I can't put him in that position."

"Look, you want my honest opinion? You're about a month away from giving birth. You don't need any more stress in your life. You should stay away from this case. You should probably stop working altogether. You're hardly working now anyway. Maybe you should just stop altogether. You'll at least want to take time off after the baby arrives."

"Stop working," Claudia fumed. "You're out of your mind. I'd go crazy. Besides, I can't afford to stop working."

Paul looked at her dubiously.

Claudia felt the tears coming again and scorned her lack of self-control. "I'm beginning to think this was a big mistake," she said, unsure exactly what she was referring to.

Paul reached over and squeezed her hand. "I don't know what you're upset about. Things are looking great. The protests outside the U.S. Attorneys office are continuing and the numbers are growing everyday. We finally got an editorial in the *Washington Times*, and even the *National Journal* published editorials in your favor. Most of the other media coverage is going your way, with the exception of Fox News and the religious channels. And now Weymouth has scheduled oversight hearings. In the last week I've been on PBS *News Hour*, *Cross Fire*, NPR, MSNBC and C-SPAN, plus a whole host of other shows I can't keep track of."

"I know — my mother has watched all of them. I can't bear to. She says you're great — very telegenic."

"So what's bothering you?" Paul asked kindly but with a bit of impatience in his voice.

"I don't want to stop working. I don't want to be a stay-at-home mom. This was the biggest case of my career and I'll be damned if I'm going to drop it because of pregnancy or because some unethical prosecutor brings a bogus charge against me."

Paul nodded sympathetically. "Under the circumstances, I can understand why you feel that way," he said kindly. "But you have other considerations now besides yourself. And frankly, other things that are more important than representing Emad Khadonry. He's already got a big firm representing him and there are several more that would love to step in if they want out."

His words stung but she knew that he was right and it made her sad. She had spent her life fighting to be taken seriously as a woman, believing with every fiber of her being that women could be as successful as men in their chosen careers, and here she was losing out on the biggest case of her career because she was pregnant. It seemed like a personal failure somehow.

"Is this new offer because of the hearings?" Claudia asked.

"In part, but I think the daily protests have been effective, too. They're just getting too much bad press for going after you. Let's face it, the fact that you're pregnant, whether you like it or not, makes you more sympathetic."

She groaned. He took a long drink of the tea, draining the glass. "Even if you take the deal, Weymouth is going to hold the hearings. Unless they dismiss Emad's case, which I don't think they'll do. Not yet anyway."

Suddenly Claudia wanted nothing more than to take a nap. Talking about the case always made her sleepy. Her head raced with all the possible outcomes. She wanted Paul to go. He must have sensed her distress because he said, "I should get going." As he stood to leave he said, "Do I have your word that you'll at least discuss it with Emad."

Claudia didn't say anything. "Claudia," he said, "I want you to promise me."

"Okay, alright," she said. "If I'm going to say no, I'll talk to him first."

"Thank you," he said, giving her a quick hug before leaving.

43. Meeting with Emad

Claudia woke from a nightmare, cold sweat covering her legs and arms making her chilled and clammy. In her dream, she had been on trial and the jury was coming into the courtroom to deliver its verdict when she woke, a scream stuck in her throat. She wrote the details of the dream in the journal she kept by her bedside, trying to decipher their meaning.

She did not feel afraid of the charges against her. Convinced they were bogus, she could not believe any jury would convict her. She worried more about Emad's case. Post September 11, the anti-Arab sentiment ran high, and she believed a talented prosecutor could capitalize on that fear to obtain a conviction. She worried Emad's new lawyers were not adequately representing him, because she believed no one worked as hard as she did for her clients.

But maybe she should worry more about the case against her. Maybe a jury would not see the facts in the same way she did. And if she was convicted, would a judge send her, a seasoned and respected lawyer, to prison, simply because she went a little out of her way to help her client? Probably not, but she had done enough jury trials and seen enough clients sentenced to know that anything could happen. Clients she had been sure would be convicted were found not guilty and clients she was sure were innocent were convicted and sentenced to long prison terms. She even had one client who had been sentenced to death.

The thing she hated more than anything, the thing that drove her to be a public defender, was her hatred of government abusing its power. When the government overreached, bringing charges against someone who was really innocent or bringing more serious charges than the facts warranted, she tried to do everything in her power to fight them. She didn't want to do anything to assist them in their game. Now that it was her life, how could she do less than what she would do for a client? She wanted to go to trial, regardless of how much stress and disruption it caused her.

But now she had this other person-to-be to think about. Paul was right. She had no business representing Emad now anyway. She should just take the deal and get on with her life, forget about asking Emad's opinion.

Rita Jane and Audrey definitely wanted her to take the deal, but they knew her too well to tell her so. "Whatever you think is best," was all they would say when she asked them what she should do. They knew that if she knew that they were trying to pressure her, she would do exactly the opposite of what they wanted.

In despair, she read her horoscope looking for guidance. When it gave her none, she remembered her promise to Paul that she would talk with Emad. She called his new lawyers and asked their permission to meet with him. When they agreed she called the prison and made arrangements to visit that afternoon.

The guard led her into the 3-by-5-foot Plexiglas cubicle that served as the "contact" meeting room. It was difficult to maneuver with her big belly. Once in, she couldn't easily turn around. She watched Emad's face light up when he saw her and realized this was the first time that he had seen her visibly pregnant.

"It is so good to see you my friend," he said, trying to shake her hand with both of his cuffed together. To her surprise, Emad looked well. Much better than he had the last time she had visited. She knew the same could not be said of her.

Claudia explained to him the "deal," that all charges against her would be dismissed if she agreed not to resume representing Emad. She told him how reluctant she had been to ask him what to do, because she didn't want to put him in the position of having to decide.

He nodded as she spoke and when she finished he said, "You did the right thing to tell me." She waited for him to say more. "I think you should take the deal." She started to protest but he interrupted her, "I'm not just saying this for your sake, I'm saying it for mine, too."

A stab of hurt passed through her. She braced herself for more rejection. "We're too close, you and I. We're friends really. I think it's better to have lawyers who I don't care about so much. I am less guarded with them."

"Gee thanks," she said morosely, but she knew what he meant.

"It's not personal. You're a great lawyer and you're a great person, but right now I'd like to see you focus on your baby and get out of this mess."

She started crying and Emad looked horrified. "I hurt your feelings." He patted her on the shoulder with his shackled hands.

"It's not that," Claudia said. "I cry over everything these days."

He looked relieved. "My wife did, too," he said.

Claudia considered trying to talk him out of it, but she knew she needed to let go. She suspected it had been difficult for Emad to be so honest with her.

"Are they doing a good job for you, these big firm lawyers?"

"They're not as good as you, obviously," he said.

"Right answer," she smiled.

"There are two of them doing the work that you were doing alone. One of them is very experienced and one is very green." He smiled. "I like the green one better. She's not so jaded. The older one thinks he knows exactly how things are going to go in the case, but the younger one is open to ideas or suggestions I make. Plus, she's new to Washington and she's lonely. She comes to visit me, even on weekends. I keep telling her she needs to get a life. Sarah is starting to get jealous." He chuckled.

Claudia wondered if maybe Emad had a crush on his young lawyer, but she was comforted by the image of the nervous young lawyer visiting her client on the weekends. The idea occurred to her that maybe she should call up the lawyer and invite her to lunch — offer to mentor her. Who are you kidding, Connors, you'd probably faint if you got in a cab to go downtown for lunch. Let go.

"You'll be at the hearings?" Emad asked.

She nodded. "Even if my case is dismissed, I think Weymouth will still want me to be a witness."

"Good, my lawyers are filing a motion to get permission for me to attend the entire hearing. I doubt it will be granted, but it sure would be nice to have a week or two outside of this place."

A guard walked by and held up his right hand and mouthed the words, "Five more minutes."

Claudia started to protest, but realized she wasn't his lawyer anymore so her visits were restricted to half an hour.

"Are they treating you okay?" she asked.

He shrugged. "It's like everywhere else, there are decent guards and there are — well, to be blunt — assholes. Like that one. He's definitely a hole."

Claudia giggled at Emad's uncharacteristic language. At least he hadn't lost his sense of humor.

"Some of the inmates call me the A-rab terrorist, that's how they say it, A with a long A, rab. But some think I'm getting a bum rap. I'm not hassled much because the guards keep me in protective custody. I don't go out to the yard with the other prisoners. I eat meals in my cell. I'm basically alone all the time."

It was always difficult for Claudia to hear about what her client's lives were like in jail. It was too painful. It was especially hard with a man like Emad, a gentle man who had never done a violent act in his life. He wasn't cut out for prison life. "I wish we could get you out of here," she said. "Have your lawyers suggested doing another bail hearing?"

"They have, but they thought maybe we should wait until after the hearings. If the U.S. Attorney's office gets a lot of negative publicity, the judge might be more sympathetic."

Claudia doubted that would happen, but she said, "There's always hope," even though she wasn't sure she felt any.

The guard unlocked the door and announced that it was time for her to leave.

"Thank you, my friend, for everything," he said, bowing his head and putting his hands together.

Claudia managed a sad smile and left quickly before the tears started again.

44. Happy Hour

"I think we should pick an androgynous name like Chris or Andy so it won't matter if it's a girl or a boy." Rita Jane said to her neighbors assembled on the piazza for the regular Friday afternoon happy hour.

"How boring," Aimee said. "My parents picked a boring name, too, but at least they had the good sense to spell it differently. Kids want to be special. They don't want to have the same name as everyone else."

"Speak for yourself," Esme said. "I like my name now, but as a child I hated it. I sometimes lied and said my name was Elizabeth because I so desperately wanted a normal name."

Rita Jane was sipping a very cold Corona, which was the most delicious thing she had tasted in a long time. She had been drinking only rarely, to be in solidarity with Claudia, but she couldn't resist when Aimee offered it to her when she arrived home from work.

Rita Jane flipped through the baby name book that she had bought at the used bookstore.

"It's so hard to decide when you don't know the gender. We decided against learning the gender of the baby, though Audrey said we should find out. That way if we were disappointed we could work out our disappointment before the baby arrived."

"If you don't know the sex of the baby," Frances said, "Everyone will buy you green or yellow things. If you do know, you'll get blue or pink."

"I like green and yellow better than pink," Rita Jane said. "But what do you think about the question of finding out?"

"It makes sense to me," Frances said. "I was terribly disappointed when I learned that my first child was a boy. My husband wanted one, of course, but I really wanted a daughter. Of course, I fell in love with him once he arrived and didn't care, but it probably helped that I had some time to get used to the idea."

"Claudia's dead-set against finding out," Rita Jane said.

"Claudia is still in denial that she's pregnant," Aimee said.

Rita Jane laughed.

By 6 o'clock the piazza teemed with people catching up with their neighbors and relaxing at the end of the workweek. The humid air felt thick as pea soup. People were stripped down to shorts and T-shirts, some fanning themselves. A few of the toddlers ran around with nothing but diapers on. Some were running through the lawn sprinkler to cool down. The thought of her own child doing that some day made Rita Jane smile.

It was nearly 7 when Claudia returned from work, walking slowly and looking, as usual, exhausted. Reflexively, Rita Jane tried to hide the beer behind her back, but Claudia saw her.

"I want one of those," Claudia announced, pointing to her bottle. "I was going to have a glass of wine but that beer looks so good I'll have that instead."

While Rita Jane was thinking of what to say, Dan said, "We've got some O'Doul's. It's not bad, actually." He reached into a cooler and opened one and handed it to Claudia. Rita Jane braced herself for Claudia's response. Claudia had been a headstrong woman before the pregnancy, but as the due date grew closer, she became more and more irritable.

"Thanks Dad," she said sarcastically. "You want to know what I had for lunch, too? Why does everyone think they can tell pregnant women what to do?

Dan looked shocked.

Audrey intervened. "Claudia went to the doctor today and she said that an occasional drink was fine now that she was late in her pregnancy. In fact, she thought it might help Claudia to relax."

Rita Jane didn't want Claudia to drink regardless of whether it was okay, but maybe a beer would put Claudia in a better mood.

"It's true," Dave said. This late in the pregnancy an occasional drink is not going to hurt the baby.

"In Texas," Audrey drawled, "we believe in pregnant women drinking now and then. It helps them relax. Eases the stress."

"That explains a few things about certain people from Texas," Dan said.

Everyone laughed, breaking the tension.

"There's certainly worse things than growing up to be President," Audrey said. "I'd love my grandchild to be President."

"I can see it now," Dan said, "My own flesh and blood, the first President of the United States raised by a trio of gay parents, whose mother was a lesbian terrorist."

Claudia took a long sip from the Corona and announced, "I've got news."

Without waiting for her to continue, Dan interrupted, "They dismissed the case."

Claudia nodded. "Oh my God!" Rita Jane yelled gathering Claudia up, as well as she could, in a huge hug. Claudia was immediately surrounded by her neighbors — people hugging her, patting her on the shoulder and slapping her high-fives. Rita Jane gave her a big juicy kiss.

"How do you feel?" Dave asked, always the therapist.

"Relieved, but a little sad. I feel sad for Emad. And for myself. For all we had to go through, especially him."

"It's not over yet," Dan said. "Those bastards are going to regret the day they brought that case. To revenge," Dan said, lifting his glass for a toast.

"No, to justice," Claudia modified.

"To justice," everyone shouted in unison.

45. Rita Jane Gets Discovered

Rita Jane was finishing up her lunch shift, looking forward to an afternoon of painting in her studio, when Paul stopped her.

"Rita Jane, I'd like you to meet my friend, Peter LaRochelle. He's in the corner booth."

She hadn't had a chance to paint seriously for months and had been trying hard to get back into a regular routine. She didn't want to be distracted and end up in a long conversation with someone she didn't even know.

"I'm really in a hurry to get home," Rita Jane said. "Can it wait?"

"No," Paul said.

Reluctantly, Rita Jane followed Paul to the table and shook hands with a small man, neatly dressed, who looked like he might be an accountant. He smelled like patchouli, which didn't fit with his formal attire

"Peter's been admiring your work," Paul said.

"What work?" Rita Jane asked.

"This piece," Peter said pointing to the picture of Emad's daughter praying for her Daddy to come home from jail that Paul had hung in a corner of the restaurant.

"Thank you," Rita Jane said.

"Do you have a minute to talk," Peter asked.

"I'm kind of in a hurry," Rita Jane said, but Paul glared at her, so she sat down across from Peter. A few extra minutes wouldn't make that much difference.

Paul brought over two tall glasses of ice tea before Rita Jane had a chance to say no.

"I work for the District," Peter said. Rita Jane nodded politely wondering why she should care what this man did for a living. "I'm an artist, actually." That got Rita Jane's attention. "I'm the Curator for Art in the District of Columbia Public Buildings, or CAD for short."

"Really?" Rita Jane was curious. She had never met anyone who was both an artist and a government worker.

"I commission artists to do works of art for public buildings. There is a little known law that requires that a certain portion of all federal contracts for large public buildings must be spent on art."

"That's great," Rita Jane said, still unclear what any of this had to do with her.

"I'd like you to submit a RFP to paint a mural at a soon-to-be-built community center in the Cardozo neighborhood near U Street."

Rita Jane could hardly believe what she was hearing. She was being asked to submit a proposal to paint a public mural. This was the dream of a lifetime, but all she could think of was that in less than a month she would be a mother.

"I'm flattered. I truly am. But my partner is having a baby in less than a month. I don't think I'd have time to submit a proposal."

Paul, who had been eavesdropping nearby, called over, "I can help," he said cheerfully. "You can use slides from the 'Color of Fear' exhibit. It will be easy."

Peter took a business card from his suit jacket pocket and handed it to her. "Post-September 11 themes are very popular. Your 'Color of Fear' concept is definitely along the lines of what the committee is looking for."

"When are the proposals due?" Rita Jane asked.

"August 1." He stood and picked up his black attaché case. Then he took Rita Jane's hand and brought it to his lips and kissed it. "Enchanted," he said before departing the restaurant.

As soon as they were sure that he was safely outside, Rita Jane burst into giggles. Paul said, "He's a bit of a fruit cake, but he's a nice guy. He's done a lot to promote artists in this town. It's a good thing I had that painting on display. This may be your lucky break."

"Do you really think I'd have time?" Rita Jane asked. Already her mind was racing with possibilities for the mural.

"It'll be tough, but I'll help you. I've got loads of free time now that Claudia's case has settled. Besides, I owe you after all the hours you've put in around here."

She felt the heat and humidity suck the energy out of her as soon as she left the air-conditioned restaurant. She chose to walk home on the well-shaded Maple Street instead of the more direct path down Carroll Avenue. With each pace, she worked out the details of the proposal in her mind. She wasn't ready to go inside yet, wanting to savor the news a little longer and have time to process it herself.

The twins were playing in the sandbox when she arrived in the piazza. She sat down at an outdoor table and pulled out her sketchbook, happily sketching the children, who were oblivious to her. The thought occurred to her again that she should paint a mural on the wall of the children's room. That could be like a dress rehearsal — she could paint a smaller version of the mural on the kids' room and use that as part of her proposal submission. Now she needed a theme. She needed inspiration and help from her higher power. She finished up the sketch and wrote on the bottom, "Mural proposal," and ripped out the sheet of paper to put into her God box.

46. The Hearing Begins

It was standing room only at 120 Rayburn House Office Building, the chamber of the House Judiciary Committee. Every major network and newspaper had sent a reporter leaving few seats for the public. Fortunately, Weymouth had reserved the front row for witnesses, including Claudia and Dan, and had said they could each bring a guest to sit with them.

The air conditioning did little to cool the enormous room, crowded with hot, testy people. It felt like sitting in a car on a hot summer day with the windows closed. Dan had told them that dressing for congressional hearings was important because C-SPAN, CNN and all the major networks would be airing it live and you never knew who might see you on television.

Claudia wore one of the few maternity outfits she had bought — an off-white linen pantsuit with a light beige blouse. Dan had on an elegant gray pinstriped suit that was making him sweat. Rita Jane, oblivious to Washington conventions, and not owning any suits, wore a brightly colored flowered skirt and white T-shirt.

Rita Jane had never been to a congressional hearing before and was acting like a child in a toy store, craning her head every which way to get a better look at the ornate gilding on the ceiling and the portraits hanging on the walls. Dan acted blasé, as if these hearings were an everyday occurrence, which she supposed they were. Claudia wiggled uncomfortably on the hard wooden chair, unsure if she was nervous, or just uncomfortable.

As the hour approached, members sauntered into the chamber carrying cups, presumably filled with coffee. Weymouth arrived promptly at 10 carrying only a note pad and pen. Two staffers followed behind him awaiting his instructions. Sitting at the center of the three-dozen committee members, he appeared like a king presiding over his court. He had subpoenaed 25 witnesses and what with taking breaks to go to the floor for votes or attending committee hearings on other pressing matters, the proceeding was expected to go until at least the Fourth of July recess.

The chairman pounded his gavel and launched into a speech about the importance of the matter before them. Claudia only half listened to the rhetoric. She was watching her nemesis, the U.S. Attorney. She thought of Emad in prison and his daughter crying herself to sleep every night and rage burned through her. She was pleased to see a hint of anxiety on his chiseled face.

Several members asked to make opening statements knowing that the hearing would be on every major news station and their constituents would be watching. It was past 10:30 before the questioning began.

The first witness was William Richards, the Deputy Attorney General in charge of the Criminal Division. "Mr. Richards," the chairman boomed in his ominous voice. "Would you please tell the committee the nature of your work since September 11?"

Richards droned on about how he was the head of the terrorism unit and that his unit had been diligently investigating and prosecuting cases related to the September 11 attack or to individuals and organizations sympathetic to the people responsible for the attack.

"And one of these is Mr. Emad Khadonry."

"Yes, sir, Mr. Khadonry has been a long-time contributor to the organization Widows and Orphans, which is a front for Hamas."

"And how is this related to the September 11 attack?" Weymouth asked testily.

"Since September 11 we have compiled a list of all organizations that give money to known terrorist organizations like Hamas. Widows and Orphans is one of them. Under the PATRIOT ACT, he can be prosecuted as providing material aid."

"You still haven't told me how Hamas is connected to the September 11 attack."

"We are not just going after Al-Qaeda, but other terrorists, too. It's all part of the war on terror."

"You are comparing an organization that gives money to Widows and Orphans to Al-Qaeda?"

"No, I'm comparing Hamas to Al-Qaeda," Richards said defensively.

"How many other Americans have donated money to Widows and Orphans?" Weymouth demanded.

"I'm sure there are many, but I can't give you the exact figure."

"You haven't researched that in preparation for this hearing?" Weymouth asked accusatorily. Richards shook his head. "Would you like me to answer for you?" Weymouth asked. Without waiting for his, Weymouth said, "Two thousand, six hundred and fourteen." Richard's face reddened. He was fidgeting with a ballpoint pen. Weymouth continued. "Those are not all within your jurisdiction, of course, but within the District of Columbia there are over 100 people who have donated to the organization since September 11." Weymouth paused for affect. "I'm curious to know why you decided to prosecute Mr. Khadonry, as opposed to the other 100 people in the district."

"We had confidential information detailing his involvement with the organization that went beyond contributing money. We suspected that he might be funneling money through Widows and Orphans to fund terrorist training camps."

"Do you have proof of this?" Weymouth asked.

Richards nodded, "I do, but I can't disclose it because it's confidential."

"Not any longer," Weymouth said. The audience laughed. Richards looked like he wanted to disappear. Claudia actually felt sorry for him.

"Did you make the decision to prosecute Mr. Khadonry?" Weymouth asked. Richards hesitated. "Please answer the question," Weymouth said again raising his voice.

 He shook his head from side to side.

"Let the record reflect that the witness is shaking his head no," Weymouth said. "So the decision was made at a higher pay grade, eh?" Weymouth asked, his voice softening.

Richards nodded again. Weymouth snapped, "I'm going to have to ask you to speak up, sir, so that everything can be recorded for the record."

"I'm sorry," Richards said. "I was asked to bring the case by someone high up in the Justice Department."

Weymouth paused to let that last remark sink in. He nodded his head. "And who was that?"

"Bai Quoung, Special Assistant to the Attorney General. Or rather, he was. He has since taken an appointment at a law school somewhere. I think Georgetown."

"Did Mr. Quoung recommend prosecuting anyone else?"

"Yes, but so far we have not finished grand jury proceedings, so the information is not public."

Weymouth cleared his throat. He took a sip of water and returned to questioning in an angry tone. "Is it possible that your office was motivated by the fact that Mr. Khadonry has been involved in anti-war protests?"

Richards flinched. "Of course not." A buzz filled the room. Photographers flashed pictures and reporters scribbled furiously on their notepads.

"Right," Weymouth said. "No further questioning."

Other members picked up where Weymouth had left off. The Democrats had a field day attacking Richards. Some of the more conservative Republicans tried to rehabilitate Richards by tossing him softball questions, but even they were hesitant to make Weymouth look bad. Angering the Chairman could result in retaliation. Chairmen were notorious for holding up bills of members who publicly crossed them.

At 12:30 Weymouth broke for lunch. Claudia was nibbling on a cracker in the hallway when Dan tapped her arm. "Weymouth wants to conference with us." Claudia and Dan met him in his office behind closed doors. Rita Jane left to go to the cafeteria to stand in line and order lunch for the three of them.

Weymouth was waiting in his office with his door open. No staff was present.

"I'd like to call you as a witness, Dan," Weymouth said, dispensing with formalities. "I'd like you to talk about the sneak and peak search the FBI did on your place. They were likely looking for political affiliations of yours and it makes Martin's claim that they don't consider things like that seem ridiculous."

Claudia looked at Dan who was nervously rubbing his hands on his pants. "That's okay with you, isn't it?" Weymouth demanded.

Dan looked at Claudia as if searching for permission and she nodded and steeled herself. "There's something you should know, Congressman." Weymouth's eyebrows shot up but he didn't say anything. "They were searching my apartment because of my relationship with Claudia. They were looking for information about her."

Weymouth burst out laughing. Dan looked mortified, but then Claudia started laughing and Dan eventually joined in, too. When Weymouth had finally regained his composure he gasped, "How scandalous. The lobbyist for OutReach had a heterosexual affair. The media will have a field day with that." Then his face grew serious and he looked at Claudia, "You're not. Because of him are you?"

Claudia nodded.

"This is getting weirder by the minute," Weymouth said.

Claudia and Dan both nodded.

"Okay, I've got to think about this. The reporters may get a hold of this story and investigate until they find something. If the FBI knew about your affair it may come out."

Neither Claudia nor Dan said anything, but she suspected he was dreading that outcome as much as she was.

"I'll think about it some more," Weymouth repeated. "I'm not going to call you today, Claudia, so you are free to leave. Of course, you are welcome to stay."

"Thank you," she said. Weymouth stood up, walked to the door, and opened it for them. "Thank you very much," he said, shaking their hands. After they left, Weymouth closed the heavy door behind him, but Claudia thought she heard him laughing inside.

47. Claudia Testifies

On the third day of the hearing, Chairman Weymouth finally summoned her to testify. Dan had been attending every minute of the hearings, but after the first morning Claudia had been waiting by the phone. Weymouth had promised to give her at least two hours notice before she had to be at Rayburn. So she had watched the hearings from the television at her office, getting very little work done.

On the day he finally called her, Claudia had worn the "blueberry" dress. Although she still felt like an overripe blueberry in it, she cared very little. At this stage in her pregnancy, comfort trumped appearance any day of the week. Besides, the dress reminded her of her mother. Audrey had returned to Texas and she missed her. Wearing the dress reminded her of her mother's support. Plus, if her mother watched the hearings, she'd be happy to see that Claudia was wearing the dress.

She tried unsuccessfully to reach Rita Jane from her cellphone on the cab ride to the Hill, which was fine, because she didn't really want Rita Jane to watch her testify anyway.

By the time she took her place at the heavy oak witness table, sweat was clinging to the back of her neck. Her bare thighs stuck to the wooden chair. She dearly wished she were anywhere but where she was. When Weymouth told her to begin, she took a deep breath, pulled the microphone closer, and prayed she wouldn't throw up or say anything too embarrassing.

Weymouth asked the questions in a way that enabled her to explain what she had done for her client and why she had done it. She answered him directly, looking straight at him, trying not to think about the fact that the room was packed with spectators and dozens of reporters. She was getting into the rhythm of the questions, feeling more confident, when Weymouth paused and took a sip of water. Claudia felt her stomach turn.

"Miss Connors, why do you believe the U.S. Attorney's office chose to prosecute you?"

Claudia hesitated, unsure of what Weymouth was getting at. She took a slow sip of water buying time to think of what answer he wanted. Then she answered, "I can't say for sure, but I believe they did not want me to represent Mr. Emad. By charging me as an accessory, they forced me off his case."

Weymouth nodded. "Why would they do that?"

"Because I was something of a zealot about this case."

"Can you explain?" Weymouth asked.

Claudia nodded. "I knew Mr. Emad personally. I considered him a friend. He spent time in my community." She paused, "I was involved in political activities with him."

Weymouth interrupted her, "Such as?"

"We were both part of an anti-war organizing committee."

"Did you attend meetings together?"

"Yes."

"Were some of those meetings at your community?"

"Yes."

"Anything else you'd like to add?" Weymouth asked, with a tone that suggested there was some other information he was looking for.

"We had organized a support committee for Emad. Kind of a defense committee."

"Did the U.S. Attorney's Office know about these activities?"

"I hadn't thought so then, but now I suspect that they did."

"Why do you say that?"

Claudia hesitated, wanting to explain about the FBI visits without getting into her relationship with Dan. "The FBI visited our community on several occasions ostensibly to find out information about me."

"What kind of information?"

"Information to help make their case against me, I suppose."

"How many times did they visit?"

"At least twice."

"Can you describe those visits?" he asked. Claudia realized this was her opportunity to talk about the break-in at Dan's house without Dan having to do so. If this was a real trial that information would have been inadmissible as hearsay, but this wasn't a real trial, and besides, Weymouth was in charge.

"Once they executed a delayed-notification search warrant on Dan Canavan's apartment."

"Can you explain what that is?"

"It's a sneak-and-peek search. A black-bag job. They went into his house when he wasn't there and looked around, but Dan came home early from work and found them there."

There were gasps in the audience. Claudia continued. "Another time we were having a community work day and two officers — the same two that went into Dan's place — set up surveillance right in front of our community."

"Really, in broad daylight?"

"Yes. One of our members became suspicious and asked them what they were doing. When she found out they were FBI she invited them to lunch."

Laughter filled the room.

"Did they join you for lunch?"

"No, they declined."

"Were you present that day?" Weymouth asked.

"No, I was inside my home resting. Pregnancy exhausts me," Claudia said. A murmur of understanding went through the audience. Claudia relaxed a bit. Things were going well.

"Ms. Connors," Weymouth asked, "is Emad Khadonry a terrorist?"

She knew this question, which would also be inadmissible in court, must be infuriating Martin. She smiled inwardly but outwardly put on her best lawyerly voice and said, "No, sir. Emad is a law-abiding citizen. This so-called 'terrorist' investigation is a colossal waste of time and money. It would be laughable if it weren't so tragic. Emad's young daughter hasn't seen her Daddy in seven months!" A buzz filled the room.

"One more question," Weymouth said. "Are you a terrorist?"

"No, sir."

"Thank you, that's all the questions I have," Weymouth said.

Claudia stood up to leave when she felt a stab of pain so sharp she gasped. Her legs felt wobbly so she leaned on the table. She fell back into her seat as she vaguely heard Weymouth announce that the hearing would be in recess for 15 minutes.

Dan was at her side with a cup of water looking at her with an expression of mixed excitement and horror. "Is it time?" he whispered urgently.

"It can't be. It's not due for another two weeks," Claudia said.

Weymouth asked her, "Are you alright?"

She nodded bravely but sucked in her breath as another stab of pain coursed through her body.

"I think we should take her to the hospital," Dan said frantically.

Weymouth looked at him sympathetically. "Dan, I've been through this a few times already. Let's not overreact. Help me take her into my office and we'll call her doctor and see what he advises."

Claudia walked jerkily to Weymouth's office braced on either side by Dan and the congressman. As soon as they eased her onto the couch in Weymouth's office, Dan was on the phone to her doctor who advised that they bring Claudia into her office for a check up. He immediately called Dave for a ride to the doctor's and called Rita Jane and told her to meet them there.

Weymouth returned to the hearing after promising Dan that he would not call him as a witness that day. Weymouth also called the Capitol Police and obtained permission for Dave to drive his car into the secured area at the rear of the Rayburn Building, an area that had been restricted to the general public since September 11. Weymouth also sent a security guard who offered to help escort Claudia to the car.

Dan insisted on going to the doctor's office even though Claudia urged him to stay and watch the hearing. It took Dave almost an hour to maneuver the traffic on Capitol Hill so that by the time they pulled up to the entrance to the Georgetown University Professional Building, Rita Jane was already there looking anxious.

Claudia insisted that Dan wait outside while the doctor examined her but let him return to hear her advice. "I'd like to admit you to the hospital. You appear to be in the beginning stages of labor, but your cervix is not dilated and your water hasn't broken. You'll need to be on complete bed rest for the remainder of your pregnancy. You could stay at home but that would mean someone else would have to wait on you hand and foot because I mean complete bed rest. I recommend that you go into the hospital so we can make sure you are properly cared for."

The doctor left the room giving them privacy to discuss their options. Claudia began to protest but Rita Jane interrupted her, "Please listen to what she's saying, Claudia. For the baby's sake."

"I agree," Dan said vehemently.

"I'm not even going to ask you," she said to Dave. "You're a doctor. I know your kind always stick together."

Dave smiled, "Try to think of it as a vacation."

She felt such weariness she didn't have the strength to argue anymore. "I'll get Georgia to bring over some files. You guys better bring me some good books to read or I'll go out of my mind," she said resignedly. The doctor sent for an orderly with a wheelchair to push her over to the hospital. At her insistence, the others left to go back to work, promising to return later with comfortable clothes and books. As she waited for the orderly, she thought of all the people who had a stake in her life now, who were personally affected by the decisions she made, and who felt that they had a right to have a say in those decisions, a thought that both comforted and annoyed her.

48. Dan Testifies

Catching a cab from the hospital, Dan and Rita Jane held on for dear life as the cabbie expertly maneuvered through Georgetown traffic.

"Watch out," Rita Jane screamed as the driver ran a red light, narrowly missing a crossing pedestrian.

"It's better if you don't watch," Dan said. "I usually close my eyes and pretend I'm somewhere else."

On Pennsylvania Avenue all traffic was stopped for blocks as a presidential motorcade passed. Sirens screeched as a dozen police motorcycles and cars led a line of several large black cars with tinted windshields away from the White House.

Dan looked at his watch and cursed the traffic.

"On days like this I fantasize about living in a cabin on a lake in some remote place, like Maine."

"You'd last about five minutes," Rita Jane said. "You'd be bored out of your mind without the gossip and intrigue of Washington."

Although sitting in a traffic jam was not exactly fun, at least she was out of the hospital, where she had spent most of her time since Claudia was admitted. She took Dan's advice and closed her eyes. She felt lighter than she had in a long time. For months she had been comparing herself with Claudia, wishing she were the pregnant one. Each time Claudia vomited or complained about being exhausted, Rita Jane imagined that her body would have tolerated pregnancy better. Now the jealousy was gone, replaced with real concern for Claudia and the baby.

The cab dropped them at the Independence Avenue entrance at 9:55 and they pushed their way to the head of the security line and sprinted to the Judiciary Committee hearing room just as Weymouth was beginning his opening remarks.

Weymouth called Dan to the witness table and began asking him about the FBI visits. Rita Jane knew that Claudia had already been asked about them and wondered why the Chairman was asking them again. He then asked Dan where he worked and he asked him to describe Out-Reach.

As soon as Weymouth finished questioning Dan, Congressman Blake, who looked like a cross between Smoky the Bear and Humpty Dumpty said, "Excuse me, Mr. Chairman, I'd like to ask this witness a few questions with your permission."

Rita Jane racked her memory for where she had heard of Blake and remembered that OutReach had quoted him as saying that the answer to the problem of homosexuality was for gay people to accept Jesus Christ as their Lord and Savior.

Blake looked disdainfully at Dan who attempted a look of nonchalance, but Rita Jane knew he was nervous. "Mr. Canavan. I understand from your testimony that you are a ho-mo-sex-ual?" He said it slowly, articulating each syllable.

Dan hesitated. "Yes, that is correct."

"Yet isn't it true that you had a sexual relationship with Claudia Connors?"

The room stirred and Rita Jane said a quick prayer for Dan to keep his cool. "It wasn't exactly a relationship," Dan said, sounding ridiculous, even to himself.

"Oh really," Blake said dramatically. "What would you call it?"

"We're friends," Dan said simply.

"But you had sex with her," Blake persisted.

"One time," Dan answered.

"I see," Blake said.

"If it's only one time, it doesn't count?" A burst of laughter escaped from the audience. Weymouth pounded the desk with his gavel.

"I don't see the point of this line of questioning," Weymouth interrupted. "Please stick to relevant questions."

"This is relevant, Mr. Chairman," Blake said. "This man is trying to give this committee the impression that the FBI was unfairly harassing him, when in fact the agents were well within their rights to search his house."

"I allowed that question," Weymouth said, "But I hardly think whether Mr. Canavan has one-night stands is relevant to our inquiry."

"It goes to the question of his char-ac-ter," Blake said. "What kind of man impregnates his friend and then leaves her to have the child on her own?"

Weymouth said, "Out of order. The last remark will be stricken from the record." He turned the full force of his wrath on Blake. "You may ask questions but you may not engage in character assassination. Do you understand?"

"I'll rephrase it," Blake said smugly. "Isn't it true that you impregnated Claudia Connors and deserted her, forcing her to raise the child on her own?"

Rita Jane was so furious she wanted to stand up and scream that Claudia hadn't even wanted to have the baby, that it was Dan who had been willing to raise it. Dan cleared his throat and took a deep breath.

"It is not true. I have not abandoned Claudia Connors. We are not married, but I will support her and the child."

"Is this your idea of family values, Mr. Canavan?"

There was so much commotion in the room, few heard his answer. Rita Jane had wanted to run up to the desk and hug Dan, and then go punch Blake in the nose. She was grateful when Weymouth announced a two-hour recess for lunch.

They went to Tortilla Coast, the Mexican restaurant behind the Rayburn Building that was always swimming with staffers and lobbyists. Rita Jane, who never drank at lunch, ordered a large Margarita. Dan sipped iced tea and picked at his food, too upset to eat anything. Rita Jane ate the entire basket of tortilla chips, alternating the sweet taste of the drink with the salty taste of the chips.

"At least the worst is over," Dan said. "The worst has come out."

"It was so hard to sit there and be quiet. I wanted to stand up and yell at Blake that you hadn't abandoned your baby, you had saved it."

"I don't think that would have helped matters," Dan said. But then he smiled. "It would have made a good headline, though. 'Gay Catholic man saves his unborn child from abortion by a pregnant lesbian terrorist'."

They burst into hysterical laughter — the kind that made your stomach hurt — drawing attention from the other patrons. Before they left, Rita Jane had managed to get Dan to eat half of a black bean burrito, convincing him that he needed to keep up his strength.

They walked back to the Rayburn Building together. As they arrived at D Street, Rita Jane heard someone call Dan's name. She assumed it was a reporter.

"I'm going inside to get a seat," Rita Jane said leaving Dan. "Good luck."

Rita Jane walked past the attractive man and smiled at him, but he didn't notice her. She hadn't gone 10 feet before she heard the shot. She turned to see Dan on the ground, blood pouring from his head.

49. The News

From her bed at Georgetown Hospital, Claudia watched Dan testify and cursed the television set. At one point she yelled so loudly a nurse came in and asked if she was okay.

Outraged by Blake's accusation that Dan had gotten her pregnant and then abandoned her, she wanted to insist that Weymouth call her again as a witness so that she could tell the truth: That if it hadn't been for Dan and Rita Jane, she would have had an abortion. Feeling guilty, she put her hands on her belly and apologized to "The Child" reassuring him/her that she was glad that she hadn't made that decision.

Claudia turned off the television in disgust. She had promised Rita Jane that she would practice some form of meditation or deep relaxation every day. Rita Jane had bought her a tape of Swami Satchidananda leading a guided meditation. Claudia had never meditated regularly, but Rita Jane had read an article about the benefits of mediation for expectant mothers and had wheedled her until she agreed to give it a try. Claudia doubted whether it would help her, but figured it wouldn't hurt her.

The soothing voice of the Swami was interrupted by the phone ringing. She decided to ignore it. "Now imagine that you are in a beautiful place," the voice was saying when a nurse scurried into her room, "You have an urgent phone call," she said. "We're transferring it now."

Annoyed at being interrupted, she said haughtily, "I'm meditating."

"I think you should take this call," she said quietly.

Fear pushed through Claudia's foggy brain. Something had happened to Rita Jane. She was relieved to hear Rita Jane's voice, but she couldn't understand anything she was saying. "Are you okay?" she asked her.

Rita Jane was sobbing hysterically. After a minute, Paul came on the phone and said simply, "Dan's been shot."

"What, when?" she screamed in disbelief. "Is he alright?"

"No, but at least he's still alive. He's been taken to Georgetown. See what you can find out about his condition. We're on our way now."

* * *

When Rita Jane arrived, she ran to Claudia and squeezed her so hard it hurt. Her streaked makeup made her eyes look like a raccoon's and her curly hair sprung wildly in all directions. She looked a bit mad, Claudia thought.

"He can't die. He just can't. Oh God, he can't die," she collapsed on Claudia's bed sobbing hysterically. "I don't know what I'll do if he dies. He's my best friend."

Claudia said nothing, but stroked her hair, quietly, like her mother had done to calm her when she was a little girl. "He's not going to die," Claudia said firmly, realizing she couldn't face that possibility either.

"I've been such a jerk," Rita Jane confessed. "I'm so sorry."

"What are you talking about?" Claudia said.

"I've been so jealous of you. I wanted so much to be pregnant and it has been so hard listening to your complaints, and taking care of you when you were sick, because I wanted to be pregnant, and you didn't. I thought it wasn't fair. I've been so selfish." Her chest heaved as she struggled to breathe. Claudia feared she was hyperventilating.

"It's okay." Claudia stroked Rita Jane's hair. "You haven't been selfish. You've been great. I couldn't have gotten though this without you."

Rita Jane continued sobbing. Claudia kept stroking her hair. "It doesn't matter now. Everything is going to be okay."

How odd life is, Claudia thought. The last thing she had wanted was to be pregnant. She had disliked being pregnant so much that it never occurred to her that Rita Jane would be jealous of her. But now that she had confessed to it, the idea made perfect sense. How could I have been so blind? Claudia wondered.

Rita Jane cried until she fell asleep. Claudia reached into the pocket of Rita Jane's jean jacket and pulled out her cellphone. She scrolled down to the entry for the Spencers and dialed the number. Claudia relaxed when she heard Leigh, preferring to deal with her rather than the doctor.

"Can you come to GW Hospital? Your daughter needs you."

"Is she okay," Leigh asked.

"She just needs her mom, that's all."

50. The Waiting is the Hardest Part

"Well, he's still alive," the surgeon told the assembled group of Dan's family and friends who were waiting anxiously for any news. "He has survived the surgery. We've repaired the damage from the bullet, but he is still in critical condition. We've induced a coma. The next 48 hours are crucial. He's young. He's healthy. He's got a good chance of surviving," the doctor finished on an optimistic note before rushing off to his next task.

Dan's entire family had been notified and had been visiting in shifts because the ICU only permitted one visitor at a time. Mrs. Canavan refused to leave Dan's side, except to let other people who she deemed suitable, visit, and then she insisted that they promise to get her immediately if there were any changes in his condition.

Audrey had returned from Texas. What should have been a wonderful family reunion on the occasion of the baby's birth had become a somber wait.

Rita Jane made a detour along the way to the small chapel before returning to Claudia's room. Since the shooting, she had been lighting candles daily to the Virgin Mary, praying for Dan's recovery. The small chapel smelled of cheap incense, but at least she had the place to herself. She knelt down at the front pew and dutifully folded her hands and bowed her head. "Dear God," she prayed silently. "I can't believe you are letting this happen. Things were finally going well. Claudia's case was dismissed. Dan found a great boyfriend. My parents were coming around to the baby idea and now this. How could you let this horrible homophobic lunatic ruin our lives?" Tears were stuck in her throat and her breathing was shallow and labored.

"I know it's not your fault. I know I should be grateful that he's still alive. At least there's hope, but I just don't understand why someone would want to kill Dan. He's the nicest guy. He's so caring and loving. Why is there so much hate in the world?"

She waited for an answer, but none came. Instead she cried out her rage and pain and fear. How could she live without Dan who had been the one person, above all others, who had always listened to her, loved her, encouraged her, cherished her and just been there for her?

Back at Claudia's room, all the networks were carrying around-the-clock coverage of the shocking story. First, the revelations that Dan had fathered a child with a lesbian, who had been charged with providing material support to her terrorist client, and then the news that he had been shot during a recess from the hearing where these revelations had been made. It was such a wonderful combination of drama, intrigue, and passion that the media outlets would keep the story running for days.

The shooter had calmly turned himself in to Capitol Police saying that he had done his duty and rid the world of a homosexual sinner. No charges had been brought yet while police waited to see whether Dan would live.

When they couldn't stand the television anymore, they turned it off. They both dozed a while, Rita Jane sitting beside Claudia in the Naugahyde chair, holding her hand.

She heard her mother's voice calling her name and thought she must be dreaming, but when she opened her eyes her parents were there, carrying a large arrangement of plants and cut flowers, arranged in a beautiful bowl. She started crying.

"What're you doing here?" Rita Jane asked.

"Claudia called and told us what has been going on. We wanted to come by and offer our support."

Rita Jane couldn't stop crying, it was as though all of the pain, disappointment, joy, fear, love, beauty and ugliness that had been trapped inside her now had to be released.

"I'm glad you're here," she said. She found that she meant it.

51. A Visit from Weymouth

The day after the shooting, Weymouth arrived in Claudia's room bearing a large bouquet of flowers. As always, he was impeccably dressed and clean-shaven, but his skin was ashen, and his eyes swollen. He looked like he hadn't slept in days.

Claudia introduced him to Audrey who took the flowers and went to look for a vase. Weymouth sat down in the chair next to Claudia's bed and grabbed her hand, "I feel so terrible," he said. He looked on the verge of tears, his broad shoulders shaking. "I didn't want him to testify," he sobbed. "I should have refused to call him as a witness."

Claudia interrupted him. "It wasn't your fault. You can't blame yourself."

"But if he had been here at the hospital instead of at the hearing, he would still be alive."

"He is alive," Rita Jane said, horrified at the thought that anyone had given up on Dan so soon. "I know Dan. He's a survivor. If anyone can survive this, it's him."

"Rita Jane's right. He's going to survive. We have to believe that."

Audrey had returned with the flowers prettily arranged.

Seeing Weymouth she put the flowers down, and stuck out her hand, "Audrey Connors, I'm Claudia's momma."

"Nice to meet you," Weymouth said taking her hand. "You have a remarkable daughter."

"I do indeed."

"I heard what you said to Claudia, and she's right. You can't blame yourself. Dan wanted to testify. Wild horses couldn't have kept that boy away. And he's got everything to live for now. He's going to be a daddy."

Weymouth looked hopeful. "I hope you're right," he said softly."

Rita Jane and Claudia looked away, discomforted by seeing Weymouth, who had always seemed so strong and impenetrable, bear his soul. Powerful men were only human, after all, and could suffer like the rest of us.

Just as quickly as he let his guard down, he put it up again.

"I came by to tell you that I'm holding a press conference at 4 o'clock this afternoon. I believe the networks will be covering it. Please try to watch it if you can."

Rita Jane couldn't imagine why he would be holding a press conference, but she didn't really care. "Would you like to see Dan?" she asked softly. "They allow visitors into his room one at a time. Someone is with him all the time — usually his mother or Dave — but I'm sure they wouldn't mind leaving so that you could visit."

"I'd like that," he said.

Rita Jane escorted him to the ICU. He walked like an old man, heavily and slowly as though he were dreading what he would see.

When they arrived, the nurse told her Dave and Mrs. Canavan had gone to get some coffee. Paul was in with Dan, but agreed to leave so Weymouth could visit. Rita Jane asked for a moment with Dan first. She sat down beside her friend, reaching for his hand, which had an IV line going into it.

"You'll never guess who's here to see you, Dan," she said. "Congressman Weymouth. I knew you'd be thrilled to get a visit from the Chairman, although I suspect you'd pick a different outfit to wear. Don't worry, though, you look fine. That hospital gown suits you."

Weymouth entered and Rita Jane said goodbye to her friend, kissing him on the hand, as it was impossible to find his cheek with the oxygen mask and layers of bandages wrapped around his head.

"He's ready for you," Rita Jane said to Weymouth who made an attempt at a smile. He touched her hand gratefully and she smiled.

Weymouth got down on one knee and leaned over the bed with his head bowed as if in prayer. Rita Jane and Paul watched through the window. Weymouth said something to him, but Rita Jane couldn't make out the words. Weymouth bowed his head and clutched his hands together as though praying to God to intervene. Watching him made Rita Jane cry again. Paul put his arm around her and squeezed her tight. Rita Jane hoped God was listening.

Dave returned from the cafeteria with several cups of coffee and smiled when he saw Weymouth. "Dan would be pleased," he said sadly. Rita Jane nodded.

In less than five minutes Weymouth emerged from the room. He thanked everyone for allowing him the time with Dan, and reminded everyone to watch the 4 o'clock press conference that afternoon.

52. The Press Conference

Anticipating a large number of visitors in Claudia's room to watch the press conference, Audrey had emptied the wastebaskets, scrubbed the toilet, wiped down the bathroom sink, and picked all the dead and drying flowers from the various bouquets that covered every surface of the room.

"There are people who are paid to do that momma," she said, laughing at her mother.

"You know I can't stand to just wait."

"I feel guilty just sitting here," Rita Jane said. "Can I do anything to help?"

"Help Claudia change into a clean shirt and shorts. And do something with her hair. It looks wild."

Audrey had gone around to other patients' rooms asking to borrow their chairs so had managed to squeeze six into the small space, but they had to keep the door to the room open to do so.

At 3:30 they turned on C-SPAN 1, to make sure they didn't miss any of the news conference. A reporter was interviewing Ken Parker who said that Weymouth had never called for a press conference without disclosing the topic. Parker guessed that he was going to announce a special piece of legislation related to the shooting, such as making it a federal offense to kill someone because of their testimony at a congressional hearing.

Dan's father had managed to convince Dave to leave Dan's side, but only on the condition that Dan's mother would call immediately if anything happened. Paul and Aimee had also come by to visit Dan, so they tagged along, too. Leigh had come to visit Rita Jane and Claudia.

At 4:00, the camera panned to an image of the Capitol Building, and then showed a throng of reporters with cameras and notebooks in hand. Weymouth stepped forward to the microphone.

"Good afternoon. Thank you for coming. I have prepared a brief statement that I will read and then answer questions," he said his face expressionless.

"Two days ago, after testifying at an oversight hearing in my committee, Dan Canavan was shot outside the Rayburn House Office Building by someone who claimed he did not like his position on gay issues. Dan Canavan is an extremely talented advocate and lobbyist and cares passionately about protecting the civil and human rights of all people.

"I got to know Dan when he was lobbying the SOFA bill. Most lobbyists who work on this issue would not have bothered to lobby me.

I'm a Republican, and they work with Democrats. Dan was different. He sought me out and asked for my help. I believe that it was his public involvement in this issue that led to his shooting.

"Dan could have made a lot of money working for a big K-Street lobbying firm, but instead he chose to use his law degree to work for a nonprofit organization working to end discrimination against gay and lesbian people.

"Institutionalized discrimination is still very much alive and well in the United States. Gay people, with a few exceptions, do not have the right to marry. This fact means that in a majority of states they cannot legally adopt children together, share health benefits or make end-of-life decisions. This legally sanctioned discrimination makes it socially acceptable to treat gay people as second-class citizens. It also leads some misguided people to believe that they can use violence against gay people.

"The only way for laws to change is for people to change and that is why today I am choosing to publicly announce that I, too, am a homosexual. Although I am married and have three children, I have always been gay. My wife, who is my best friend, knows this about me, but married me anyway. Dan Canavan learned about my true identity and instead of publicly outing me, he privately approached me and asked for my support in trying to oppose SOFA.

"I always thought that it was okay for me to have my public career and my private sexual identity. I rationalized, as do many others, that whomever I chose to love is nobody's business. Now I realize how wrong I was.

"I believe I have done a good job representing the citizens of the Fourth Congressional District in Mississippi. I hope my constituents will re-elect me, but if they choose not to then I am willing to accept that outcome. There are more important issues at stake than my political career. What is at stake is creating a safe society for all citizens, whatever their race, nationality, gender or sexual orientation. Any questions."

There was a pause of several seconds before the media pounced on him.

"Are you coming out of the closet because you feel guilty about Dan Canavan's shooting?"

"I am coming out of the closet because I believe it might prevent future shootings."

"Did you have an affair with Dan Canavan?"

"No."

"Do you believe it is your fault that Dan Canavan was shot?"

"No."

"Is Dan going to survive?"

"It is unclear at this point if he will or not."

"Did Dan Canavan father a child with Claudia Connors, a lesbian?"

"I am not here to talk about anyone else."

"Are you going to get a divorce?"

"Absolutely not. My wife and I love each other and love our children. We aren't the only married couple who doesn't sleep together."

This remark got a laugh from the reporters and gave Weymouth the break he needed to wrap things up. "Thank you very much for coming. I have to get back to work now."

Claudia turned down the volume on the commentators offering their opinions about why Weymouth had done what he had done. Everyone looked at each other, unsure of what to say.

"Unbelievable," Dave said.

"Incredible," Rita Jane said.

"That poor man," Audrey said. "It must be weighing heavily on his soul."

"Dan would be proud," Claudia said.

53. The Baby

Rita Jane felt something tug on her arm, waking her from where she had fallen asleep on a chair next to Claudia's bed.

"I think my water broke," Claudia announced calmly.

Rita Jane ran to the nurse's station yelling, "Help, help," as though there was a true emergency, and not just another pregnant woman going into labor.

The nurse called the doctor who arrived in under a half an hour. She measured Claudia's cervix and declared it to be 6 centimeters dilated. In moments, a stretcher arrived, and attendants maneuvered a moaning Claudia off the bed and onto the stretcher. Audrey and Rita Jane followed as they pushed the stretcher down a long hallway, onto an elevator and into the delivery room.

Audrey and Rita Jane stood on either side of Claudia, holding her hands, rubbing her back and giving her words of encouragement. Rita Jane was officially the coach, but it was soon clear that Audrey, having already had four children, knew how to anticipate what Claudia needed better than Rita Jane.

Rita Jane mostly held Claudia's hand and let her squeeze as tight as she needed to during the contractions. Claudia's cries of pain disturbed Rita Jane deeply. When a particularly bad pain struck, Rita Jane ran into the hallway looking for someone to help Claudia. The nurse offered an epidural, but Claudia didn't want any painkillers. She bravely endured each contraction, and Rita Jane felt pride and love as she watched her partner endure the pain.

After several hours of active labor, Claudia fell asleep. Rita Jane offered to go to the cafeteria for coffee. She stopped by the ICU. Dave was alone with Dan. He left Dan to go talk to her.

"She's in labor," Rita Jane said.

"How's it going?"

"It's pretty awful. I don't know what's normal. How long can this go on?"

"With a first baby, a long time."

"What's that mean?"

"Well, I've heard of labor lasting up to three days. But they wouldn't let Claudia go on that long. At her age, she's a high-risk. If she doesn't deliver within 24 hours, they'll perform a cesarean."

"Do you mind if I go in for a minute?" Rita Jane asked. Dave nodded, and slumped down in the chair, looking as though he would fall asleep right there.

Rita Jane sat down next to her friend and took his hand. Keyed up on adrenaline, she felt both exhausted and hyper-alert.

"It's started, Dan," she whispered. "She's having the baby. God I wish you were with us. You have so much more patience than me. I just want this to be over with. I want all of this to be over with. I want to wake up and have the baby here, and have you sitting up in bed, all better, holding the baby."

She stroked his arm, avoiding the tubes connecting him to life. "You better not die on me," she said, more angrily than she had intended. "I mean it."

She concentrated with all her might on the image of Dan, alive, healthy, happy, holding the child. With all the power at her disposal, she willed her friend to live. Sitting on the chair next to him, clasping both of her hands around his, she bent her head and prayed.

She returned to the delivery room feeling somewhat calmer. Claudia was still sleeping intermittently. Rita Jane sent Audrey out to take a break, and settled in next to her partner, waiting. The doctor had also left the room to check on another patient.

She must have dozed herself, because the next thing she remembered was Claudia saying, "The baby's coming." And sure enough, there was the top of the head, and the doctor was telling Claudia to push and Audrey was holding Claudia's hand and reminding her to breath, and Rita Jane was looking on in amazement. Claudia rallied a last burst of strength pushing as hard as she could, and the next thing they knew there was a bloody, screaming, baby boy. All three women gasped at the child. Rita Jane had been convinced that it was going to be a girl, but then she realized a boy was perfect. She looked at Claudia who said, "Now we know what to name the baby."

Rita Jane nodded.

The doctor cut the umbilical cord and passed the baby to Claudia who held him close to her heart. "Hello, Daniel Canavan Connors Spencer. Welcome to the world."

Rita Jane left the delivery room to tell her family and friends, who had been anxiously awaiting the news. "It's a boy," she said proudly. He's beautiful, and Claudia is fine, too."

Her mother hugged her. "Congratulations. That is great news. Now you need to go get some rest."

"I need to go tell Dan first," Rita Jane said. "Will you come with me?"

As they walked through the maze of corridors between obstetrics and ICU, Rita Jane realized there would never be a better time to tell her mother about Claudia.

"Mom, you know before when I said that I wasn't a lesbian. Well, I'm still not sure if I am, but Claudia is my girlfriend. Or partner. Whatever you want to call it."

"We figured that out, dear." Leigh said. "We didn't believe you were going to raise a child with a stranger."

"But I didn't lie to you," Rita Jane insisted. "At your house I was telling you the truth. We weren't together then."

Her mother murmured, "Uh huh."

"I swear to God, I wasn't lying," Rita Jane said, but realized she didn't have the energy to argue further. "It doesn't matter. I'm glad you're here."

"Me, too."

They arrived at Dan's room. He looked amazingly peaceful despite the tubes and machines that connected him to life. Dave saw her through the glass window and left the room.

"It's a boy," she said. "We named him Daniel Canavan Connors Spencer."

"That's a wonderful name," Dave said.

"Do you mind if I tell him?" Rita Jane asked.

"Of course not," Dave said.

Rita Jane crossed herself reflexively before entering Dan's room, a gesture that startled her. She sat down next to his side and took his hand.

"I've got good news," she began. "Claudia had the baby. It's a boy. We named him after you." She fought back tears. "Listen Dan, you have got to get better. We need you, and your son needs a father. You have absolutely got to get better. Do you hear me?"

Dan lay unresponsive.

"I mean it Dan. I absolutely will not have you go and die on me right now. You've got to get better."

The tears were close to coming. She stood up to leave and when she bent over to kiss him, she could have sworn she saw his eyelids flickering.

Epilogue

54. Moving Day

Rita Jane took a last look around her former home. Amanda was returning from India next week and Rita Jane wanted the place to look perfect for her homecoming. Rita Jane hadn't really lived in her rented home for months. Even before Danny's birth, she had spent most of her time at Claudia's place and that had only increased after the birth. Still, it had been nice to know that she had her own place to retreat to when life seemed too hectic. She would miss it, but at least she still had her studio.

She stopped by Dan's house to check on Danny, who was sleeping soundly on Dan's stomach. Dan himself was dozing in his favorite recliner with the television turned on to a college football game. His recovery was going well, but he hadn't been back to work yet and he still slept a lot. Taking care of Danny was the perfect occupation for him since they both seemed to sleep most of the day. Dave was cooking soup. Pots and pans covered every counter surface and the aroma of garlic and onions permeated the air.

"Isn't this the scene of domesticity?" Rita Jane asked.

"I love a man who can cook," Dan said. "There are definitely benefits to getting shot. I haven't had to cook a meal for myself in three months."

"Don't get any ideas about doing that again," Rita Jane said.

"I keep telling him he doesn't have to get shot for me to cook for him. I'll cook for him even if he's healthy," Dave said.

"Isn't he the best?" Dan said with a dreamy expression on his face.

"Do you want me to take him now? I've just got one more load to move out of Amanda's."

"We'll keep him as long as you'd like," Dan said. "He's happy right where he is."

Rita Jane dragged the cart stacked with boxes up the elevator. "It's my last load," she said to Claudia who was unloading groceries. "You're stuck with me now."

"What are you talking about — stuck with you? I'm the luckiest woman alive. Where's Danny?"

"He's with the boys. He's fast asleep on Dan's chest and I hated to disturb him. Plus, Dan didn't really want him to go."

"Does that mean we have the afternoon free?"

"If we want it," Rita Jane said. "What did you have in mind? A matinee? A hike? It's a beautiful day outside.

"I was thinking of something that we could do at home — a little indoor recreation shall we say?"

"Sounds like a plan," Rita Jane said. They took each other's hands and went upstairs leaving the groceries and boxes to be unpacked later.